THE
RAMPANT
REAPER

THE RAMPANT REAPER

MARLYS MILLHISER

ST. MARTIN'S MINOTAUR

NEW YORK

www.minotaurbooks.com

Library of Congress Cataloging-in-Publication Data

Millhiser, Marlys.
 The rampant reaper : a Charlie Greene mystery / Marlys Millhiser.— 1st ed.
  p. cm.
 ISBN 0-312-29096-9
  1. Greene, Charlie (Fictitious character)—Fiction. 2. Nursing home patients—Crimes against—Fiction. 3. Women detectives Iowa—Fiction. 4. Literary agents—Fiction. 5. Iowa—Fiction. I. Title.

PS3563.I4225 R36 2002
813'.54—dc21

2001058854

First Edition: July 2002

10 9 8 7 6 5 4 3 2 1

For aging children of the elderly everywhere

THE
RAMPANT
REAPER

CHAPTER 1

◆

M ONSTER TREES STRETCHED a shroud across the
sunlight and Charlie Greene in the sad little graveyard.
Spores of dying leaves and turned earth moved thick on the
air. The earth was so black she imagined it seethed with im-
patience to decay or to grow anything that came near. A hungry, spongy earth that sucked at her boot heels.

In clear sunlight on the other side of a wire fence, giant
harvesting machines and grain trucks longer than railroad cars
rumbled and exhaled gassy breath to provide sustenance for
the living. Charlemagne Catherine Greene stood at her
mother's side to provide solace for the dead? Why *was* she
here?

Still dressed in their airplane clothes, they looked as out
of place as belly dancers at a church supper.

Moss in burnt-orange splotches, like a creeping rust, nearly
covered the bases of gray gravestones. No little flat-to-the-
ground bronze identifiers here that you could run a riding
mower over, nor much grass to mow, what with all the shade.

There were obelisks tall and short, pointed stretched-out
pagodalike things, slabs rounded at the top, large and small.
And the small white lambs, heartbreaking in number, denot-
ing the young and the very young and the stillborn. This might
be a small cemetery, but it was a crowded one.

Charlie, in tight black jeans, short black-leather jacket over
a silk cranberry blouse, and black boots with high, square
heels, figured she looked, here, like the type to jump on the
back of some ancient, bald, bearded hippy's motorcycle.

1

Funny, in L.A. she'd felt fairly fashionable in this outfit, more like the type to drive off in a Porsche with a young hunk. Edwina Greene's tailored black suit screamed expensive. The whole effect spoiled by sensible shoes. At least she wasn't sinking into the soil.

The gloom was not lightened by the number of mourners in wheelchairs hacking up God-knew-what to drown out the minister bravely trying to minister. Between the hacking oldsters and the graying children behind their wheelchairs, the minister and the marshal were closer to her age than anyone but those innocents long rotted away under the white lambs.

The oldsters demanded to know when could they take their nap, eat, go to the bathroom, or simply get the hell out of here—who was it being planted anyway? Their children, Charlie figured, counted the days until they could escape to Arizona for the winter.

She knew who was the marshal because he leaned against a Jeep Cherokee wearing a George W. grin to perfection, and on the side of the blood-red vehicle supporting him and his grin, MYRTLE MARSHALL stood out dramatically in white.

The minister, obvious because she officiated, wore a long, flowing skirt and a knowing if benign cast as she picked up a handful of that hungry black dirt. She said something Charlie couldn't hear over the honking, snorting, hacking of the geezers in wheelchairs, the pointed questions of the hearing-impaired of both sexes, and the harvesting machinery roaring on the other side of the fence.

Dead leaves swooped and swayed in a gentle, gliding fall to touch down and crunch brittle underfoot as the uneasy and demented alike shifted in their discomfort.

Everything but the leaves seemed to go silent, every eye that could see turned to Charlie Greene, and even the good-natured marshal stopped grinning when a mewling sounded in Charlie's purse.

If you want to know what it's like to feel truly out of place, forget to turn off your cellular at a funeral.

Charlie's mother walked stone-cold silent to the rental car parked along the road outside the Myrtle Cemetery. Two handicap vans passed them loaded with the wheelchair folks. Some of their gray-haired children looked over their shoulders at the Greenes. They were about Edwina's age, the women were dressed in a combination of skirt lengths and sensible shoes, some in dressy pants. Their husbands in white or light shirts, no ties or coats. The day was warm once you left the gravestones.

Charlie looked back to see the Myrtle marshal filling in Great-aunt Gertie's grave. Charlie walked in sunlight, he shoveled in deep shade. Stephen King'd have a blast with this.

"God, I'm sorry about the cell—it just seems like I've been rushing around all day and haven't caught up with my head yet. I didn't mean to embarrass you, honest."

Charlie's mother turned with tears in her eyes. "Don't sweat that, Charlie. For once, this isn't about us."

What isn't about us? I fly from Long Beach to LAX to Minneapolis and take the vomit comet to some place called Mason City and we rent a car for another place called Myrtle where *your* great-aunt died. I'm adopted. I'm not related to her. Do you have any idea of what I'm missing back home and at work? How important can this be?

But Charlie couldn't remember seeing her mother in tears since Charlie's father, Howard, died, and she was too stunned to voice her angst. And stunned by Myrtle, Iowa, too. The marshal had taken off his lumberjack shirt.

Charlie worked in Beverly Hills on Wilshire at the firm of Congdon and Morse Representation, Inc., a Hollywood talent agency, as their sole literary agent, and that call had come from a new, exciting, and valued client. It was one of the many reasons she should not be in Myrtle. Charlie had sucked up her heels from the ravenous dirt to crawl off behind a really big flat, bending-over slab tombstone to answer the call. She

3

hadn't been this humiliated since she realized nobody was going to ask a pregnant teen to the prom. She'd had to make whispered excuses to Shirley Birkett, the latest successor to Danielle Steel, and would have to find time real soon to answer that call more fully.

Jesus, we're talking bucks here, careers even.

But somehow, looking at the people of Myrtle, she didn't think she'd bring all that up over coffee. And there was coffee, with three different kinds of carrot cake, in the basement at the tiny Methodist Church. Here, people even came up to talk with Edwina, who still looked shockingly exotic. Imagine how her daughter looked.

"Edwina, what's happened to you? You were always so lank—I mean . . . studious. Did you finally find God?"

"Cancer finally found me," Charlie's mother answered politely. She certainly had changed since her mastectomy. Even Charlie couldn't believe how much. "Aunt Abigail, I'd like you to meet my daughter, Charlemagne Catherine Greene."

Aunt Abigail—how many aunts were there around here?—looked Charlie up and down and sideways over half-glasses. She was taller than both Charlie and Edwina, arrow-straight and bone-thin. Her navy-blue dress had a startling-white lace collar. Her cheeks had sags where once had been bags.

"So, it's you, is it?" Aunt Abigail had to be ancient, but her movements were as swift and sure as her dislike when she turned away and strode to the other side of the room.

"God, Mom, I didn't know how to dress—this was all so quick. And all you said was the weather was changeable in Iowa in October."

"It's not you, honey. It's her. Remember that. Sorry I had to bring you and on such short notice. But there are things you need to know. Now, let's both stop being sorry. It can get you suffocated here."

Charlie's mom hadn't called her "honey" since she gave birth at sixteen. Edwina, a professor of biology, lived in Boul-

4

der. Charlie lived in Long Beach as the unwed mother of a trying, gorgeous teenage daughter, Libby.

"Oh, Edwina, I'm sorry about Aunt Abigail. But I guess we both know what we're facing here." This was Cousin Helen, who had stood off away from them at the burial of Aunt Gertie but who now hugged Edwina, and Charlie, too. She smelled pleasantly of black soil and garlic. "I know this has got to be culture shock coming in from the real world, but I am so grateful. I haven't told her anything. I was waiting for you guys to help me out."

The basement was chilly. Charlie's leather jacket didn't seem enough. She took one bite of carrot cake and put its paper plate with the plastic fork on a table. She hugged a paper cup of hot, watered-down coffee for solace. Others seemed to draw courage from Cousin Helen and approached Charlie's mom, most remaining distant from but curious about Edwina's daughter.

They tended to be short, middle-aged to senior citizen types, their elders deposited someplace by the handicap van. The men had white foreheads where the sun had not reached under baseball caps. The women looked sort of like laid-back soccer grandmoms, if there were such things.

But before they could really warm up to the exotic Greenes, Great-aunt Abigail announced soundly and surely from across the room, "Gertrude died old and sick and cursed. And we all know why." The glaring-white collar rose as the old lady's arm lifted, and, a finger pointing at the guests, she whirled to face the interlopers and glared directly at Charley. "Because of her. It was murder."

5

CHAPTER 2

✦

*C*HARLIE STOOD OUTSIDE the church, remote from the small band of people standing around her mother. She knew Edwina was from Iowa, but she'd rarely heard of Myrtle and never of these relatives. Edwina had never brought Charlie back to visit and Charlie'd never wondered why. Well, boy, did she now.

She was a busy career woman and didn't have much time to waste wondering. She knew her father had had a previous family, but Howard had never chosen to invite them to the house. Charlie hadn't wondered about that either.

You're thirty-four years old, Charlie Greene—washed-up by Hollywood standards—but still as self-involved as a teenager.

Two more church spires rose among splendid scarlet, burnished-orange, gold, and russet trees. They were glorious in the sunlight against the depth of sky and scattered puffs of clouds as white as Great-aunt Abigail's collar. Looked like a painting, a fake Hollywood backdrop.

Just because you've never been to Iowa doesn't mean it can't be beautiful. Little bit out of our element, aren't we?

How could a place like this produce a Great-aunt Abigail?

Your mother needs you now, and she has all the answers, and she was there for you after the accident. Took six weeks off work to nurse you. Even lost her boyfriend because of you. You owe much of your prized independence to her.

Totally without her permission, Charlie's conscience was

growing stronger as she grew older, thus making her weaker. Didn't make sense.

I was there for her after her mastectomy, Charlie fought back, but she was beginning to see the lovely red trees through tears and suddenly realized she wasn't alone after all.

"You really hurt for the passing of old Gertie? Well, don't. She didn't know who she was or why and didn't give a damn either. Not for, oh, like—" the Myrtle marshal pursed his lips and squinted at the cloud puffs "—I'd say ten, fifteen years now."

"Really?" Charlie wiped a cheek. Hollywood literary agents don't cry. Well, not in public. She was so self-involved she hadn't even heard him approach. "That long?"

"Oh, yeah. Took her a whole Myrtle minute to die, poor thing. But she didn't mind because she didn't know. So if you look at it that way, a Myrtle minute's not that bad. In the long run." His last sentence cracked him up so hard that even Charlie's grin found her. He stuck out his hand. "You're Charlie Greene. Del Brunsvold."

"Was Gertie your mom or aunt or somebody? I mean, I noticed you filling in the grave as we were leaving."

"This is Myrtle where the marshal is the sexton, and I plow the streets in winter, too. Hey, we all got to make a living. Oh, my. You could wipe out half the town with that smile," said Del, the marshal of Myrtle who plowed the streets. "I'd have to put you in jail, you know. If I had one."

Charlie and the marshal were both laughing when Edwina and Cousin Helen joined them. Cousin Helen looked startled, to put it mildly. There was no end to the social faux pas Charlie could commit in Myrtle, Iowa.

---❖---

"Go slow," Edwina said. "I want to see this."

Charlie, driving the rental car, was scared—her mother's voice had gone hollow like she'd never heard it do before.

But she didn't have to be reminded to go slow—Charlie wanted to see this, too.

The main street of Myrtle was actually called Main Street. And it was paved, sort of. The asphalt had crumbled away at the edges, leaving pothole parking along the high concrete curb and sidewalk. The sidewalk was wide but only on the side of Main Street that had stores—a few boarded over, others with windows out and sills and sashes loose and crooked like warped, vacant eyes. Crumbling foundations and thresholds presided over cracked, humped sidewalks.

The other side of Main Street was mostly empty lots, the city garage, and the Town Hall. One of the lots was scored by a long trench that Helen explained was a cave-in that the worthless Delwood better get filled in before someone broke a neck stumbling into it.

"What caved in?"

"We all figure it was from mining the white rock around here for buildings and roads in the old days."

On the store side of the street, signs read THE MYRTLE HOME AND FARM HISTORY MUSEUM and MYRTLE LIBRARY, and there was a grocery store, too. All were closed, the grocery store had been for years. The Myrtle Post Office—

"Charlie, stop."

Charlie already had.

"What's happened to the pool hall?"

"Not much but the name, I understand," Cousin Helen answered from the backseat. She was showing them the way out of town to "the farm" so they could unpack. "I've never been in it, of course."

Charlie was laughing again. This was certainly being a strange day. Crying, laughing, feeling sorely out of place. "Viagra's Bar and Grill?"

"Kenny Cowper's back in town. Marlin's Kenny. You probably didn't know him. He took over the place."

"I knew Marlin," Edwina said.

They turned at another abandoned grocery store, and on

8

the side road out of town stood a Sinclair station. The sign covering most of its window advertised GAS FOOD, AND VIDEOS. A block later, they crossed a beautiful white-stone bridge—made out of the local rock—and were on a road between fields that stretched to the horizon.

A dusty road of white crushed rock that coated the black Lumina. Charlie pulled out to pass one of those huge shiny-green harvesting machines—burdened with claws and chutes—that invariably seemed to be pulled by old dirty pickups and far too slowly. "Don't people in Iowa know there aren't three 'e's in deer?"

"Some of them don't know there can be three 'e's in Greene," Edwina said dryly.

There was only silence from the backseat until Cousin Helen relented. "John Deere is a trade name, Charlie. Everybody knows that. And Edwina, a lot of us younger folks feel bad about how you were treated. It doesn't look like it, but times have changed in Myrtle. You'll see. Next turn is ours and to the left. Second farm to the right."

Edwina ordered a stop here, too, when Charlie was about to turn into the drive of the second farm to the right. "My God, what's happened to the trees?"

"It's called 'Family Farms,'" Helen answered with a sigh. "Told you things had changed."

"I buy their products all the time at Von's." Charlie pointed to a little sign that managed to fit a young, slim family, happy cows, pigs, and chickens all in the same picture with a barn.

It was a long drive, with a few buildings and a windmill at its end. "Used to be big maples and oaks along the driveway. Buildings were shaded by more, and there was a regular forest behind them." Edwina had tears in her voice now. "Half the buildings are gone."

"Oh, yeah. Like Uncle Elmo says, what the home place needs now is a real good tornado." Helen's tone held more than a modicum of stoic sarcasm. "Trees don't grow profits every growing season, don't ya know?"

Great, there's an uncle, too. How much family did Edwina have here, and how could she have hidden it this long? Charlie, however, was beginning to guess why.

She was sure that her mother's parents were dead, and Edwina had always claimed to be an only child.

The driveway to the home place was two rutted mud tracks through high, dried-up weeds in the middle that scraped and scratched at the underside of the Lumina with bristle sounds to make your teeth grit. In other words, it was not much in use. Why should it be? There was nothing at the end of it but some foundations, a house, a few sheds, a giant barn falling apart, and the windmill unaware of a swift October breeze. The house was wood like the barn, both showing white paint worn through to gray patches. The front porch took up the whole face of the house and sagged at both ends like a frown. Helen had Charlie drive around to the backdoor, where the back stoop sagged, too. "Couldn't we stay in a motel or bed-and-breakfast?"

"No such things around close. It's not as bad as it looks."

"It'll only be a night or two," Edwina added and opened the car door.

Well, it was too that bad—the kitchen floor as warped as the front porch and back stoop, the October breeze that didn't interest the windmill whistling around the window frames and into the room. A stained gas cooking stove took up half a wall, and a round table in the middle of the room wore a tablecloth stuck on with thumb tacks.

"I don't think so," Charlie said over the din of a football game on a television in the next room. "I've been humiliated, scorned, and made to feel like a slug. I'm not sleeping here tonight."

Edwina said, "No, you haven't, you just imagine it, and that should make you feel guilty enough to do what's expected of you."

Cousin Helen yelled, "Elmo, turn that damned thing off. You got company."

Charlie said, "I never heard of these people until today. How should I know what they expect, and why should I care?"

"You know—" Charlie's mother studied her closely "—maybe I didn't do such a bad job of raising you after all."

And Charlie looked back really close for the first time this trip. "Edwina? You've done something to your face. What—"

"—not just any game. It's the Vikings versus the Packers." But the football game silenced in the next room. "And I wouldn't go to that old bat's funeral if the dish was dead and there weren't no game."

There were honest-to-god grooves in the wood flooring where foot traffic had worn a path and where out walked a man with a cane, followed by Helen, who nearly ran into him when he stopped short at the sight of the two women standing in his kitchen. "Ain't neither one of them two our little Edwina, I can tell you."

"Hello, Uncle Elmo."

He wore a silly grin filled with stained teeth too straight to be real for his generation, a few wisps of gray hair, and oversized bib overalls like the ones young girls wore these days, but his were more sturdy and had more pockets. He leaned the cane against the refrigerator and hobbled over to peer into Charlie's mom's face, turning his head to one side as if suspicious.

"God love ya, little girl, I never said you could turn into such a good-looking woman." He smelled of cigar and beer, but Edwina didn't seem to mind as she disappeared into his hug. "What took ya so long to come home?"

And then—

"I know. You don't have to tell me. Nobody meaner to women than their womenfolk. Well, I'm sure glad to see you. And this has got to be your little Charlemagne Catherine. Ain't she a beauty, now?"

11

"Uncle Elmo—" Helen handed him his cane "—Aunt Abigail announced at the church this afternoon that Aunt Gertie was murdered."

"Well now, that's not so far-fetched. Awful lot of folks died in that place lately."

"The Oaks is a nursing home. They're supposed to." Cousin Helen had tightly curled hair of an indiscernible color, which probably meant she colored it herself—sort of a pale, orangey-gold color like she'd been doing it too long. Her face was broad with a big smile and her body heavy-boned, plus she had a chronic sniff and thick eyeglasses. "Gertie was supposed to have died many, many years ago."

"Yeah—those are the ones been going. Could be someone's giving them a little extra shove. Wouldn't surprise me none. Nope." Uncle Elmo put his arm around Charlie's shoulders and gave her a squeeze and a wink.

"Did anybody tell the marshal?" Charlie asked.

"Delwood Brunsvold?" Helen's jaw dropped for a moment. She was a mouth breather, so you weren't sure if she was done talking or, as in this case, slack-mouthed with astonishment. "What good would that do?"

CHAPTER 3

✦

"Why doesn't the windmill turn in the wind?" Charlie asked Uncle Elmo as they sat on the droopy stoop drinking Budweiser.

"Froze up. Nobody young enough to crawl up there and oil the bearings anymore. I did it for years." He turned to look down at her with a thinking-hard squint. "You afraid of heights, pretty little Charlie?"

"Terrified."

"Yeah, these young folks just can't cut the mustard. Shame, too."

Edwina and Helen had driven off in the rental to bring back dinner.

"What did you mean about women being meaner to women? Who was mean to Edwina?" Besides me.

"People around here don't discuss that sort of thing, but it seems to me when a young person goes off to college, gets a good job someplace else, they get separated from their folks at home and the town. And when girls do it, they're lost forever. It's like a shunning, but nobody organizes it or talks about it. It was sort of like Edwina was getting above herself, not that anybody said so. Their attitudes said it. Edwina was plain and she was awkward, and her place in the pecking order was set by that even though her folks had the money to send her to the university and she had the brains to make good on it. Hard to explain because we don't talk about it."

"I think you explain it very well. It's been in the air ever since we got here. Being different is threatening. Those who are different feel threatened, too. People do that to each other everywhere, women especially because they're more vulnerable and subtle and backhanded about it. But what kind of work can people find around here, where the marshal digs graves and plows streets?"

"Matter of fact, we have three major industries and they're all owned by one man. He went off to college and after a while, came back home and took over the family businesses and they flourish. That's Gentle Oaks, the grain elevator, and The Station. Without Harvey Rochester, town of Myrtle'd a died years ago. Oops, you'd better get rid of that beer can. Here comes your mother and the family with the dinner. Ladies in Myrtle get their jollies eating, not drinking spirits. Prohibition was a real lively event around here in the old days, you can bet."

The family came in two pickups and an ancient Buick, as well as the rental. And they didn't bring commercial carryout. They brought covered bowls and flat pans for the oven and saucepans for the stove top. The kitchen range was soon giving off horrific gas smells to warm up the food, and the "ladies" were setting out the plates and table service from a buffet onto a beautiful old claw-foot table that took up ninety percent of the dining room. It reminded Charlie of an Italian family's apartment in Manhattan in the building where she and Libby had lived before moving to California. But there was no wine, no pasta, no garlic, no salad greens, no vivid arguing, gesturing, hugging, or laughter here. A few chuckles were all.

By the time Charlie sat down next to Edwina at dinner, three more carloads of family had arrived—from faraway places called Nora Springs and Floyd and Fertile. Really. Charlie was treated with nothing but a curious, distant kindness. But for once, she was so grateful to be sitting next to her mother she could have cried.

Again? What time of the month is it? Ever since the accident, her body had been screwed up menstrualogically. In

14

L.A., that word would have gotten laughs. She didn't think it would play in Myrtle.

The reason she was so glad to be close to Edwina at this particular table was that when she reached for her fork, her mother elbowed her in the ribs, only recently healed, mind you, but the gesture gave her time to notice that everyone else was instead bowing their heads.

Uncle Elmo delivered grace while bowls of creamy mashed potatoes, creamed peas with pearl onions, scalloped corn, gravies of every kind steamed comfort into the air. There were platters of sliced ham like on the Family Farm commercials, fried chicken that reeked of real butter, a beef stew that burbled odors from a crock pot plugged in with a cord separating Charlie from the man next to her. And platters of flaky dinner rolls, lime Jell-O with pineapple and carrot bits and marshmallows. Still out in the kitchen were four kinds of carrot cake and true homemade pies with meringue on top and pans of brownies. We are talking maybe five o'clock in the afternoon here. In Charlie's time, it was three. She didn't know if this was lunch or dinner.

Uncle Elmo's prayer was short and to the point. "Dear God, grace this table with love, not envy, hunger, not revenge. And most of all gusty appetites, not petty ones. Now these two women here have traveled from the Rocky Mountains and the Pacific Ocean to rejoin our family in time of need. Let us, Lord, support them as their incredible journeys here support our own. Let us not be petty, let us enjoy thy bountiful feast. Amen."

Charlie had no idea how all these people related. Two very elderly, very tiny ladies had come in the very big Buick. Elmo had whispered that they were sisters and "maiden" ladies. Did that mean they'd never had sex? Or just never married? They dressed in dresses, hose, little hats, and ate like birds.

Charlie took an instant liking to Helen's husband Buz, a big man whose stomach hid his belt and whose robust sense of humor nothing could hide. He was responsible for what chuckling there was.

The men wanted to talk about the football game, the women about distant children and grandchildren. They had to wipe buttery crumbs off their fingers before handing the endless family photos around the table—the men passing them on to the women with barely a glance, the women exclaiming how much little Derek looked like Grandpa Staudt did once, or Art's Ronnie.

From the endless bowls and plates passed before her, Charlie selected a fried-chicken breast, mashed potatoes and chicken gravy, creamed peas, and a flaky dinner roll with real butter to put on it. She couldn't remember the last time she'd had fried chicken—it usually came grilled, dry, boneless, skinless, tasteless now. Everything on her plate was so good she ate it all—something she never did. Well, this *was* a stressful situation.

"How long did it take you to drive clear from California?" one of the maidens asked Charlie during a lull in the football and grandchildren, just as Charlie savored the last of the real milk-chicken gravy. There had to have been a pound of butter on her plate alone.

"I flew from LAX to Minneapolis."

"And I from DIA to Minneapolis, and then we flew to Mason City together and rented a car," Edwina said.

"Isn't that terribly expensive?" the other maiden asked.

"We both work," Charlie explained. "Missing too much of that can be even more expensive. We can't afford the time off to drive this far."

"Yeah, just wait till this stock market crashes," Elmo said. "Everybody'll have more time than they want and no money to live on."

Helen and many of the women under, say, sixty-five, assured Charlie they worked, too. "Farmers and their wives have to have outside jobs these days."

Having seen the humongous John Deere harvesting machines on the roads, Charlie could see why.

"Helen and Buz took two weeks to make it to Tucson last year," Elmo said. "When are you leaving this year?"

Edwina dropped her fork and stared at Cousin Helen, who rolled her eyes and said, "Well, we have a right to a life, too."

While the other ladies gathered in the kitchen to wash the special china and silver kept at the home place and the men sat down in front of the TV in the room off the dining room, Charlie and Edwina crept upstairs to unpack and settle down. Theirs was a small room with twin beds and heaps of thick comforters. The one bathroom in this house was downstairs off the kitchen.

"Be thankful," Edwina said. "It used to be in the backyard."

Charlie discovered that her cellular didn't connect from here—it hadn't from the back stoop, either. She'd have to wait until she got back to Myrtle to contact her new and valued client, so she confronted her mother. Hell, neither of them could afford this time off or wanted to be here.

"What is it Helen wants you to help her with? Why get upset if she and Buz winter in Arizona, and how can she take that much time off if she works? Are we being had? Is that why I had to come? You're my mom, but I need answers. There's a bad secret here, isn't there?"

Edwina grabbed the pillow off the bed she was sitting on and sobbed into it.

"Tell me what's going on. Hell, if they're really killing off helpless old people, I don't want to stay around here, and I don't want you to, either." Charlie grabbed some Kleenex and handed them to her mom when she turned over. That's when Charlie realized what was so different about Edwina's face. No bifocals and bags underneath and no droops above. She had a hollow look there she never had before.

From Charlie's earliest memories of her mother, Edwina had been studious and dowdy, like a university professor and mother, widow and grandmother should be. But a couple of years ago, Edwina had a mastectomy for breast cancer and it changed her forever. Suddenly her dumpy figure straightened and slimmed, her lank hair was colored and styled, and front teeth capped. And for a short while, she even dated a younger man.

"It's Great-aunt Abigail."

"That doesn't surprise me. Is she your great-aunt or mine?"

"Mine. She'd be your great-great-aunt if—"

"If I weren't adopted. I have no problem with being adopted, you know that."

"Then how come your father and I were always Howard and Edwina instead of Mom and Dad?"

"That was rebellion, not—"

"Charlie, you're over thirty, with a child of your own. And poor Howard's been dead for eighteen years. When do you stop rebelling?"

"I notice a clever switch in the subject matter. Edwina, we aren't responsible for old people dying, and certainly not for the Wicked Witch of the Midwest, Great-aunt Abigail. Whatever is going on here, I don't like it. You keep saying it's not about us, but we are the people being treated way weird."

CHAPTER 4

CHARLIE'S LEATHER JACKET felt good that evening when she and Edwina prowled outside to get away from the television blaring inside and the ancient, dried-up smell of the home place.

Everyone had left before seven to get home to their television shows. Before they left, the women had all the dishes washed by hand and put back in the buffet in the dining room and the leftovers covered with plastic wrap and in the refrigerator. Except for the pies, which were supposed to sit out. People didn't pause over dinner at the home place.

"This had a high railing all around," Edwina said of the front porch, where the main entrance to the house was boarded over and a sign read USE BACK DOOR. "And we had family reunions in the shade of trees all over the front yard." She kicked at a stump that must have been three feet across. "There used to be seven or eight picnic tables, old wooden ones with benches, and Grandpa Staudt would reserve one of them to carve watermelons and that table would get so gummy flies would stick to it, and we kids could run and yell and spit seeds and get as messy as we wanted."

After seeing the table inside today, Charlie didn't even want to imagine what there might have been to eat on the other tables out here back then. No trees, no grass—just weeds, a broken picnic table or two, just pieces now. The television was noisy clear out here. Canned laughter from some sitcom almost drowned out Uncle Elmo's snoring. One window flashed weird lightning in colors.

Charlie desperately wanted to jump into the rental car and head for Mason City and a hotel. If it had an airport, it had hotels. Not that it was much of an airport—runways for commuter puddle-jumpers and small private planes, no Concourses or Jetways. But Edwina was so busy dealing with her issues, Charlie couldn't bring herself to play hardball right now.

Dry grasses and harvested stalks rustled in the fields all around like a sea of stealthy footsteps. The crippled barn and the stilled windmill stood as vast shadow ribs in the half-light.

Edwina and her issues continued around to the back of the house. "The barn was always full of cows and cats and pigs and pigeons. There're still pigeons. You can hear them from here. I had my eyes done."

"I noticed. There's not even a shower in that bathroom in there, Mom."

Edwina stood on top of a mound. "This was the root cellar, with shelves for home-canned goods and potatoes and apples, and it was where you headed at the approach of a tornado."

"Like in *The Wizard of Oz.* You had them done above and below." Why are you doing this? At your age, who cares? It's not like you're in the movies. "Did you get the laser job, too? Or did you get contacts?"

"Laser. I still need reading glasses, but it's the first time in my life I haven't worn eyeglasses all the time, can get up in the night to go to the bathroom without them. It's a miracle what they can do now."

"Hey, you're talking to the bionic woman here."

"Headaches gone?"

"Yeah, and the hearing blackouts are getting fewer and fewer. And the dizzy spells." Careful, mother of mine, we're talking about something important here without confrontation. She remembered Uncle Elmo's words and wondered if before she was even born, her relationship with Edwina had

20

been forged on the home place, where important things weren't discussed. Way weird.

"And there were geese, huge geese—used to scare the shit out of me. And this was the chicken house and this the machine shed." They were stepping over foundations, walking toward the barn. The wind grew chillier and the windmill made not a creak, but every board in the barn—only every other one was about all that was left—groaned and rasped like it was twisting, tortured.

"Had some facial hair lasered away, too, and I'm glad."

"You know, I really, really need to return a phone call, and it's Florida and I don't feel good about using Uncle Elmo's phone."

"I'm spending your and Libby's inheritance on myself."

"You don't owe us an inheritance. We're doing fine." And you've already done so much for us, dammit, I can't bring myself to just go off and leave you here. "But I sure do want to."

"Sure do want to what?"

"Nothing. Just—"

"Just talking to yourself. You know, I swear you did that the minute you could talk. Like you never bothered to learn to walk. Just took off running. Always at cross purposes, as I remember." Standing inside the barn looking at the holes in the roof and all around the walls, she added, "Sign of rebellion, I think I read somewhere."

Resenting Edwina for every affront and discomfort, Charlie had a lukewarm bath in the giant tub that had no shower (all that family dishwashing had depleted the resources of an ancient hot-water heater) and slept soundly until about midnight, when the brisk October breeze that made weeds and harvested stalks sound like an army of stealthy footsteps marching, marched into the room despite the fact that no window was open. Charlie reached down to the foot of the bed to draw up another dusty down comforter and slept until morning.

At which time Uncle Elmo had hot if weak coffee brewed, and Charlie had a piece of lemon-meringue pie for breakfast. He had mashed potatoes and a dinner roll. Edwina had coffee and a headache.

❖

"Shirley, I am sorry, but I was at a funeral—well, a graveside service—and when I finally got a chance to return your call, I was apparently too far away from a tower to use the cellular." They were approaching the stone bridge at the entrance to Myrtle, Charlie driving again. The bridge crossed a fair-sized river with that white, almost marblelike stone along its banks. "This is the first chance I've had." Jeesh, agents have families, you know. Edwina was not handling this Iowa situation at all well.

And poor Shirley Birkett was even worse off. She had been asked to speak at a writers' conference in Denver—her first book not even out yet—and had sat in on a series of panels held by independent booksellers and media and print reviewers on how to promote one's book. "I thought that's what publishers did."

By this time, Charlie's hot new author was sobbing and difficult to understand. And Myrtle was glorious in the morning sun.

"What are those trees with all the red and orange and gold leaves?" Charlie asked Edwina as softly as she could so as not to further distress the next Danielle Steel. She'd seen them in New England, too.

"Maples. Go straight here."

It seemed that authors were not only expected to get in a book a year, but must line up their own media interviews and book reviews by hounding authors who'd been interviewed to put in a word for them, must hound publishers for bound galleys—if they're not bound, they should bind them themselves. They should send chocolate and thank-you notes to all interviewers, reviewers, and independent bookstores that give them an autograph party. Oh, and send galleys early because a book is old news a week after publication and it takes a month or more to line up reviewers and then get reviews into print.

"My book's out in three weeks and nobody has sent me any galleys."

This sun-dappled, peaceful hamlet, presided over by a huge blue bulb on Granddaddy Longlegs spindles, resembled its main street at close quarters. For every well-kept and orderly lawn and house, there were two lots where the buildings had white paint peeling like at the home place—two-tone where patches of exposed wood had weathered to gray. Many corrugated-metal roofs replaced the old shingled ones, the result contradictory. Charlie didn't see any doublewides, though.

"And I should be sure to take wine and cookies and cheese to the autograph parties. And set these parties up myself by going into each independent bookstore and politely requesting a moment with the owner. And in a small town, it's a good idea to set up an interview with the local weekly newspaper first by myself. Then the bookstore can coordinate the signing. Don't expect the bookstore to line up the interview."

"What's the gaudy blue blob up there?" Charlie whispered to her mother. It had MYRTLE lettered on it.

"Water tower. Stop here a moment."

Charlie pulled over to the side of the road and realized she hadn't met or passed another moving car since she'd crossed the stone bridge. Edwina stared at a large Victorian. She was sort of biting on her knuckles, so Charlie figured her mother was dealing with still more issues. Rags of water-stained wallpaper fluttered in the breeze instead of curtains, not a shard of window glass left, windows and doors gaping wounds of eyes and mouths. It was the kind of house remnant that didn't need a ghost to be haunted. Charlie shivered and turned back to her author.

"... helps to publish a nonfiction book while I'm at it. It will increase fiction sales. And I'm supposed to fly myself all over the country. I don't have that kind of money, and if I spend all my time organizing these things, when do I research and write the next book? I don't have a life now, and I'm pregnant again."

Charlie had an acid-reflux moment. Lemon-meringue pie tasted better going down. "Well, look at it this way. It's your book. Your only one—the publisher has hundreds to worry about. Maybe you could do some things like that locally. Your publicist in New York doesn't know the review and media people there as well as you do."

"Oh, that's another thing—I should hire my own publicist. Don't count on my publisher's publicists. And Charlie, I just moved here. I don't know anybody."

"Maybe your husband could help out, free you up some at home so you could travel—figure out ways to do promotion. The best publicists in the business are often spouses because you're their only client. Shirley, you signed a great contract for a new author, and there was some stipulation for promo money."

"Well, I don't know where it went. And my husband is helping out by earning the living. Don't publishers do anything? Oh, and I should upgrade my Web page with new and interesting material at least every two weeks and write and send out my own newsletter and keep track of all fan mail and e-mail names and addresses so I can notify them of new books and signings in their area as well as participate in the numerous chat rooms available to writers on the Internet half the night."

"Consider that the publisher has given you a break hundreds of thousands of writers are waiting for by printing your novel and lending the credence of their name to give it validity. What you do with this golden opportunity is up to you.

24

You're really in business for yourself and that takes an enormous commitment."

"Charlie? I quit." And the Danielle Steel of Tampa, Florida, hung up on her agent.

"Edwina, I swear I'll never take on another book author. I'm sticking to screenwriters from now on. They usually have some clue about the reality of the industry."

"You've been saying that ever since you went to L.A. and got a big head. I liked you better in New York." Charlie's mom was beginning to sound like herself again.

Edwina had paid for Libby's childcare as well as Charlie's out-of-state college tuition and living expenses in hopes that Charlie would become a high-school English teacher. Instead, Charlie went into a low-paying editorial job in D.C., which required more subsidizing, and then on to a literary agency in Manhattan, which required a lot more subsidizing. It wasn't until Charlie was hired away by Congdon and Morse Representation in Beverly Hills that she began to pay her little family's way in the world. She owed her mother too much for comfort.

"So, is this the house where you lived with your parents?" Charlie started the Lumina.

"No, Charlie, this is the house where you were born."

Charlie let the engine die and looked again at Edwina Greene and the haunted house that didn't need a ghost.

CHAPTER 5

✦

ARE YOU TRYING to tell me that I'm from Myrtle, too? Is that why I had to come here with you?"

"In a way, Charlie. In a way."

"But you said you adopted me from an agency in Boulder."

"Just let me sort some things out. I can't believe you had no interest in this before now. At the end of this road, turn right."

Charlie'd always figured one family was complication enough in this life and hadn't been that curious about probably some poor embarrassed pregnant teenager. Charlie was a lot more interested in friends and her status among them and the allurements of life in general. Until she became a poor embarrassed pregnant teenager.

This road ended at a white rock wall resplendent in a wine-red ivy intent upon covering it completely one year soon. The crushed rock of the road narrowed to pass through a gate and beneath an ornate wrought-iron arch in which GENTLE OAKS was lettered in among curlicues and metal leaves. The crushed rock in and around Myrtle was white like the bridge at its entrance instead of rock-colored, which Charlie thought of as gray like the tombstones in Myrtle's crowded little graveyard.

Gentle Oaks, Uncle Elmo had explained, was one of the three viable businesses owned by Harvey Rochester, native son who'd returned to make good. "Smart man, but he talks funny."

Gentle Oaks, judged by its drive, should have been a fabulous mansion. It was, instead, the last stop for many before the Myrtle Cemetery. Unlike the grain elevator and the rail-road station, converted into a restaurant—the other two businesses of Harvey's—Gentle Oaks was labor-intensive and the largest employer in town. And Myrtle was lucky for it, because in most small towns around, the women had to travel to a monolithic hospital system in Mason City for work. Ice and snow storms could make that a worry.

Uncle Elmo was a wealth of information. Since Edwina had gone reticent on her again and on her place of birth, she would ask him when they got back to the home place instead of badgering the woman beside her. Charlie was never sure whether love among the three generations of her female family was really displaced fierce loyalty or loyal fierceness. Talk about dysfunctional.

Edwina could control her progress down memory lane at least long enough to confirm that the trees towering over the drive were oaks. They looked suspiciously like half of those at the cemetery. Humongous, with black bark and huge brown leaves with knobby fingers. The other half of the grave-yard's forest were maples with huge leaves and jagged fingers. The drive circled around a center island where ornate, stilled fountains had filled with leaves instead of water and stone lawn ornaments posed as if for sale—deer, racoon, bear, squirrel, duck. No plastic and no flamingoes.

The building curled a semicircle around the end of the drive opposite the island with lawn ornaments. A one-story brick, it had bright white pillars holding up the porch roof, and matching shutters at the paned windows, sort of a colonial ranch house-motel hybrid. There were French windows and doors, and the porch was lined with empty wicker lawn fur-niture, white with bright floral cushions and a scattering of brown leaves. The oaks, soaring over the place like a Disney nightmare, didn't look gentle to Charlie. Perhaps it was her mood, this being a somber place on a somber trip.

The help and service trucks must park behind the build-ing—but there were no NO PARKING signs on the drive, so

Charlie pulled up right out front behind the marshal's Jeep. Maybe his grin would lighten up her day.

The small lobby, decorated in pleasant pastels, had chairs and a couple of sofas, silk-flower arrangements, and the closed door to the administrator's office. There was no reception desk, so they opened the double doors at the back of the lobby and were met with two women rushing out—one in a wheelchair—and the overriding stench of human feces and the startling blare of an alarm. When they turned back into the lobby to get a breath of air, the wheelchair lady grinned a mouth missing half its teeth and took a magazine from one of the end tables.

Cousin Helen was next through the door. "Oh, it's only you, Gladys." She turned back inside and held the door open to reach behind it and the alarm blessedly silenced. "Sorry about this," she told Edwina. "It's just nuts today. And tonight's the full moon."

"Should we not have opened the door?" Charlie asked.

"It's not you gals. It's Gladys and her ankle bracelet that set off the alarm."

Gladys had a lovely head of gray-streaked hair and a leg in a knee cast, extended out in front of her on a sort of plank. Her other leg was bent at the knee, that foot on a foot rest, and around its ankle she wore a black band with an oblong box on it. She grinned even wider and as Cousin Helen turned away from her, slipped her magazine up her skirt and reached for another. "I have three boyfriends, honey, how about you?"

"There was another woman slipped through with Gladys," Charlie said.

"Oh, shit."

"We got plenty of that." Gladys clapped her hands and drool slid down over her chin. Her glasses were so dusty it was a wonder she could see. "We're gonna have fun today. It was Marlys."

"Where's that no-good Delwood when you need him?"

"His Jeep's outside," Charlie offered.

"That, I know." Helen wore white polyester pants with a blue-flowered smock almost to the knees.

"Not Marlys Dittberner?" Edwina said. "That was—"

"The very one. Welcome home, cuz." She opened the doors to let the smell out into the lobby and yelled, "Darlene, tell old Delwood to get his sweet ass out here fast."

"How can you stand it?" Charlie asked, breathing through her fingers.

"I can't believe it, Marlys Dittberner. Still alive," Edwina said.

"Oh, the smell? You get used to it. And it's worse in the morning. You got what, eighty filled adult night diapers to change? And we're fully staffed. Think what it's like out in the real world where women and junkies can get paying jobs." Cousin Helen looked like herself but didn't sound like the woman Charlie met in the church basement and ate dinner with last night. "We're usually spiffied up by nine, ten in the morning. After-lunch bowel movements are a lot less trouble. Staff can often get them on the potty chair in time. We're talking full-grown infants here, you know."

"I am a kid around here, you have to understand." The marshal of Myrtle was trying to explain to Charlie why he got no respect from Cousin Helen. They drove the streets of Myrtle looking for Marlys. "I am a forty-five-year-old kid. Kids get no respect in Myrtle."

"Even if they dig your grave and plow your streets and arrest speeders and protect your home and—"

"Nah, kids owe them that much, and hey, I even get paid for what I owe them anyway. Sweet deal all around. But, I tell ya, Charlie, I'm a little shocked you went off and left your mother back at the Oaks that way. I was only kidding about needing help looking for Marlys. Your mom seemed kind of stressed out, as in totally destroyed."

"I can't help her. She won't talk to me about anything

important. Show's me a house that looks straight out of Kosovo and tells me I was born there after telling me all my life that I was adopted at an agency in Boulder. And then clams on me. Won't explain the discrepancy."

"She might have good reason."

"I don't even know why I'm here. And it's not like we don't both have lots to do at home."

He rolled the windows down and stopped the Jeep. "Man, you're steamed. Hey, Kenny, looking for Marlys. You seen her?"

And this tall guy, must have been six foot four with a weight lifter's chest and biceps, leaned against the marshal's door and bent down to look inside. He had a jaw, and his teeth flashed in a smile that left his eyes cynical. "Marlys. Not again. Del, you're going to have to take charge of that loony bin and establish order up there. What kinda lawman are you? Who's your friend?"

"This is Charlie Greene—"

"As in?"

"Yeah. Charlie, this here's Kenny Cowper."

"As in Viagra?"

"I live on the stuff."

"Does it help?" Charlie asked politely.

"Whew. Better keep the windows down or this heap's toast. I'll spread the word on Marlys."

" 'This is Charlie Greene as in' what?" Charlie demanded as Kenny Cowper walked off. He wore a forest-green sweatshirt, Levi's, and dark hair with an excellent cut. He was one of those guys who could look at you and leave residue.

"He was insinuating you were hot enough to burn up this here vehicle."

"That part I got, Delwood. My question stands."

"Well, it's not like your visit was unexpected, you know."

"It was to me. I barely got tickets and they cost the earth. And explain to me how, in a place where no one discusses things that are important, does news like my visit get around?"

"You know, I've always wondered that myself." Del wore a red-and-blue-plaid shirt with sleeves rolled up and Dockers. His hair was sort of a medium brown with a couple of gray streaks.

"There, that's the house she was talking about. Slow down."

"I know." He stepped on the gas. "But we're looking for Marlys."

"What do you mean you know? What do you know?"

"I know it's pheasant season and there's gonna be loose ammunition flying around and I want to find Marlys before a stray bullet does. That's what I know."

"Why did my mother's Great-aunt Abigail point me out as the reason for Gertie's death? And my mom tell me Abigail is why we came to Myrtle? And my mother, who never cries, has done nothing but since we got here?"

"It's family, Charlie. No explaining it, but it's the most powerful force for good and evil too. Probably because it goes deeper than the sinkholes around this town."

"Myrtle has sinkholes? Is that why the dirt sucks?"

"This is the best dirt in the world. You can grow a full-grown tree in ten years. We don't really have sinkholes. Lots of old wells cave in and there was rock mined and then filled over to grow crops. Pays to watch children around here, though."

"You have a family?"

"Divorced. Three kids. She got everything—kids, house, car, bank account. Fine with me—she's the better parent."

"You have parents?"

"Now them I got in spades. I got my parents and three of their parents." He pulled over at a railroad trestle when a man in overalls like Uncle Elmo's came running at the Jeep.

"Looking for Marlys? Just spotted her heading down the alley toward the house." He looked across Del at Charlie. "That—?"

"Yeah. Thanks, Ben. Looks like you get your wish after all, Charlie Greene." And, siren blaring, they did a U and headed back down the road, screeching to a stop in front of the haunted house that didn't need a ghost.

CHAPTER 6

---❖---

"W HY'D YOU NEED the siren? There wasn't a car or pedestrian in sight."

"To impress a pretty woman? See if it still works? Uh-uh, none of that. Not that smile again. More lethal than a tanked-up pheasant hunter."

They were walking toward "the house," Charlie having ignored orders to stay in the Jeep. "Was I really born here?"

"That's not for me to say."

"Maybe I should ask Marlys."

"Oh, jeez, I'm not touching that sucker. Now you stay out here. Floors are rotted."

Following close on his heels, Charlie asked, "If I wouldn't stay in the car, why would I stay out of the house? Was this a whorehouse?"

"Woman ought to have more respect for the law," he muttered, turning to face her. "Can you really imagine a whore-house in the middle of Myrtle, Iowa?"

Over his shoulder, she looked into the eyes of an ancient hag with long, snow-white hair and a bright pink scalp. Charlie was looking into Libby Abigail Greene's eyes and her own, too.

"She's in there, I can tell by how you just lost your tan. Don't make a move."

"She has my eyes."

"No, you have her eyes."

"Is she my birth mother? My daughter has those eyes, too." Charlie suddenly had to pee.

"She's well over a hundred years old. You figure out the math on that one. Now stay quiet. I'm going to turn around very slowly so as not to scare her. Marlys, I've come to take you home, honey." He turned very slowly, which gave Marlys the chance to vanish.

"Nobody well over a hundred years old can move that fast." Charlie picked her way across a ruined floor in a ruined house. She felt sweaty all over. Blood sugar? That had been a problem since the accident. She'd had to learn how to snack. The fat cells on her thighs just loved it.

Charlie commuted from home in Long Beach to the agency in Beverly Hills, and one day last spring, a semi had jumped the median on the 405. Twelve people and Charlie's Toyota died. Charlie didn't.

"I don't know how she does it." Myrtle's marshal put his hands on his hips and turned a full circle, eyes searching floor, what ceiling there was, and out the extreme-open windows. "Marlys? Honey?"

"Maybe when you're well over a hundred, you don't want to be called honey."

"Yeah, too much sweet stuff, huh? Hey, you old bat. Bitty, bitty, bitty. Get your diapered ass over here this minute."

Charlie started laughing and then thought better of it.

"That didn't work either. I—hey, you okay?"

"I need food and a powder room fast. But not in that order."

Charlie was back in the Cherokee and headed toward the railroad tracks in seconds. Good thing Marlys didn't decide to cross the road.

Next to the grain elevator and mountains of shelled corn sitting all around it was The Station. An old brick railroad station right out of Norman Rockwell that had been turned into a restaurant. Charlie left the ladies' room feeling in control of her world again and had to walk through the bar to get back to Marshal Delwood, waiting at the cash register. A boy-man with a toddler on his lap, two men at the bar, and the bartender watched a sport thing on the huge TV. Everybody but the toddler and the bartender sucked on a beer.

Back at the cash register, this tall, thin woman in leisure-fit jeans and low-necked blouse laid her cigarette down in the ashtray, picked up two menus, and rasped, "Smoking or non?"

"Non," Charlie answered automatically.

"You'll be sorry." Delwood Brunsvold chuckled low and dirty.

"Do you smoke? I didn't even think."

The hostess lady led them past tables with padded captains' chairs and checkered tablecloths, stained-glass windows and outdoor carpet, past buffet steam tables to a cold, dark, windowless area way at the back, crowded with cheap metal tables, folding card-table chairs, and highchairs. Kids ran between tables on a chipped tile floor with what appeared to be mashed potatoes on their hands and chocolate pudding around their mouths and in their hair. And the smell of dirty diapers.

"I'm not hungry." Charlie backed away from a grinning brat and into the marshal of Myrtle.

"Yes you are. We'll take a table up front in the sun of a window, and the buffet, please."

"Right you are, Del. Coffee?"

"Do you have lattés?"

"Nope. But you can pour cream in it and hiss a lot if it'll make you feel better. Is this—?"

"Just pour coffee and orange juice fast and stop being a smartass, okay?"

"Whatever you say, Officer Sweetle."

"Officer Sweetle?" The orange juice was half sugar additive and certainly not fresh-squeezed, but Charlie felt better in minutes. They sat at a table for two in the light of a stained-glass window. "What's that noise?"

"Church bells. We got here just in time before the church crowd. Sunday brunch, Charlie Greene. You can have lunch or breakfast or both." He leaned closer and frowned, sat back and considered. "Those teeth can't be real. I heard about your accident. Are those caps or dentures? Don't worry—whatever they are, they light up the room."

"Edwina was into orthodontists when I grew up. Hated it then, love it now. You do know how to make a woman feel good, don't you?"

"Let's get some food in you before you turn my head, okay?"

"What about Marlys and the pheasant hunters?"

"She'll keep for a while longer. I'm the law and I say we move."

"How did you know about my accident? There're people living on my street in Long Beach who don't know who I am." But even Charlie forgot her question when faced with the salad bars and steam tables at The Station.

You could get cabbage or macaroni or potatoes in your mayonnaise at the salad bar. The rest was Jell-O with fruit, canned fruit cocktail, or cold peas and cheese cubes with mayonnaise. Or you could top off a wilted piece of iceberg lettuce with chicken salad, ham salad, or egg salad in mayonnaise.

For breakfast, there were scrambled eggs, sausage, bacon, potatoes, waffles, pancakes, and cinnamon rolls. For lunch, creamed soup, bean soup, scalloped potatoes, mashed potatoes, fried chicken, fried fish, barbequed ribs, dinner rolls, overcooked mixed vegetables floating in butter sauce, and at the very end—well-done roast beef au jus and ham and a guy to slice them as you wanted.

Charlie went through the line with an empty plate and went back to start over. She selected small amounts of egg salad, hashbrowns, a dinner roll and a slice of ham. The dessert table across the room on the way back offered apple pie, pecan pie, and carrot cake—she didn't count the kinds. Del was already seated before a heaped plate and scrutinized her choices. She ordered a glass of milk to go with the coffee.

"I get it. You're diabetic."

"No, just not used to all the mayo and fried stuff. You should have seen the dinner last night at the home place. And I was on a lot of drugs after the accident. It's taking my system a while to get over them. *And* fat's about as popular as gray hair in Hollywood." She'd forgotten how good mayonnaise tasted. "So where are the ex and the kids?"

"Des Moines."

"Ah, you did leave home and go to the big city."

"Oh, yeah. Iowa State, Des Moines, family—and then everything went bust and I came home. I love it here. I get to play Marshal, look for Marlys, talk to dead folks out at the cemetery, got two snowmobiles, hunt pheasants, look for Marlys, play with my snowplow—it's just a dump truck with a blade on the front but it's really big, makes lots of noise."

"And be Officer Sweetle, too. What more could a man want?"

They were trying to ignore a woman at the next table who couldn't extricate herself from the captain's chair. Finally, Delwood went over to hold the chair down. "Now you push with your arms, Mrs. Lansky. They just don't make these things big enough."

"Guess I'll have to go on a diet," she said ruefully.

Mr. Lansky, skinny of course, stared at the ceiling. The girl with them sat on a folding chair from the nonsmoking pit. More of her hung over each side than rested on the seat.

"Do you eat here often?" Charlie asked Del when he sat down again.

The hostess had the captain's chair moved against the wall and a folding chair replacing it before Mrs. Lansky returned with her second helping.

"Well, Station's only open evenings and for brunch on Sunday. There's a little café in the schoolhouse for breakfast and lunch every day but Sunday. I eat with my folks now and then. And Viagra's is open for lunch and dinner every day." He glanced over at the double backsides at the Lansky table. "Maybe I won't have that piece of pecan pie after all."

"How can such a small town support all these eateries?"

"The Station draws from the towns around and the farms—what's left of them. So does Viagra's, and the population's aging fast here. Women get to be a certain age and have some money, they don't want to cook anymore. And there's no McDonald's this side of Mason City."

"Are any of your people at Gentle Oaks?" Charlie asked as they stepped outside.

"Two grandparents and a great-aunt."

"That why you were up there this morning?"

"No, as a matter of fact." He pulled out his cell phone. "Better see if the coroner's shown yet. Had another death last night."

Charlie took the opportunity to check her own voice mail. A call from Larry, her assistant at the office. One from Mitch Hilsten, superstar. And one from Libby Abigail Greene, who never would have had that middle name if Charlie had met its origin.

Libby's was a simple, "Hi, Mom, everything's fine here. Just wondering how you and Grandma are doing in Iowa. And *what* you and Grandma are doing in Iowa. Have fun, love ya."

That kid had been nothing but trouble since her conception—and yet that voice alone could bring a constriction to the back of Charlie's throat that took her breath away. That kid was a senior in high school and would soon fly the nest. Charlie so wanted to be there, not here.

Charlie's hair was sort of a light bronze and uncontrollably curly. Libby's was platinum-blonde and straight, but both drew looks of surprise when they took off their sunglasses around strangers—their eyes were dark, almost black. Like Marlys Dittberner's.

CHAPTER 7

✦

"D O YOU ALWAYS call the coroner when someone dies at Gentle Oaks?" Charlie asked the marshal. They were driving around looking for Marlys again. "I mean, isn't a nursing home where people go to die?"

"First time since I been marshal, I've called the coroner for anything. But you have to understand that the Oaks is not your regular nursing home. And it's the only place in town that's got more business than it can handle. They've had to send people to Mason City because there just weren't any more beds."

"Frankly, with the diet and exercise regime around here, I'm surprised anyone lives long enough to get to Gentle Oaks."

"It's a mystery, for sure. People go in there at death's door but don't die. For years and years, they don't die. Lose a lot of weight. Had the water tested. Didn't show anything."

"Do they get better?"

"No, they just stay at death's door."

"For years and years. Doesn't make sense. People like Mrs. Lansky and her daughter can't—"

"They're from Floyd."

"Oh."

"Anyway, at the Oaks, we got more people over a hundred than anyone wants to admit. Bad for business, you know. And thirty or so of them—we got at least one of their children there, too. People just don't die there—until lately. Abigail Staudt isn't the only one wondering what's going on. We've gone eight years without a death up there, and in the last month there's been five, counting old Annie last night."

"Any similarity in the infirmities of those who died?" Charlie couldn't quite believe his story, but was worried enough about her own aging and dreading her mother's to not want to contemplate later generations.

"Oh, yeah. Vegetables, every one. Course we got a lot of those at the Oaks."

"My mother's Uncle Elmo says he doesn't doubt there's murder happening up there."

"Eight years without a death in a nursing home is unheard of, impossible. But follow that with five in a month is suspicious. According to insurance companies wanting to sell people like my folks long-term health-care policies, two years in a nursing home is usually it. Tell that to somebody in Myrtle. You have to understand, Charlie, most people in this town are in their mid-sixties to late seventies and most of them have folks at the Oaks, some more than one generation. Touchy subject here."

"How are they dying?"

"Suffocation, or what looks like it—which can be of natural causes or not. And yes, we've called for an investigation into every member of the staff. Not unknown for someone dealing with that situation every day to feel sorry for those who suffer."

"The pillow-over-the-face technique. My writers have worked that old saw to death. So, how about your folks?"

"They both look like Mrs. Lansky and her daughter. Live from one meal to the next and butter better be butter and milk better be cream. My brother and his wife are the same way. Drove my wife nuts, but I don't worry about it. When they go to the Oaks, they'll slim down a lot and they'll never die."

"Unless Marshal Brunsvold fails to solve the sudden primordial death-syndrome caper. Wow, who lives there?"

"Harvey Rochester himself. Quite a man, our Harvey. Except he talks funny. And right next door is where I live. Not as fancy, but a lot less maintenance."

Both houses sat on lots like you'd put apartment buildings on in Long Beach. Del's house was small, square, one-story smack in the center of the lot, plus flagpole with flag waving, some trees, and a few sheds at the back. Two snowmobiles sat up toward the street like lawn ornaments with mowed weeds for a lawn. It was the last house before the cornfields began.

Harvey's house stood in the front of the lot, with a screened porch on each side and curved windows at each corner upstairs and down, and an open formal porch between them. Two stories, with high ceilings and an attic by the looks of it, and probably a basement, the house extended back quite a way. There was a lot of room, but it was the curved corner windows that caught the eye. The house and the outbuildings were of that white-painted wood with the gray beginning to weather through in spots.

"Your accident didn't leave any dents or permanent injuries at all? You don't even have a limp."

"Didn't I tell you? I'm the bionic woman now. So why is it I and my daughter have Marlys Dittberner's eyes?"

"Charlie, you've got to understand, people here don't talk about things like that." He turned the Cherokee around and started back down the street. There were lots of houses on big lots with snowmobiles for lawn ornaments, she noticed now.

"Then how come everybody knows these things? Everybody but me."

"You kind of find out things that nobody talks about by rumor, hints, innuendos, and such—piece them together over the years and end up knowing what everybody else knows by living here. But direct questions will just get you put off. People aren't direct about some kinds of things in small towns—important things, scary ones, embarrassing things, intensely personal things, family things. Or stuff that could cause un-

41

known results. People are cautious. This is Myrtle, not Minneapolis."

"I don't live here. I don't have years to find out anything."

"What's this bionic woman business? You have mechanical parts—powerful ones?"

"That is a very direct, personal, important, and potentially scary question. How can you ask it?"

"Because you don't live here. You're not one of us."

"Then why do I have Marlys' eyes?"

"Because she's your great—" Marshal Delwood was saved by his cellular. Marlys had been sighted on the road to the cemetery. He switched on the siren and floored the pedal.

"Don't you think that might scare her? The siren? Or at least alert her?"

He turned it off and slowed down. "I get carried away. It's so much fun being marshal."

"I'd hate to be out when you're plowing the streets."

"You sound like my mother."

"Great what?"

"Great-grandmother. And you did not hear that from me."

"I heard a rumor on the wind, or was it an innuendo?"

Nothing in Myrtle is far from anything else, which still did not explain how Marlys could move so fast, but they were already at the gates of the dark little graveyard with the sucking soil.

"Wouldn't it be better if we parked here and walked in? Less threatening for her?"

He stopped the red Jeep under the entrance arch that announced they were entering the MYRTLE CEMETERY. "Okay, bionic Charlie, you call the shots. Your way isn't as much fun as mine, you know."

The marshal grabbed his cellular, Charlie her purse, and they slid to the ground without slamming the car doors. They walked to the sides of the white-rock-graveled one-lane drive into the shade and still-gliding dead leaves. Maple leaves, because of those finger jags, catch on your clothes and hair. They also make it impossible to sneak because once fallen, they crunch right along with the oak leaves.

"There she is," Charlie whispered and pointed to the lone standing figure ahead whose hair blew in the wind. The rest were tombstones. "Don't call her honey, okay?"

This guy was no rocket scientist but he was endearing and fun—he grimaced, wrinkled his nose at her, and gave her the bird.

And then his cellular went off and he was just another guy. "Got to go, coroner's at the Oaks," he whispered, Charlie thought, with somewhat unnecessary jubilance. "You're running this show. You keep track of her till I get back. Don't let your great-grandmother out of your sight. Meanwhile, I'll check on your mother for you." The dork stuck out his tongue but backed the Cherokee away with proper decorum.

Her supposed great-grandmother (Charlie didn't trust marshals or anyone named Delwood, no matter how cute) watched her careful approach without pulling a disappearing act, pulling out a long knife, or an ax even.

At close range, Marlys's eyes were rheumy and full of veins. Charlie wondered how much they could see without eyeglasses. Charlie wore contact lenses to see the ancient woman at all. And she had the odd feeling that she could be more vulnerable than this creature somewhere from her past who knew the secret innuendos, hints, and rumors of generations of people who didn't discuss that which was too important to trust. She studied Charlie from head to toe and before turning away, declared, "Top dollar, just like I foretold. Too bad."

"Does that mean I'm related to you? Have some value?"

"Course not. But we're both related to Gertie here." They stood side by side at Great-aunt Gertie's grave—Gertrude Staudt—where the rich, hungry dirt was so newly turned it trembled. With insects? Worms? Charlie's overactive imagination? She'd had vision aberrations since the accident, which often meant the onset of a migraine, but few since the titanium plate had been implanted in her neck. "God, I want to go home."

"Be careful what you ask for." The shaky finger of the creature beside Charlie pointed at the fresh dirt at their toes. "Gertie said the same thing, over and over and over. And got her wish." There was a live brain behind that statement, and that was possibly scarier than the vomit comet taking two passes to land at the Mason City airport because of wind turbulence on the runway. "You wear your pants that tight, honey, you'll cut off your female rhythms. Skirts are better." She raised hers, dropped her soiled diapers, stepped out of them, and squatted on Gertie to pee forever and sighed. "So good to be out of that place. You won't try to take me back, will you? Why would you have that right?"

"But you'd be warm and fed—"

"And dead at the Oaks. I don't mind being dead out here." Several oak leaves had caught in her flowing hair like dried flowers. She was stick-thin, her dress hung on her, reached to mid-calf. She wore a pink sweater to match her scalp, and tennies with anklets, one white and one green. Now that the diaper was gone, Charlie was sure that was all she wore.

"Tell me about Gertie."

"There was four sisters, Gertrude, Abigail, and Annabel. Augusta died of scarlet fever as a wee child."

"Annabel was Annie." Charlie shivered.

Marlys nodded. She didn't appear chilly at all. She just trembled from age. "Now, there's one."

"Abigail."

"They was beautiful and proud and pure. Never married. Just broke hearts right and left. Couldn't find nobody pure enough for 'em. Become quite a burden on nieces and nephews' wives. Course, pure is how you look at it. What you know." She cackled. Her lower bridge was gone, but she spoke clearly without it.

"Big family."

"Oh, yeah. Staudts tried to populate the whole town. Except for the sisters, they bred like mice. The sisters all become schoolmarms and all taught at the school. Ruled the place. Almost ruled the town. Railed against bootlegging and fornication." Marlys raised her arms toward the sky, hidden behind the towering trees and their dead and dying leaves. "They was so righteous everybody waited for a rumor, maybe even a truth, they could find disgusting. Mind, nobody came out and said that."

This old woman was breaking the unspoken law in Myrtle, Iowa, about keeping the unspeakable unspoken. She was leading her quarry away from Gertie's grave and the soiled diaper. They moved from shade to shadow to deeper shadow. Charlie seriously wouldn't want to be caught here at night without a flashlight. The gravestones from all different time periods and of all different shapes and sizes were a dark gray except for that odd encroaching moss and the white lambs of the children's graves where, strangely, no moss grew.

"Marlys, you and I have very similar eyes. Why is that? Am I descended from a Dittberner?"

"That's my married name." The old black eyes turned knowing and amused. "We all bred like mice, truth be known. Three, four families in this whole town made it what it is. Most was Germans, Norwegians, and the Cowpers. Too much inbreeding makes for strange history."

"What about Harvey Rochester?"

"His mother was a Cowper. His father was a Rochester."

"Who was Myrtle?"

"You're standing on her. See for yourself."

45

CHAPTER 8

✦

M YRTLE WAS ALL the name on the stone. It was the bent-over, tall, oblong slab rounded at the top that Charlie had ducked behind, embarrassed when her cellular had gone off. "She died before the Civil War."

"Old town. Old graveyard. Old people. So sue us."

"Was she kind of like a founding mother?"

"You could say that. If you couldn't think of a better reason."

"She was only eighteen when she died." Libby's age, gulp.

"People didn't use to live to retire and beyond and beyond some more in them days."

"Marlys, do you think there's a murderer up at Gentle Oaks killing the helpless?" Charlie had jumped off the grave when the old woman told her she was standing on Myrtle, actually jumped up off the grave because it was quite an indentation. Not surprising when you thought of how long ago it was filled with Myrtle and then with sucking dirt. The reason the stone was bent over could possibly be the bare tree root crossing just in front of it—probably right over Myrtle's head.

Charlie decided to think of other things, until the ancient Marlys Dittberner said, "Whole place is a contract with the devil. Most folks won't even come up and visit you there because they know their time's coming next. It's our curse, the devil's dram. It's spreading, I hear—but it's always been this way in Myrtle. You look at the dates on these stones, girl. People live long here. Myrtle, she left a curse on this town—

46

been dying since she was murdered, but can't die. You ought to take your mother and get out of here while you can. Them that stay are doomed."

"But how do you explain Del Brunsvold coming back to his roots here? And Kenny Cowper?"

Marlys Dittberner kicked daintily at the bare oak root above Myrtle's head and looked directly at Charlie. "Dumb explains most folks if you think on it too long."

Charlie was about to ask how Myrtle was murdered when the mewling in her purse distracted her just long enough to lose Marlys again. To regular people who were not tone deaf, it might have sounded like music, but to Charlie it sounded like a sick cat, extreme sick. It was Mitch Hilsten, big-deal superstar.

"My God, Charlie, I've been trying to get you for two days. What are you doing?"

"Looking for Marlys. If I were a writer, I'd have a ball with this place."

"What place?"

"Myrtle, Iowa. Edwina and I are looking into the welfare of seriously ancient relatives."

"Charlie, tell me no one's been murdered in Myrtle."

"Myrtle for one."

Charlie roamed among tombstones and indentations that had been people checking out the dates on the stones and looking for Marlys while Mitch Hilsten explained why he'd hardly be out of town for his new project because most of it was interiors and much of the exteriors could be shot on the lot or in redwood forests in California.

"Tell me you didn't take on Bambo, please? That's so corny." Why didn't he get engaged to some vacuous starlet again and leave Charlie alone?

"Hey, deer are popular and they are everywhere. What's the matter with Bambo?"

"Mitch, you know deer aren't aggressive unless they're in

47

rut. You're a conservationist." He wasn't dangerous in rut even. But he was good.

"Birds weren't either until Hitchcock got ahold of them."

"Talk to you later. Busy now. Bye."

"Charlie? Be careful. It's not only the full moon, but your vulnerable time of the month."

"Pervert." She hung up and looked for Marlys, who was plenty strange herself. The sucking dirt was after Charlie's boots again.

Bartusek, Sievertsen, Wyborny, Auchmoody, Hogoboom, Fellwoek, Longbotham, Enabnit, Nimglet, Talgoth, Bublitz, Streblow, Stubbe, Overgaard, Truex. All kinds of people here who weren't Cowpers or Staudts or Norwegian, either. Lots more than three or four families for sure represented here. Marlys was nuts. Charlie went back to the Staudts' section—it was pronounced "stout"—and the dirty diaper which supported the idea that Marlys lacked screws, and then started looking for Edwina's parents. But she couldn't remember their first names. Edwina had mentioned them by name surely in Charlie's youth, or was it just Mom and Dad?

So she started looking for Marlys again without much hope, wandering among the dead in the dark under the trees until she got so depressed she gave up and headed back to town and Gentle Oaks. She saw a couple, whose butts would never fit on an airplane in the coach class, raking leaves in their front yard. They nodded as she passed. Many, if not most, of the people she saw at the cemetery and church yesterday were not obese, many quite slim. It was just that those who were heavy were so unbelievably enormous—they were the unforgettable ones, and you went away remembering only them.

The sun was warm enough away from the Myrtle Cemetery that Charlie hooked her leather jacket over her shoulder by a thumb and enjoyed the colors and lack of people and traffic. There's a lot to be said for a small town. *Was* it only the job opportunities that drove the young to the cities? Or the guilt thing as well?

Because of her teen pregnancy and her father's heart attack and death before Libby's birth, Charlie had lived a life drowned with guilt. But she was beginning to get an inkling here in Myrtle, Iowa, as to how heavy a guilt load could really get—especially for previous generations caught up in old ways. The shunning could come about simply because you got above yourself, dared to step out of the prescribed pecking order. Edwina—a strong, competent, often grating woman—could be reduced to childhood helplessness by a look back here at the place of her roots. Even after years of ignoring those roots and Myrtle, even after having formed her own life, family, career.

Myrtle was beautiful today, despite sizable shoddy patches of neglect, and had been yesterday, too. Edwina had rarely spoken of Iowa that Charlie could remember, but when she did, it had been with a shudder and often about relentless, bug-ridden, smothering humidity and heat in summer and bone-chilling cold in winter. Charlie's mom had three fingers on one hand that would turn white on the ends when they got cold just putting away frozen groceries. She never tired of telling Charlie it was caused by frostbite from walking to school in an Iowa winter wearing heavy mittens, while Charlie ran off to school bareheaded without gloves or boots because fashionable kids didn't wear jerky stuff. Charlie lived only a block and a half from her grade school, for godsake.

She passed a derelict Solemn Lutheran Church that looked rather cheerful with the sun shining through all the holes and the bright colors of the maples around it.

She could hear footsteps behind her on the white rock drive to Gentle Oaks, but didn't turn and look. With any luck, poor, demented Marlys Dittberner had been curious enough to follow her.

But when she reached the white columns holding up the porch roof, it was the deep and unmistakable voice of Kenny Cowper behind her that said, "I'll say one thing for you Auchmoodys—you sure know how to move right in a pair of jeans."

Charlie's gut knew a dangerous man when her eyes saw one, ears heard one. An if-it-looks-too-good-to-be-true-it-probably-is kind of thing. Her inner voice reminded her of what Mitch Hilsten had said a short time ago—she was particularly vulnerable right now and it had little to do with the full moon, but a lot to do with her female rhythms, as Marlys put it. There were certain times of certain months when Charlie didn't go out at night. And it wasn't only to protect herself.

He held the outer door for her and she stepped in, but he didn't follow. She turned to see him facing the drive with hands on hips. He appeared to be breathing deeply. It wasn't until she'd crossed the lobby that she realized he too had Charlie's, Libby's, and Marlys's almost black eyes. Was one of Charlie's progenitors a Cowper? But his hair was so dark—brown, not black, but dark—and he had a pronounced widow's peak. Inbreeding? Different traits appear? Could inbreeding explain the unreasonably long-lived people here even when they're at death's door?

Charlie carefully opened the inner door this time, nobody flew out and no alarm startled the quiet of the place. Now the odor was of cooked food rather than what it would become later. She'd turned toward a nurses' station when a clanking sounded behind her and a raspy voice said, "Got a match?"

Something hard poked the middle of her back. "No."

"Got a cigarette?"

"No." Nobody would have a gun in a nursing home, would they? Sure what it felt like.

"You smoke?"

"No." Charlie whirled to find a small man pointing a cane at her.

"Can I borrow a cigarette?"

"I don't have any. I don't smoke. Now leave me alone."

He wore overalls way too short for him and a shapeless

pinstripe suit jacket that looked like gangster-era Chicago. So did his hat. And shapeless slippers with white socks. His ankles were enormous.

"Well, you don't have to get nasty about it." The clanking started up again the minute he did. "Tart."

"Sherman, you get back here with that silverware." An RN, by her badge, came around the curve in the hallway and passed Charlie to grab his arm. "Hi. You must be the girl from L.A. Come on in the dining room. Got to unload his socks."

"The silverware?"

"Yeah. Wouldn't mind so much but he steals the dirty stuff off the trays before we can get to it. Before I went into nursing, I used to work in a preschool and believe me, it was easier than this."

"Is he an Auchmoody or a Dittberner or—"

"Sherman's a Rochester—and a disgusting one. This is awful, old man. Look at your socks. Ought to be ashamed of yourself."

"Ciga-riga-roo?" A florid lady howled from across the room—the only person left except for the busboy who came to put Sherman's stolen goods in a pan with water.

"Harvey's father?"

"Grandfather. His father blew his own head off with a hunting rifle out in a field. Very moody, the Rochesters. Isn't that right, Sherman?"

"Head was all over the place," Sherman said gleefully. His ankles had shrunk to sticks.

"Like in *Jane Eyre*?"

"Never heard it. That in Iowa?" Her badge identified her as Mary Lou Hogoboom. Her butt wouldn't fit in coach either.

"Ciga-riga-roooo?"

"Off to see the wizaaard." A large-screen TV hung from the ceiling in one corner. Only the busboy paid attention to

51

Judy Garland skipping down the yellow brick road with men dressed like animal, tin, and straw.

"I was looking for my mother—Edwina."

"I know. She and Helen are around here somewhere. All the aides are busy getting the residents off their potty chairs and down for naps right now. I have to smoke Flo and Sherman and me. Come with us and I'll show you where they might be. Or we'll come across somebody who knows."

The smoker was a glassed-in porch at the back of the building, heated in winter, with screens all around to air it out. There were several windows along the hall here looking down on loading docks and employee parking. There must be a walkout basement below at least this section of the building. Edwina, Cousin Helen, Marshal Del, and Kenny Cowper stood watching a gurney with a covered figure on it get its legs folded so it could slide into a Floyd County Sheriff's Department van. Great-aunt Annabel, no doubt.

CHAPTER 9

✦ ——

*C*OUSIN HELEN, CHARLIE, and Edwina stood in the hall gazing into the smoker, mostly at Kenny Cowper, who squatted next to a woman in a wheelchair. She puffed on a cigarette in one hand and patted him on the head with the other. Even squatting, he was taller than she was in her wheelchair and she had to reach up to pat him.

"That his mother?" Charlie asked.

"Grandmother," Helen said with a sniff. "Mother remarried when his dad got run over by a combine. She moved off to Florida. Can you imagine?"

"Yes, absolutely," Charlie's mom answered. "Definitely absolutely."

The residents may have been shuffled off of potty chairs to their beds for naps, but it seemed that televisions were tuned to blasting in every room up and down the hall. Helen explained that it helped the inmates feel less alone. "They don't really hear it, and it helps the staff with a pretty dreary job, too."

Something tugged at Charlie's jacket sleeve and she looked down to see Gladys and her extended leg and wheelchair. "He's one of my five boyfriends." She pointed to Kenny, who turned to look at them all standing there admiring him. He winked at Gladys and turned back to his grandmother. "See? Told you, didn't I? We talk dirty together. How many boyfriends do you have?"

"Not a one, Gladys. I stand in awe of you."

"Least you can stand."

"Edwina, I keep telling you, Iowa's not so bad—just your memory of it. Our memories do not improve with age, you know. And you look wonderful, but we both know you aren't getting any younger."

"If Iowa is so wonderful, why do you and Buz go to Tucson for three months during the winter?"

"Because I have to get away from this and you-know-who or go nuts. It's not Iowa. And we've raised four children. It's time for us now."

There was a growling behind them and everybody but Gladys turned when a pretty young aide in tears shouted, "Fatty Staudt and Fatty Truex are at it again. I quit."

"Disgusting old geezers," Gladys pronounced the two grinning, skeletal men racing after the young aide in their wheelchairs by paddling with their feet on the floor rather than rolling the wheels with their hands. "I don't know what they see in her, do you?"

"Your mom and Helen are sort of the last of the female line in the responsible generation, them responsible for the last generation and all before that," Uncle Elmo explained to Charlie as Cousin Helen and Edwina fought it out in the kitchen at the home place. "All you folks who go off to California, or whose parents do, don't know what's going on back at the home places in the country. What's happening is the old folks are stacking up knee-deep, what's happening."

They kicked around, literally, inside the rickety barn, stirred up mice and dust and probably memories for him and her mother, who was too busy fending off guilt and cousins to enjoy them. Charlie was beginning to see why she was needed here. Edwina needed her help in a gargantuan struggle with guilt instilled in a childhood so long ago that she couldn't remember half of it. But the residue clung like Kenny Cowper.

"Every generation—" Uncle Elmo looked up at disgruntled pigeons in the rafters and the sky between the roof that

54

was there and the roof that wasn't "—people live longer and more of them live longer. Always been people over a hundred—just damn few."

"But all those women here at the dinner last night, surely they don't need Edwina, too. They live here. She hasn't for years."

"They all got other branches of older Staudts and in-laws to see to. Your mom and Helen are all that's left of the direct issue of the Myrtle Staudts."

"Why does it have to be women? Look at the marshal."

"Doesn't have to be women, but they're more likely to live long enough to see the older generations cared for properly. They're also more responsible as a general rule for seeing to the needs of others."

"And more responsive to the agonies of guilt if they don't."

"Imagine a California girl learning about real life. Miracle. Women don't do what's expected, they don't get to enjoy life anyway—might as well knuckle under. And the marshal went off and left a wife and three children when his folks were and are still seeing to the past generations. Plus which, he's got a sister-in-law in town."

"So what's Edwina's guilt-ridden role in all this family stuff?"

"Someone's got to see to Abigail. And nobody wants anything to do with her and her bossy piety. Spent the last sixty years making enemies of her family and the town. Helen's got her hands full with me and a bunch of Staudts at the Oaks. Time your mother took on her fair share."

"She works full time, what can she do? She's got at least five more years before retirement and could work longer—which she probably will. She loves her work."

"She's widowed. Her child is grown and on her own. Who better? She's going to put rats and bats before family?" Edwina was a professor of biology at the University of Colorado, specializing in rats and bats of the high desert plateau.

"Her job means nothing because she's a woman. Time she

gets ahold of reality and her role. Don't you see how ridiculous that sounds to the modern world? She could lose what is meaningful in her life, and her means of paying for her retirement. And her mind as well. Who would want to live with Great-aunt Abigail, for godsake?"

"Don't matter. Edwina was born and raised here. It's in her blood to do the right thing. You already did what was in your blood."

❖

It was early evening when Charlie and Edwina drove Cousin Helen home. Apparently, Helen didn't drive. Buz drove her to work and back. Theirs was a nice house for Myrtle, well kept. And not three blocks from the entrance to the Oaks. They weren't invited in.

Edwina had changed since her confrontation in the kitchen at the home place. It was in the air and her mood had lifted, while Charlie's had tanked. Charlie wanted out of here.

"I smell french fries," Edwina said when they drove down Main Street. "Let's have a beer and bar food at Viagra's before we head back to that ramshackle place and Uncle Elmo's snoring. What do you say, Daughter?"

"I say absolutely, Mother, extreme absolutely. Maybe we can pick up a six-pack for Uncle Elmo. He's about out."

Viagra's was full of pheasant hunters—lots of plaid jackets and matching caps—several admiring each other's kill pulled out of cloth sacks. The TV above the bar played a sport show about pheasant hunting, starring guys in plaid jackets and matching caps.

On one side of the TV flashed a lighted sign of the Budweiser bull frog. On the other was an enlarged photo in black and white with a bunch of guys standing around, leaning on, and hanging out of an ancient vintage automobile. Their clothes reminded Charlie of Sherman Rochester's coat. Their hats pushed back at jaunty angles and cigarettes in hand reminded her even more of old Sherman.

Of the living here, one woman with tight jeans and a loose grin played pool with the guys. The rest were guys. There was one empty booth, and the Greenes took it just as Kenny Cowper came down a flight of stairs at the back of the room, lit from behind by a bare bulb he'd had to almost double over to avoid. The place had gone silent except for the television, and Kenny followed the direction of the gaze and smirks in the rest of the room. The place smelled like french fries, beer, and secondhand smoke.

Kenny skirted the pool table to their booth. The slow smile spreading across his teeth actually reached his eyes this time. "What can I do for you ladies?"

"We're women, Squirt," Charlie's mother told him, and his smile turned into a laugh.

He hit the palm of one hand with the fist of the other. "Goddam, I knew that."

Then he slid in beside Edwina. "So you do remember me."

"Taken me all day to sort you out. You couldn't have been more than three or four the only other time we've met."

"Five, actually. I didn't start growing till about ten. Know how I remember you? You called me 'Squirt' in front of a bunch of guys. They called me that until I got so big, they didn't dare."

"You wouldn't hurt anybody," Edwina said softly, and Charlie stared at this "woman" she called mother. Well, okay, when she forgot, she did.

"Yeah, but you get big enough—nobody dares find that out. Specials tonight—and there are two specials every night and that's all there is, so we don't need menus—are walleyed pike or pork tenderloin on a sesame-seed bun with fries and a salad. What'll it be, women?"

Charlie ordered the pike and Edwina the tenderloin and whatever was on draft. The beer of course came right away and they each took two healthy gulps, leaned back into the booth, which had head-high backs, and sighed. "Might not be heaven, but like Squirt said, it's all there is."

"That laser surgery did wonders. You're not even walleyed anymore. When did you have it done?"

"Before I took six weeks out of my life and living to nurse you back to humanity after the accident. You didn't even notice. Your neighbors did, and Libby, but I swore them to secrecy. I've got this theory, Charlie. People see what they expect to see, not what's there. Besides, you were dealing with a lot of your own problems at that time."

"Okay, so why are you so changed after that knockdown drag-out with Cousin Helen? Sounded to me like you were losing big time. 'Just because you move across the country doesn't mean you cancel out your responsibilities to the people who came before you, who nurtured you, cuz.' Stuff like that. You were eating guilt and then all of a sudden you were back in control."

"Because, Charlie, I rose from the sea of despond with a wonderful idea."

"About what to do with Great Witch Abigail? Edwina, as your only daughter and the mother of your only granddaughter, I forbid you to give up the only life you have and come back here to take care of Abigail Staudt. She can go live at Gentle Oaks like everybody else."

"That's just it, Charlie, she can't. She's old, but she's not ill mentally or physically. Boulder, however, has independent-living facilities for the elderly that watch out for the frail and encourage their independence for as long as possible. She's not dying. She's not senile. She's just old."

"Don't they have places like that in Mason City?"

"Probably, but there's a passel of Staudts needing seeing to there, too, and the number of young people who've skipped off to other places makes it hard."

"They're expecting you to come back and take care of her. Live here. Give up your work and everything."

"You and I both know that won't happen. If Howard were alive, they wouldn't even think to ask it."

"Would you be able to even stand having her in Boulder?"

"Just down the hill from the university there's a place called the Good Samaritan, with an eight- or nine-story apartment building for seniors and one floor of assisted-living for those who need more, plus a nursing home attached for those who need the most. For the apartment dwellers, there are scheduled activities, a dining room, in-room cooking facilities, bus trips. Everything she'll need. Once a week I could walk down from the labs to have lunch with her and that would be it. And she could hurl accusations, opinions, and self-righteousness every which way and nobody would care because they're not from Myrtle and she's nobody to them. Kind of sweet, huh?"

Somehow, Charlie had the feeling that this would backfire, but was so glad Edwina had a positive thought she didn't relay that feeling. She'd much prefer to get her mother out of here without Great-aunt Abigail Staudt.

CHAPTER 10

✦

THEY ORDERED ANOTHER beer when their sandwiches arrived and discovered the salad was the lettuce, onion, and tomato garnish on the buns with the pike and the pork. And probably the ketchup that came with the fries.

"You've got to try a bite of this—used to be served at hamburger joints and drive-ins everywhere. Haven't seen them since I left Iowa." Edwina cut a hunk off one end of her sandwich and Charlie did the same with hers to exchange.

"Kenny Cowper's body does not look like he maintains it on deep-fried stuff like this." Although Charlie had to admit it was the best deep-fat-fried "stuff" she'd ever eaten—crispy, crunchy, salty, and hot through. The fish tasted like freshwater, the pork like pig, and the fries like a thicker version of McDonald's.

"Know what another delicious irony is? Ladies don't drink beer in pool halls in Myrtle. And I'm going to suggest shipping Great-aunt Abigail off to the outside world, where tonight will prove that foreign ladies do drink beer in pool halls. That ought to get some of the guilt turned in the other direction, cause some consternation in the other camp. We should have dinner here tomorrow night, too."

"We have to catch the eight a.m. vomit comet to Minneapolis the next day. Can't we spend tomorrow night in Mason City?" And get a decent shower? How do people who don't have showers wash their hair?

Marshal Delwood swept in on a cold wind, waved at a few

60

of the "boys" who called out to him, and shoved in beside Charlie. "So where the hell is Marlys?"

"I don't know, Marshal Sweety. Lost her in the cemetery, like I told you."

"Well, I figured you'd gone back looking for her. Since you lost her."

"Why would I do that?"

"Don't you feel any responsibility?"

Actually, she did, but Myrtle was not the place to let anybody know that. Poor old woman was wearing nothing but a thin dress, sweater, and tennis shoes the last time Charlie saw her. "You're the marshal, that's your job."

"Here you are in the pool hall swilling beer and that poor old lady's out there? It's supposed to freeze hard tonight. Know that?"

Charlie took another bite of pike burger which she absolutely didn't want—it was twice as big as she could eat and her capacity valve was about to revolt. "I'm not one of you. She's your responsibility. I don't live here, remember? So what are you doing sitting in the pool hall when you could be out freezing your butt doing your job? What's the matter with you?"

That elicited a two thumbs-up from Edwina, an accolade Charlie couldn't remember ever receiving from her mother.

"You are not normal, lady." He had the nerve to grab a french fry off her plate and dip it in her ketchup.

"Oh, come on, Brunsvold." Kenny Cowper walked up with a glass of beer of his own and one for the marshal of Myrtle. It was like he just appeared suddenly up out of the floor, which, with someone his size and magnetic charge, was an impossibility. He slid in beside Edwina. "Last time you lost Marlys, she'd slipped into Orlyn Sievertsen's doghouse between his Labrador and Saint Bernard. All three were warm as toast next morning, and Orlyn's dogs have been howling nights ever since 'cause they want Marlys back. Admit it. Marlys Dittberner is crazy. But she's not dumb, and certainly not

61

helpless. Meanwhile, women, I would just like to point out that your real sin here in Myrtle is to come into my pool hall and piss off my clientele by ignoring the whispered jokes, smirks, leers, winks, and nod-nods around you. Have you no shame? Sitting here totally absorbed in your own conversation? It is incredibly rude, self-involved, self-important, unfeeling, and—"

"Above ourselves." Charlie winked at her mom.

The marshal shook his head in disgust and poured more ketchup for Charlie's fries. "Don't look at me like that. You're the one wouldn't let me have pecan pie for brunch."

Charlie was so stuffed she couldn't get through a third of the second beer and Delwood Brunsvold went through her fries in minutes. She'd just handed him the rest of her sandwich when Ben, the same guy who stopped them this morning, rushed in with almost the identical question as then. "Marshal, you looking for Marlys? I just saw her next door and she's buck-naked. Gettin' cold out there."

If Charlie didn't know better, she'd have thought this whole scene was scripted.

It had been a long time since Charlie Greene had seen her breath frost the air and felt a stinging nip at the end of her nose. But the rest of her was warm, if bloated. The law in Myrtle had declared that everyone stay in Viagra's except Ben, himself, and Kenny Cowper so as not to frighten Marlys.

The jeers this time were not for Charlie and her mother.

"Whose army's going to frighten Marlys Dittberner?"

"You need help, boy, you call."

But everyone except Charlie followed Marshal Del's orders.

"This woman's trouble."

"I noticed." Kenny reached around a partition, grabbed his jacket, and put it over Charlie's shoulders. "Southern California girls got water for blood. Hot water, but still—"

His down jacket came to below her knees and she was glad of it. She and Ben stood waiting for the marshal and the owner of that jacket to act out in the doorway.

"Against the law to have open liquor containers on the sidewalk, and glass ones at that, in this here town of Myrtle," said Delwood and raised his glass to Kenny's face. Okay, reached.

"Well, nobody ever told me that and I own the damn pool hall."

"No lie. It's on the books."

"Myrtle's got books?"

But they both emptied their glass glasses, nodded in agreement, handed the glass containers to Charlie, and walked off. "Come along, Ben."

Charlie handed the beer glasses over to Ben, who stood looking at them. The guy who owned the damn pool hall and the guy who upheld the law were sort of giggling at each other until she slid in between their chumminess. "Maybe we should go find Orlyn's dogs?"

It was dark, but you could see the sky through parts of the roof of the two-story derelict next door. The guys had decided on a new tack. They each had hold of one of her arms, which made for a lopsided tableau.

"So what do you think, Charlie? Does Marlys need an agent?"

"Actually, I think Marlys needs a manager."

"What about Abigail Staudt?"

"She's going to love Boulder, where everyone is more opinionated than she is, if not more righteous. They're great arguers there. They'll love her, too. They can turn guilt on its head. You know, all that sun in Colorado makes people weird."

"She can't leave Myrtle."

"Then she's still Myrtle's problem, isn't she?"

"They make women meaner every year," said the marshal.

"Don't Marlys . . . oh, Jesus." The barkeep let go of Charlie's arm barely in time to catch the naked form that fell from the ruin of the second story.

"If there's an ordinance that disallows glass containers on the sidewalks, why isn't there one that makes landlords shore up ruins or tear them down instead?" Charlie took off Kenny's jacket and threw it over Marlys Dittberner. She smelled better naked.

" 'Ordinance?' 'Disallows?' " the marshal said. "Man, you valley girls talk like lawyers."

"Marlys owns this building. Was once her grocery store—times got bad, they used to deliver even. By horse and wagon. So much history in these little backwaters, all being lost to senility, Alzheimer's, agribusiness, and the Grim Reaper."

"For a Myrtle boy, you talk funny," Charlie said right behind Kenny.

They carefully traversed the rotted flooring, moonlight through the rooftop and second floor lighting their way.

"You must not have met Mr. Rochester yet," the barkeep said, his voice coming from his feet.

"Oh, shit, I forgot this is the full moon. Hang onto her tight, Kenny." Del followed behind Charlie, who was watching the creepy play of shadow and blackout on the floor. Almost gave her vertigo.

A dog howled across the street. The floorboards creaked beneath their feet like the barn out at the home place. Marlys groaned. Charlie missed Kenny Cowper's jacket. It was freaking-cold out here, especially when the wind whistled through the holes in the building.

At the back of the store, they stepped out another hole onto a cement loading dock with cement stairs down to the alley, went past the exhaust fan of Viagra's kitchen spewing french-fry odors, up a wooden staircase to a balcony, and into Kenny's home. It was mostly one enormous room with shoulder-high bookcases—well, shoulder-high on Kenny—dividing it into sections for sleeping, office, workout equipment, an entertainment center and lounge along one wall, kitchen and eating space between and along windows overlooking Myrtle and Main Street. The enclosing wall space was decorated with old grainy photos of the pool hall, the railroad station, and more guys lounging around ancient autos or playing baseball. The bathroom and a closet were closed off at the rear.

"Very nice," Charlie, who should have been fussing over poor Marlys, said.

"My whole family used to live up here with my grandparents." Kenny laid Marlys on a couch and wrapped her in a blanket. "I sort of like it better this way."

Marshal Brunsvold was on his cellular to Gentle Oaks. "Yeah, we got Marlys—tried to do herself in again. I don't think she's hurt much. I'll be bringing her up."

"Why wouldn't you let her kill herself if she wants to? Can't be much fun being alive at the Oaks."

"Against the law," the marshal said without hesitation. "I'll drive the car around to the alley side so we don't have to depress the revelers in your fine establishment, Ken. If you'll just carry her down for me."

"That law must be on those books he was talking about. First time I've heard of them." That smile, slow and easy and knowing, reminded Charlie of a cat stretching. Oh, boy.

Marlys decided to get feisty about the time Marshal Sweetie's Cherokee came to a stop in the alley, so Charlie drove it while he hung on to the ancient woman with Charlie's eyes.

"This is insane," Charlie said as she pulled into the semicircle in front of Gentle Oaks, where the leaves were falling big-time now in an icy wind and the moon loomed large and bright and orangey. Marlys growled low in her throat and the law growled back.

"Del."

"Sorry, I get carried away when the moon's full, too. Specially the harvest moon because it means football and snowmobiling and pheasant hunting and Halloween. Right, Marlys?" He chuckled low and evil, and Marlys copied that sound with a little too much gravel but even more evil. "Besides, watching you and Kenny look at each other could steam up all North Iowa."

"How long has he been back from the outside world?"

"About eight, nine months now. He likes Myrtle a lot better than your mom."

They both literally wrestled a frail, little old Marlys Dittberner into the nursing home's outer doors, losing the blanket on the way—Charlie was briefly reminded of the famous photograph of a fleeing girl, mouth gaping in a scream, napalmed in Vietnam—when the inner doors opened at them in an horrendous roar of rage. Not the doors—the two guys in wheelchairs.

CHAPTER 11

*I*F CHARLIE WAS getting a little spooked by the moonlight leaking through a ruined grocery store that once delivered by horse-drawn wagon, it was nothing compared to Gentle Oaks at the full of a harvest moon.

"What do you people do around here for Halloween?" she asked the marshal as they wrestled a naked-again Marlys through careening wheelchair lunatics, but that awful alarm system drowned out her voice.

Fatty Staudt and Fatty Truex were trying to arm-wrestle each other out of their wheelchairs. Their hospital gowns opened in the back and swung free among flailing arms. Even bare-gummed, they could voice vile expletives over the alarm, but their snarls were slurred and hissy. Wouldn't you think the testosterone would have worn out by now, even if they hadn't?

Charlie was looking for the doohickey to turn off the alarm when a bare, hairy arm came down in front of her face and did it for her. The doohickey was a cream-colored box beside the door, and the hand at the end of the arm curled its fingers under it to turn it off. The hairy arm belonged to Richard Burton in his younger days when he was alive—the moody, broody, smoldering Richard Burton. Just one problem, his eyes were almost black, like Charlie's.

"Just *what* do you think you're doing?" he thundered in a stage voice with accents suggesting the British, but trained for Broadway. "And who the hell are you, anyway?"

"Jane Erye?" Please tell me you're not Harvey Rochester

or I'll pee my pants right here and now. "You talk funny."

"You notice that, too?" Marlys Dittberner stopped struggling to look up into Charlie's face. "Ain't normal, huh?"

Marlys had had a double mastectomy with no attempt at a rebuild. That's why she didn't wear a bra. Made sense. This woman made sense in a lot of ways Charlie really didn't want to deal with.

"Help me, help me, please help me," a woman's voice pleaded from somewhere close and then screamed. At least the TVs were off.

"What are you doing here, Harvey?" Del wanted to know.

Marlys groaned and peed on the floor. Charlie groaned and crossed her legs.

An enormous fat Siamese with long hair waddled down the hall, sniffed the wet spot on the carpet and then hissed at Harvey.

"Dolores, get thee hence," Mr. Rochester intoned and pointed behind him, where Charlie spied the saving grace of the universal sign for ladies' room.

She left Marlys with the marshal—"Don't lose her this time, dammit"—and made it in time but barely because of an all-consuming hysterical bout of laughter. Whoever said the nice old Midwest was boring and predictable hadn't visited Myrtle, Iowa.

Charlie was still giggling when she and the marshal and the Jeep Cherokee circled the drive and roared out to the main road. Del explained Harvey's presence there was due to the weekend staff and the full moon. "Residents get really violent sometimes and they're always understaffed on weekends— temporary help. Can't sedate or restrain the residents anymore. Most you can do is antidepressants or anxiety drugs, and then only on doctors' orders. Temporaries get hit around a few times, they just walk off the job. Sometimes even Harvey Rochester has to step in and help out. And he's the boss."

"Why does he act like an actor?"

"He is an actor. Or he was. Spent years in New York. Never saw him on TV or anything, but we all figured he must be acting."

"Actors, artists of any kind, tend not to be good businessmen. They use different sides of the brain or something."

"I don't know, old Harvey's a pretty good businessman. Must mean he's a bad actor, huh?" Delwood laughed at his own double entendre—when it hit him.

"What kind of a cat is Dolores?"

"Tomcat."

It was raining by the time they reached Viagra's. The Lumina was gone.

"Edwina must have left without me."

"What kind of daughter goes off and leaves her mother in a pool hall, anyway?"

"An adult daughter. And I was driving this heap so you could restrain Marlys Dittberner, remember? So you can take me out to the home place, Marshal Sweetie."

"Marshal." Ben whoever ran up to the Jeep, "Kenny wants you should take a case of Bud out to Elmo when you take Miss Greene home. Her mother left with their car. I'll run get him."

"What is he, the town crier?"

"Watchman."

"Myrtle has a watchman?"

"It's on the books."

"What's he do—never mind."

"Gets paid for it, too."

"Now stop that."

Kenny came out of Viagra's carrying a big box like it was a feather, slid it onto the backseat, and looked at Charlie closely.

Clutch.

"That the warmest coat you brought? Wait a minute," he said and went back into the pool hall.

"I was going to take Uncle Elmo a six-pack but—"

"Kenny keeps him in beer. If he runs out, he'll drive his pickup into town. Family keeps him in food and cigars. We take care of our own."

"Why shouldn't he drive into town?"

"No license, him or the pickup. Macular degeneration in his eyes. Legally blind."

"This is the most depressing place I've ever been in. How come I do so much laughing here?"

"I think maybe your answer came before your question," Kenny said, crawling in beside the Budweiser and handing his knee-length jacket over the seatback to Charlie. "What do you think?"

"Who invited you, Cowper? You have a business to run, you know."

Charlie noticed the Cherokee was the only vehicle, parked or otherwise, on Main Street, or what she could see of it. There were no streetlights in Myrtle.

"Weather report emptied the pool hall half-hour ago. Front moving in. Myrtle rolls up the sidewalks by nine anyway. But it was a fast exodus tonight."

"Snow?" Charlie asked.

"Ice," both men answered at once. Kenny added, "And I felt it my duty to protect the only law-enforcement individual for many miles—his virtue, you know."

"Well, I'm glad I've got a ticket out of here at eight o'clock Tuesday morning."

Both men chuckled.

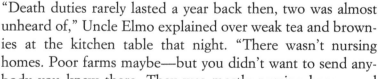

"Death duties rarely lasted a year back then, two was almost unheard of," Uncle Elmo explained over weak tea and brownies at the kitchen table that night. "There wasn't nursing homes. Poor farms maybe—but you didn't want to send anybody you knew there. They was mostly nursing homes and loony bins. Women took on the chore for love and as a duty

and out of guilt and often in hopes of money to support themselves and their children. Weren't many jobs for them outside
the home. Might be unspoken, but there was always a daughter discouraged from romance and marriage. That was the one
meant to see to the parents so the others could go on with
their lives. When women started working and earning their
own way, the system broke down. Ain't no fixing it now. Can't
blame desperate people for trying, though."

"I couldn't come back here to live. I hated it here. I still
do." Edwina was all sad again.

"You was always such a pliable young thing. Husband
gone and you getting toward retirement age, we figured maybe
coming home would sound good. Didn't realize you'd
changed so much. Abigail's lived here all her life—couldn't
send her off to Boulder."

"Why? Nobody here can stand her anyway," Charlie said.
"She gets righteous with people out there, they'll just shun
her. Sounds like justice for all."

Elmo Staudt had a big nose with a heavily veined bulb at
the end and a rather endearing rascally gleam in those blue
eyes that didn't see well enough to get a driver's license.
"More like vengeance. Vengeance ain't right. What *do* you
plan to do when you retire, Edwina?"

"I've been kind of thinking about Prescott, Arizona, for
part of the year."

"I didn't know that, but it seems perfect," Charlie said—
anywhere but Long Beach. "I have a writer there who flies
out of the little local airport to the Phoenix airport and then
anywhere. He really likes it."

"What could you do there you can't do here?"

"Almost everything I like and want to do."

"You could walk the desert to your heart's content." Charlie was beginning to see why they were marooned out here at
the home place with Uncle Elmo and not in Helen and Buz's
nicer house in town. These two had a relationship from Edwina's childhood nobody else in the family did.

"And I'd like to do some traveling, and there's a book I want to write—I probably won't have time to get to until then—on the function of intestinal diseases among the *Dipodomys ordii*."

"You won't be writing no highfalutin books around Abigail Staudt, I tell you. Schoolteaching either. And what would you do with her anyway when you went to this Prescott place?"

"Mom's not a schoolteacher. She's a university professor, for godsake."

"I wasn't going to have her living with me, Uncle Elmo. I'd put her in the Towers. It has independent-living apartments for the elderly and it's not far from campus."

"She wouldn't know anybody. What if she got sick? And that would cost money."

"There's a nursing home attached. And she'd have to get to know people, and yes, it would cost money. With both sisters gone, she can't be destitute. If she is, we'll all just have to pitch in and help, won't we? Since we're all family."

The Greenes trudged upstairs to their icy bedroom, leaving Uncle Elmo Staudt staring after them, flabbergasted.

"Do pack rats really have intestinal diseases?" Charlie asked her mother, pulling up all three comforters and putting Kenny Cowper's big coat on top of the pile.

"Everybody does."

"After tonight, I'm not spending another night in this house, Edwina, and that's that." All she slept in was a man's T-shirt, and she could see her breath on the air up here. "And I'm not letting them put the screws to you. You don't owe these people anything for making you feel like a toad when you were growing up."

"It's not that simple, Charlie."

"Your parents are dead, right? You had no brothers or sisters. Let the cousins take care of their own."

"My parents are buried not far from Great-aunt Gertie. I'll show you tomorrow. But you saw Fatty Staudt at Gentle

Oaks today. Well, he's my grandfather. He was Edward Staudt the First, my father was Edward Staudt the Second, and I was supposed to be Edward Staudt the Third. Thus Edwina. The long-awaited brother never arrived—a great disappointment to the family."

"Edwina, that is so dumb. It's not like there was a throne to inherit."

"And the final blow was that I married Howard Greene, a lapsed Jew, and eventually adopted you."

CHAPTER 12

THE SUN WAS so hot on her bare skin Charlie had trouble breathing. It beat through the rounded corner window of Harvey Rochester's living room. She and Kenny Cowper rolled on Harvey's lush carpet next to a black grand piano. It was probably the most painfully erotic moment in her life, but she wasn't exactly fighting him off. Leaf shadows played on the window and across the carpet and on Kenny Cowper.

"Told you it was her," Great-aunt Abigail hissed above them, and the piano bench was full of Harvey Rochester, pounding out something broody and moody and violent. There were two women with Abigail, all three in period dress—like the Civil War era or something. All three pointed down at her, and Kenny disappeared and Charlie was suddenly cold. By this time, she'd figured out it was a dream but damn near came anyway. Can women do that?

"Can women do what?" Her mother stood over her. She'd pulled the covers off Charlie and had a towel wrapped around her head. "You were having a bad dream. Hurry up, I've got a tub running for you."

"What'd I say, did I say anything?" Oh, jeesh.

"You were just moaning and groaning and wondering if women could do something. Now get down there before the tub runs over—real hot water, Charlie. You can wash your hair in the tub. There's a saucepan you can dip it up with, pour it over to rinse. Hurry."

"Wash my hair in the bathwater? Gross."

But after Charlie's "nightmare," she really needed a bath and her head was a total itch, so she did as she was told. The water was hot and the deep tub spilled over a little when she displaced some of that water. She got shampoo in her eyes from rinsing with a saucepan and the towels were thin to nothing and the room a refrigerator once she was out of the water, but she did feel much refreshed.

Edwina had a little travel hairdryer. Charlie didn't carry one anymore because she always stayed in upscale hotels where they were attached to the bathroom wall.

Uncle Elmo had decided to take them out to breakfast at the Schoolhouse Café in town. He found an ankle-length coat that made Edwina look like a fireplug, and escorted them out onto the back stoop.

"I think I better drive, Uncle Elmo," Charlie said, blinked, and looked again, squinting in the sunlight glinting off ice. Everything was as before but coated with shiny ice. Every dead blade of grass or weed or fence post or wire shimmered with beauty. And the skeleton barn most of all because of its mass and incompleteness, strange and saggy shadow angles and holes. This was not thin ice either. Weed blades and harvest stubble were three times their size and clacking against each other in the wind. Fence wires drooped with the weight, and a wire to the house from a pole along the driveway was barely a foot off the ground.

"Where's the car?" Charlie stepped off the stoop and landed on her ass in seconds.

"Put it in the barn—" Uncle Elmo helped her up "—because of the storm. It's still some shelter if not a lot. Your mother and I'll meet you at the gate. Careful how you step now."

Charlie pretended she was ice-skating, which she was, but on boot bottoms. Her hair hadn't quite dried at the roots and she imagined it was freezing upon her scalp, sending icy tendrils down to her nerve endings.

Jesus, Greene, will you pay attention? This is not your average slippery.

Where have you been? Charlie asked her inner voice. Is that what's been missing here?

Not as fascinated with the marshal and the barkeep as you, babe. Besides, Myrtle, Iowa, has been dominating the guilt scene. Not much I could add.

The rest of the world spoke in zillions of tiny cracking and clacking sounds. Was this what it sounded like inside a deep freeze or an ice-cube tray? She fell only twice more before reaching the barn, hoping all the way that the Lumina would start. She'd never driven a Chevy before. It was parked next to an ancient pickup of indeterminate color, and started after a couple of turnovers.

Charlie would forever be grateful for whatever instinct or fantasy or hovering protective angel told her to back the black rental out of the barn right away instead of sitting there a while to let it warm up. Because she'd no sooner cleared the barn door than the barn collapsed in shivering stages of shimmering ice-coated pieces of wood, finally too old to hold up under the weight. Charlie sat there staring at the dazzling explosion—many of the ice shards striking the windshield, some painting rainbow hues in the sunlight—thinking of Marlys Dittberner.

When the crystal dust settled, the tailgate of Uncle Elmo's pickup was all of it that showed through the humps of rubble. Edwina walked like an old-lady-on-ice on the ice and on the arm of her surefooted uncle—maybe it was the cane. Elmo had to be seventy-five at least, and if the great-aunts were his aunts, he was right—whole generations of the elderly *were* stacking up in Myrtle. And Edwina, who was herself a grandmother, had a grandfather still living. Again, thinking of Marlys with a hunch that she already had the key to something here, Charlie got out to help inspect the Lumina. When they wiped away the ice and wood dust, a few scratches showed on its hood and roof, no major dents.

"Not too bad. Better than you being under it when the roof came down, little Charlie." Elmo Staudt stood looking at the barn that wasn't. "Always figured it'd be the wind that took it. Or some kids'd set fire to it some night. But we don't hardly have any of them anymore. Now it's just me and the house that stands between the home place and the Family Farms."

Edwina and Charlie instinctively put an arm around him. "Oh, don't fuss, it don't matter. Old pile of junk." But there was a catch in his voice and he didn't move away from them. "Used to sit on the back stoop and listen to the wind whistle through the rafters and old boards creak like they was all playing a tune together. Sometimes I'd think I could still hear the bellow of cows wanting milking, and the hogs grunting and snorting."

"Don't forget the geese." Edwina had a catch in her voice, too.

"Oh, yeah. You always was scared of them geese." But his chuckle was hollow. "Well, let's get some breakfast. They have real good coffee at the Schoolhouse Café. I could sure use some."

Charlie only slid the Chevy Lumina off the drive once, managed to get it back on without anybody having to get out and push, but with a lot of advice from her elders. She hadn't driven on ice in years. And never had she seen such an expanse of it as when she turned onto the road to Myrtle. It was one solid, smooth, shiny sheet of ice, and the little snow that had accompanied it had blown off to shallow riffs in deep ditches. The sun's glare, so pretty on the exploding barn, was blinding here, even with Southern California-strength sunglasses.

"Now take it real slow, Charlie," Uncle Elmo said calmly, "and don't spook, but there's a mighty big tractor coming up behind us. Let him pass. He's got traction on that old Oliver, Lyle does. He just don't have rubber tires. People always tease him about that museum piece but he can chop up this ice a little for us and you can follow in his tracks."

Charlie hadn't even thought to look in the rearview mirror—once out at the home place, you felt all alone in the world. But the earth seemed to rumble now. "I thought you couldn't see."

"I can see out of the sides of my eyes, just the middle that's dark." Cold swept into the car as he lowered his window and yelled, "Morning, Darla. Fine day, ain't it? Old Lyle's taking his granddaughter to work."

This huge iron wheel jounced past Charlie's window and the rumble became a vibration that tickled her ears. When it pulled back in front of them, this fireplug resembling Edwina waved back at them. It was a padded person standing on a tractor, holding onto the seated driver. Charlie had never seen anything like this, not even in the movies. The closest she could tag it was like *Fargo* meets *Grapes of Wrath*.

The museum piece had great iron ridges that broke the ice into chunks that spewed out from all around the wheels. The machine was mostly wheels, and Elmo called the metal ridges "lugs."

"Does Darla work at the City Hall?"

"Oh, no. She's been to college. She's the social director at the Oaks. Social workers make good money."

"They do?" Charlie and her mother said, barely out of sync.

"Oh, yeah. Lot better than schoolteachers, from what I hear."

"Mom is a university professor and research scientist," Charlie insisted. "Not a schoolteacher."

The Oliver, Darla, and her dad were ka-chunking way out ahead of them and Charlie was glad for their damage to the ice in her path, when one of the loose chunks threw the rental sideways enough to veer her across the road and into the opposing ditch in less than a breath, facing back toward the home place.

When she saw the semi ka-chunk over the meridian, going the other way between north and south on the 405 and heading straight for the Toyota after taking out a few SUVs in front of her, it was too late to change lanes. Or was it?

She heard herself screaming and cursing as she wormed the little crushable Toyota over between two other SUVs. The one in front of her climbed the semi's hood. She managed another worm into the next lane over, where traffic was really slowing down, and then to the next. There Charlie and her beloved Toyota joined—she couldn't tell how many—cars and trucks and everything in between in a crunch that shoved it all into what looked like a grassy ditch, where the dependable old gray Toyota bent its rib cage in the middle, and Charlie, too.

Darla was one of those bouncy, cheerful people it was impossible to appreciate before morning coffee. She stood next to Charlie and Edwina as Lyle Lempky pulled the Lumina out of the ditch with his ice-crunching Oliver, and Uncle Elmo behind the wheel. Charlie was just coming out of a nightmare daze. Her mom explained her recent accident to an effervescent Darla, who counseled Edwina to find some good counseling for her daughter. And the sun went behind a cloud bank big enough to swallow the earth.

Darla didn't even blink. The glittery ice world had become *Dr. Zhivago* meets *One Flew Over the Cuckoo's Nest*, and this bubbly person didn't register it. And she had to go to work at Gentle Oaks, for godsake.

Uncle Elmo drove them into Myrtle and breakfast. Neither Charlie nor her mom objected when he explained, "I don't have a license and I can't see, but I can drive on ice, you better believe."

At the Schoolhouse Café, located in a three-story brick building that had once been Myrtle's school, the center of the community that was now the Community Center, the menu was written on the blackboard and everyone nodded at Elmo and stared at the Greenes.

On the way in, Edwina had pointed out classrooms where she had attended school. One had a preschool sign on the door. Uncle Elmo said it had closed for lack of young. Ballet and piano studios had closed for lack of grade-schoolers.

"Garden club still does good in summer, senior citizens' activity center thrives. Exercise for active elders closed, but day care for senile elders goes great guns when they can get somebody young enough to staff it," Elmo told them and ordered a double order of eggs, scrambled with melted cheese on top, biscuits and sausage gravy, and bacon. If they'd left him flabbergasted last night, he'd just returned the favor this morning and he knew it. He gave a mighty, satisfied grin and announced, "Doing everything I know how to kill myself before I end up at the Oaks."

CHAPTER 13

*C*HARLIE SUCKED THANKFULLY at the coffee, while Uncle Elmo complained that eating eggs by the ton didn't seem to make his cholesterol go up. "Used to like oatmeal a lot but won't eat it now. Might save my life. Smoke all the cigars I can stand, enjoy all the beer I can hold. What more can I do? I'm not churchy but I'm religious enough to feel bad about shooting myself. Upbringing and all. It's the curse of Myrtle. Your folks did right in leaving young, Edwina."

There were booths along the inside wall and tables of various sizes in the center of the room. The tall windows on the outside wall showed a gray sky where the clouds had coalesced into one big downer.

"How'd they die?" Charlie could hear the listlessness in her voice. She hadn't relived her accident for three months, thought that part of the nightmare over, gone off the antidepressants and anti-anxiety drugs because they leveled her out too much, took the terror out of life but the joy and excitement, too.

"Ol' Eddie dropped dead of a heart attack at fifty-five," Elmo said wistfully. "What a way to go. Prime of life. Wasn't even sick more 'en a few minutes. And Elsie? How'd she go?"

"Breast cancer at fifty. Not such a good way to go." Edwina sat back as a huge bowl of oatmeal was set before her. "Do you remember when you were very young, visiting them in Albuquerque, Charlie?"

"Were they the ones with the cool tile floors and cute birds with antennalike things running around their backyard?"

"Gambel's quail, yeah. You must have been about four. My mother was already dying but didn't show it much. None of us knew, actually."

"She had you at eighteen?" Charlie asked after some quick figuring. "I thought that was the generation that married late because of the Depression."

"Both families had money," Elmo said.

"And my mother was pregnant with me," Edwina said.

Charlie said, "I ordered *an* egg. I got two. And toast. I got potatoes, too."

"Eggs come in the plural here and with potatoes now. Don't sweat it." Edwina was still staring at all that oatmeal. "You may need some extra calories before we're through this."

They compromised by ordering an extra plate and bowl and sharing each other's breakfasts. Hey, oatmeal wasn't so bad. With all that brown sugar and cream, sawdust would have been good. The orange juice tasted like Tang, the toast was Wonder bread, but the coffee, though not Starbucks, had a kick. They all mellowed some. And Charlie decided to ignore the stares from the booths across the room and the depressing cold sky outside the tall windows and ask some hard questions. She figured she'd better before she sank back into the sea of morass ignited by Myrtle and issues on aging she had no desire to look into and the icy, damp cold out there. She'd have given anything for the marshal's grin that promised nothing but made you feel good.

"So how is it everyone in Myrtle knows I was in an auto accident last spring when I barely heard of Myrtle until a few days ago? And I want a straight answer—clear, direct, and to the point."

"Well, Lester Wyborny's son David lives out in Los Angeles, and he works in the movies, cameraman, you probably met him, and he always sends his mother newspaper clippings whenever your name shows up in one—or that *Hollywood*

Reporter. And she always sends him clippings on how bad a place California is and how dangerous it is to live there. Vivian's determined he'll perish by earthquake, tidal wave, stray bullets, or wildfire any day. Anyway, she hands his clippings about you around at church. From there, the news is spread by mouth. You do tend to get yourself reported up in the paper a lot. Straight enough answer?"

"Yes, thank you, Uncle Elmo. Now, next question—"

"And of course when that Mitch Hilsten fella got himself engaged to someone else, everybody in town either felt bad for you or thought you had it coming. They was about evenly divided on that one, seems to me."

Charlie spilled some coffee in her oatmeal. "You know about Mitch?"

"Everybody knows about him. He's a famous movie star. I liked him best in *Bloody Promises* and *After Hours.* He's real popular around here, you know. The Sinclair can't keep his videos in. Oh, and *Phantom of the Alpine Tunnel.* All that mountain railroad stuff. Didn't know the Colorado mountains was that beautiful."

"Actually, it was filmed in Canada. But—is that why everybody looks at me so funny and doesn't say anything?"

"You got to understand, this isn't Los Angeles. We never expected to actually see somebody who'd been between the sheets with Mitch Hilsten."

Well, if Charlie hadn't felt like she had three noses before, *that* sure as hell did it.

"In Myrtle, that makes him a he-man and you a whore," Charlie's mother said bitterly.

"So what's your next question?"

Charlie was still trying to get her breath and couldn't remember the next one, not that there weren't a bunch. "Well, Marlys Dittberner told me that there were three groups of families in Myrtle—Germans, Norwegians, and Cowpers—and that the Myrtle for whom the town is named was murdered. And she left a curse on the town, and you said the same thing just now."

"Charlie, Marlys Dittberner's more than a few pies short of a load of manure. Crazy folks are often the most clever, don't forget. But yes, Myrtle was killed."

"Who killed her?"

"Her family, the town, the times. We been paying for it ever since. Women aren't greatly valued by men in this town, or most towns, I'd bet, until the men get too old to take care of themselves and then they begrudge their helplessness and them that care for them."

"That's not a straight answer."

"In Myrtle's time, little Charlie, women weren't thought to earn their keep, so they came out owing. That's how you explained their duty to see to others first. Edwina, you explain this one—I'm paying for breakfast. But I will say Helen Bartusek drives me loony because I have to be nice to her because she cares for me."

"Cousin Helen? I thought she was a Staudt."

"Bartusek is her married name," Edwina answered. "Buz is a Bartusek. Her maiden name was—"

"What's all this 'maiden' stuff anyway?"

Charlie's mom put her hands over her face and Uncle Elmo called for the check. Charlie stared out the window at the gray sky and the black, leafless tree whose branches looked like threatening fingers. Charlie wanted to go home real bad.

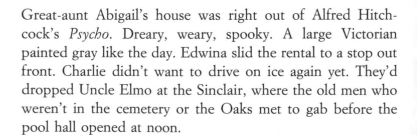

Great-aunt Abigail's house was right out of Alfred Hitchcock's *Psycho*. Dreary, weary, spooky. A large Victorian painted gray like the day. Edwina slid the rental to a stop out front. Charlie didn't want to drive on ice again yet. They'd dropped Uncle Elmo at the Sinclair, where the old men who weren't in the cemetery or the Oaks met to gab before the pool hall opened at noon.

"So, what are you going to do, offer to move her to Boulder?"

"Uncle Elmo's right, it'd probably kill her. She lives to control and judge others."

"If it killed her, she wouldn't have to go to the Oaks, right? She wouldn't have much control there either. I can't figure out how all these people are related."

"Uncle Elmo is the youngest child of Fatty Staudt or Grandpa Staudt or Edward Senior, who had three sisters that lived—Abigail, Gertrude, and Annabel. He had one daughter, Ida Mae, who is Helen's mom. She's at the Oaks. Then Edward the Second—my father—then Elmo. Ida Mae Staudt married a Truex, so Helen Bartusek, Cousin Helen, was a Truex before she married."

"So Fatty Staudt is the grandfather who carved your watermelon for family reunions out at the home place?" It didn't seem like Edwina had taken any notice of him.

"No, Fatty Staudt has become something totally unrelated to the grandfather I remember."

"Both Fatty Staudt and Fatty Truex are Helen's grandfathers? And her mother Ida Mae's there, too, and until recently, two great-aunts—Gertrude and Annabel, whose deaths are suspicious and under a coroner's investigation? I know where I'd look for the murderer—can't figure why Cousin Helen hasn't gone screaming into the cornfields before now, can you?"

"With the debt ratio, there is little money here for most. Family Farms does not pay as much as you might think. Many families in and around Myrtle had great wealth in farmland once. But one cannot spend dirt, and profit evaporates swiftly when the debt builds. The idea was that if one owned a piece of land, it would be valuable because God would not be making any more land: That it was the one thing one could never replace, and if one had a piece of it and built on it, that land would support one and one's children and their children."

Great-aunt Abigail obviously lived in two rooms of this house, the "parlor" and the kitchen. The entryway had been cold, but when they entered the parlor and the pocket doors closed behind them, it was stuffy hot. A neatly made twin bed sat off in one corner, dressers and two wardrobes alongside it, and the door to the kitchen stood open. Abigail had put on the teakettle. It whistled now, and she interrupted her lecture to go make tea. A gas-log fireplace had been installed in a real fireplace—not terribly convincingly—and Charlie, who'd thought she'd never be warm again, began to wonder if she'd ever cool down again. On an ornate side table, knitting needles stuck out of what looked to be an all-but-finished cap with what would be a rolled rim all around.

Above the fireplace was a bad painting of an incredibly ugly girl with Charlie's eyes and Libby's and Kenny Cowper's and Marlys Dittberner's and Mr. Rochester's.

Abigail came back with a silver tea service so huge she rolled it on a little table with wheels. It sat on a shiny silver tray Charlie would bet had to be polished like in the old days when women didn't have enough to do already, or had servants to polish for them. Hot tea in one gleaming pot, sugar cubes and lemon slices—except for the absence of milk, it was just like London. There were delicate cookies, cups and saucers, small plates. When you've already got three noses, you notice things.

Charlie was cheered only by the fact that the tea tasted like Lipton's, the cookies were obviously Pepperidge Farm, and there was an eye-popping-sized television in perfect alignment with the ancient woman's Lazy Boy, which of course she wasn't using now. The Towers in Boulder would have a difficult time replacing this little nest.

The lecture continued. Farmers could create their own workforce from their own loins and it would be economical because that workforce would be working for its own future families. Then the world went berserk, became unmanageable.

"Irreligious and immoral men of science invented methods of growing crops on less land. Women decided they didn't wish to wash their own dishes by hand. Farming machines became so large one went into debt so deeply that even the devil couldn't bail one out, and then computers came along to steal away one's children and their children. They could now make money without land, and purchase their food. You be careful, you women of the world. That which you bank on now could be worthless as our dirt in a few years."

In Hollywood, Charlie thought, in a few days.

"And that stock market you godless count on is merely smoke—as was the certain value and future wealth of land of which God would never make more. Those poor demented souls up at Gentle Oaks are all there on Medicaid."

Charlie'd thought listening to the evening news was depressing.

"I notice, Charlemagne Catherine Greene, your intense interest in that portrait above the mantel. I think we both know who that is, don't we, my dear? And recognize her likeness to you?"

"Myrtle?"

"Yes, our founding mother and our curse, and ultimately yours, too. She died, harlot, because she betrayed her family as you betrayed yours and as Edwina plans to betray hers."

❖

CHAPTER 14

CHARLIE AND HER mom walked out of Great-aunt Abigail's smothering house from *Psycho* into Myrtle's silent ice world. They were silent, too. For once the cold felt refreshing even though it took Charlie's breath away.

Halfway down the front sidewalk, Edwina's feet went out from under her so fast, her daughter nearly tripped over her. When she tried to help Edwina up, Charlie went down instead. They sat in this ignominious position for the longest time, cushioned by other people's "fat" coats, blinking, breathing steam into each other's face. Until Edwina, who'd been near tears ever since Great-aunt Abigail had led them into the parlor, cracked up.

Charlie had rarely heard the professor's laughter go out of control. It got so violent that Edwina had to search her purse for Kleenex to keep her nasal drainage from being an embarrassment in air cold enough to sear the lungs.

"You look so funny in that coat." She found a clean tissue for Charlie, too.

"Right. I've been thinking all day how much you look like a fireplug. You hurt?"

"No. Think we can get up?" For no known reason, that remark and their attempts to do so brought on another laughing gale and the two ended up on their knees hugging each other, but it was at least some improvement.

"Charlie, can you imagine what old Abby and the neighbors fortunate enough to be looking out their windows are thinking right now?"

That lost them whatever leverage they'd gained with the ice. "Mom, stop. I hurt."

They were on their backs again staring up at black, bare tree limbs, limned in gloomy, gray-sky light, branches like claws reaching for them. Two crows the size of condors stared down, cawing ridicule. Charlie felt laughing tears freezing on her cheeks. "Oh, please—I'm going to crack ribs again."

When they finally reached the rented Chevy, Charlie intoned, "Now repeat after me, 'I will not let that bitch ruin my life and my retirement. She's already caused too much misery and deserves no more from me."

Once inside the car, Charlie added, "And we spend tonight in a decent hotel in Mason City, before our blessed escape back to our own worlds. Where are we headed now?"

"Gentle Oaks."

"Oh, shit."

"I'll buy you a beer at Viagra's for lunch. We'll skip the special and just have french fries. Charlie, I wish I'd had the nerve to talk to Great-aunt Abigail like you did back there. I'm proud of you and Libby. Each generation works up a little bit more sass. But you build on what those of us who had less power and self-esteem did before."

"I know that, and I'll gladly take you up on Viagra's. But why do we have to go to the Oaks?"

"Hey, we're here. We're leaving soon. Whatever unfinished business we can finish before that won't come back to bite us later."

Myrtle had been sort of executed by being locked in a root cellar, similar to the home place's cellar, with some food and water and candles—all because she'd announced her intention to run off with some guy to the Wild West. He was probably a forerunner of Kenny Cowper. Because in her large family she was the least comely girl, Myrtle had been chosen as the sacrificial daughter—and should have been honored by the role since women were worth so little. No one had thought for a second that any man but a ne'er-do-well would have someone like her. So she was hidden away until such time as she would come to her senses and agree to fulfill the destiny God had designed for her in her family, the community, and the scheme of things.

Talk about shunning. No one spoke to her or saw her for two months. When the root cellar was opened, the ugly Myrtle was dead, as was her stillborn child—a son the family would greatly have appreciated if she'd been chosen for that role. Sons seemed to have been a disappointment to the Staudts for generations.

"So part of the curse of Myrtle," Charlie had said to Abigail, "is disappointing sons and disobedient daughters. Three wonderful great-aunts didn't marry and have children and it doesn't sound like they took on the eldercare either, did they? Just added to it. And they didn't provide daughters that would, right? They took on righteousness instead. Which is some sort of protection, I suppose."

Apparently, Myrtle had left a blasphemous note outlining the conditions of her curse. Again, as happened so often in Charlie's life, the real world made clear it was even crazier than Hollywood, which at least was well aware that it was not the real world.

"What did she do, write it in the dirt floor in blood by candlelight after miscarrying? Any society that merciless deserves a worse curse than that. They were like the Taliban."

"The Taliban are heathens." Great Aunt Abigail had set down her tea cup, suggesting the audience granted was now over.

"If I'd been Myrtle, I'd have turned all you maiden Staudts into fat prostitutes with harelips and crossed eyes. The lesson here is that no amount of self-righteousness justifies such evil cruelty."

"No, slut. The lesson here is that those with black eyes should not spawn, and you are a perfect example of why."

"And you are a nasty, mean, helpless old woman, and my mother is far too intelligent to get caught up in your sacrificial scheme of things. You, Abby Staudt, deserve Gentle Oaks for years and years and years."

At Gentle Oaks, snowflakes began to flutter against the windshield again and the oaks looked anything but gentle. Dark and bare and gloomy, they hovered over the building as if preparing to pounce on it. The dark sky barely cleared their tops. A dark, dank, threatening atmosphere closing in on the Greenes.

Oh, get real. And you think Harvey Rochester's moody.

Well, I get carried away by atmosphere.

"I noticed."

"You noticed what?"

"I noticed how strongly I'm affected by atmosphere. And this one's a real downer."

"Just remember how beautiful you thought Myrtle and Iowa were yesterday. We won't be there long. Viagra's will cheer you up. Just hang in." But they sat staring at the bleak scene. Charlie and her mother had not gotten along well since Charlie's hormones kicked in—similar to Charlie's experience with her own daughter—and the relationship had further deteriorated with a teen pregnancy. But as selfish as Charlie knew she was, and how much she longed to be out of here, she worried about what would have happened if Edwina had come to Myrtle alone. That cry for help had been justified.

Charlie hadn't realized how far back in the family this ponderous guilt thing had gone, how steeped with it her mother's upbringing had been, had always assumed it started with her own great mistake. Did it really go all the way back to Myrtle? She was about to broach the subject of her birth mother and the dark eyes among the blue around here when Marshal Delwood roared up in his red Cherokee.

Gentle Oaks was vastly different from what it had been on the weekend. For one thing, the administrator was in. And the place bustled with staff. The temporary weekend people had been replaced by locals, who came from town, from nearby farms or, like the administrator, from Floyd. Except for the Hispanic aides. Charlie wondered how many came to work on tractors with lugs like Darla.

Elsina Miller had two large prints of Jesus in her office. They were identical and you saw one upon entering and the other upon leaving. While activity and some panic swarmed around her, she remained serene, pleasant, benign, all-knowing—like the angel that touches people on TV, but she didn't have the teeth. Nor was she as pretty or worldly-wise.

She had lots of lush brown hair with the beginnings of gray salting it and an oily streak at the crown. Her dress was flowery with a matching belt, gathered and mid-calf. Her sweater matched one of the powder-blue flowers in the dress, somehow reminding Charlie of Dona Reed on *Nick at Night*. She wore hose with tennis shoes. When she sat down and crossed her legs, you could see the tops of her knee-highs. She was slender but with the ploop of a belly beginning below the matching belt and the early rise of a hump at the base of her neck in back.

They sat on opposing couches in her office while Delwood raged on his cell phone to somebody. Elsina Miller smiled apologetically and benignly at the Greenes. There'd been another death at Gentle Oaks.

While all this was going on, the administrator studied Charlie, finally asking gently, "Are you saved, Miss Greene?"

This angel didn't begin to compare on the threat scale with Great-aunt Abigail. "I must be. Lost my Toyota in a near-death experience, you know."

"No, I didn't know."

"You didn't? Everyone else seems to." Hell, I've been between the sheets with Mitch Hilsten. You must have heard of my one claim to fame. Del's cellular reminded Charlie that she must get ahold of Larry Mann, her gorgeous secretary.

"It looks as if Jesus loves you. He spared you."

"Tell that to the twelve who died in the same accident."

"Jesus has a purpose we do not know. I wish I could convince the marshal."

"Who?" Charlie asked when Del turned off his phone and while Elsina explained that death wasn't really dying or something.

"Ida Mae—Helen's mom."

"Myrtle's curse again?" Charlie asked so the condescending administrator could explain that there was no such thing as curses and that Jesus supervised all.

Charlie began to study Elsina as a possible suspect.

The worst part was that it was Helen who had discovered her mother dead this morning.

No, the very worst part was that Cousin Helen had decided Charlie should look into the suspicious deaths recently plaguing the Gentle Oaks Health Care Center. David Wyborny had apparently been sending home to Vivian more than just Charlie's accidents and notoriety in the industry news mags. Charlie was no detective, nor had she any desire to be, but the law of nature or Murphy's law or some other ridiculous, universal, or otherwise unnecessary law seemed to dictate that if you stumbled over one dead body in your life, others would follow. In Charlie's case, rather monotonously.

Fatty Staudt, Edwina's cadaverlike grandfather who used to be fat, wheeled his wheelchair in to ask Charlie if she was done with the combining yet.

"Yes." She and Helen were having a staring match, Elsina trying to convince all that Jesus would see to everything.

"And have the boys finished the haying yet?"

"Yes."

"Let us bow our heads in prayer. Lord Jesus, we pray thee—"

"Cousin Helen, you need professional law enforcement here."

"Goddamned right," the marshal agreed.

"That old Oliver still pulling the plows?"

"Your fucking Oliver's pulling just fine. Now get your

hands off my butt, dirty old geezer." No wonder Edwina had disowned him.

But everything came to a halt when the booming voice with the Broadway modulation boomed from the lobby, "*Now* what the bloody hell?"

CHAPTER 15

CHARLIE'S DERRIERE WAS sore from more than Fatty Staudt's pinches. All that falling down must have left some ugly bruises. She and her derriere were crowded into a booth at Viagra's with Delwood beside her, Edwina and Harvey across from her, and their server, Kenny Cowper, on a chair he'd pulled up at its end. Five steins of beer and a platter of french fries lay on the table between them.

The town watchman sat at the bar with a burger, pretending not to be listening. Outside the windows, snow fell thick and straight down, with no wind, making Viagra's feel cozy and safe.

"Kenneth, my boy, you would not believe the vile invective that came from those beautiful lips. Made even me blanch. Where perchance did such a fair maiden learn such words as those you laid upon our pure and dear Elsina?"

"My mother," Charlie answered the big-time businessman of Myrtle, and all eyes switched to the other woman in the bar, even the watchman's.

"Oh, come on. There were a few there I'd never even heard." The research scientist, biology professor, and expert on rats and bats of the high desert plateau dipped a fry in ketchup and then paused with the morsel halfway to her mouth. "Of course you have to understand the context here, Squirt. We had just come from an audience with her highness."

"Abigail Staudt?" Kenny put down his stein and stared back and forth at the women. "You went straight from Abigail to Elsina? Beer's on me, women—bravery beyond the call of duty, least I can do."

"The worst part was when Gladys and Marlys applauded Charlie's performance and so excited did they become that one at least soiled her Depends. On the spot. And you know how our administrator prefers to keep her office pure, even of that sort of thing." Rochester sounded almost gleeful.

"And that horrible alarm was going off and frankly, I'd already had a big day. I totally lost it. Lucky I didn't deck somebody." Charlie savored another french fry. "Do you do the bartending and the cooking, too? These are fantastic."

The barkeep had a way of laughing at you with a total lack of expression and no sound whatever. "Nah, I've got this secret weapon."

Charlie wasn't about to touch that one. "Mr. Rochester, do you have a grand piano in your living room or parlor?"

"No, ma'am."

"You stay away from my daughter, Squirt."

"Yes, ma'am."

The marshal wasn't about to be left out. "Ken, the really worst part was when Helen Bartusek insisted Miss Greene here investigate the rash of deaths up at the Oaks. Her mother bought it last night."

"Yeah. Ida Mae, I'd heard. But what did Miss Greene here answer to that? Leaving out the vulgar language of course."

"Said that was a job for professional law enforcement."

"And Cousin Helen replied, 'We don't have any in Myrtle,' " Edwina replied. " 'But you, Charlie, have been involved in murder before and can help us.' And Charlie said, 'Only if you let my mother go.' "

"Almost biblical," Harvey said as the hamburgers arrived.

Charlie and Edwina had agreed to share one. They make the biggest buns in Iowa. Even halves would be more than either could eat.

"Mr. Cowper, how do you keep your figure with food like this?" Charlie asked.

"He runs and lifts barbells," the marshal ratted.

"Got his own special refrigerator in the kitchen here full of rabbit food. Don't crunch, he throws it out," said Myrtle's watchman-snitch from the bar stool where he was paying no attention to them. He wore a knitted cap with the edges rolled up all around.

"And my secret weapon." The proprietor of Viagra's made a special point of pointing out the thick slices of tomato and lush leaf lettuce and grilled onion on his plate and theirs.

Charlie would never know if this food was so wonderful because of special cooking, secret weapons, or the fact that her mood and the rest of the atmosphere were so miserable. Or because from somewhere there came the delightful scent of real coffee, fresh-ground.

"So Ms. Greene, have you decided to take on the case? So that your mother's family will let her go?"

"Is that real coffee? Like a skinny latté with nutmeg sprinkles?"

"You answer my question first."

"I'm my mother's family and I'm taking her out of here, dudes. No way am I going to let this happen to her because some Taliban society mistreated an ugly woman for its own purposes." That's what she'd meant to say but not how she'd meant to say it. Charlie pushed the half-filled stein of beer away.

"But she did condescend to look at the body."

"It was dead," Charlie assured them. Ida Mae Truex had been a short and very heavy woman. She was a great mound beneath the sheet. She'd been dead for a while. By the coroner's orders, they were to touch nothing if a patient was found unexpectedly dead until he arrived, since the rash of deaths was causing suspicion.

One eyelid had been open halfway, showing some clouding. Could have been death, could have been cataracts, for all Charlie knew. She wondered if someone had closed them for her after death. The nuthouse that place was last night, anything could have happened. Ida Mae could have just died a natural death and someone tried to lower her lids. Charlie didn't know what color suffocation made the skin. Ida Mae's was sort of mottled. The bedclothes were decidedly rumpled. Maybe that was normal, too.

The staff had been late getting to work what with the ice storm, and in the frenzy to take care of all the adult babies still hyped over the full moon, Ida Mae's demise had been a late discovery.

"And we have a very large staff during the week, most of whom live nearby."

"Women come cheap here," Kenny explained. "And so do the Mexicans."

"Yeah, well, I don't come cheap. Old Marlys even called me top dollar out at the cemetery before I lost her."

"I'll vouch for that," Edwina said.

"You want that latté, you have to tell what you discovered when you examined Ida Mae's body."

"I hire men, too. It's the weekends that are the devil at all long-term health-care facilities."

"We don't call it a nursing home in front of Harvey," the marshal explained. "It would be insensitive."

"Gentle Oaks, may I remind you gentlemen, is the only full-occupancy business in the county. And it thrives on more than cheap labor. It thrives on my good head for business."

"Charlie says that makes you a bad actor," the marshal offered.

"Even with a good supply of cheap labor, I don't see how you can make money at this," Charlie said. "I don't see how you can make money with Viagra's or The Station either. Look, it's noon. There's hardly anybody here."

"Ahh," intoned Mr. Rochester, "the staff at The Station does the cooking for Gentle Oaks as well. Food is transported in a van on trays in specially warmed or cooled shelf containers. And food is even cheaper than labor here. Small gold mine is what it is. Long-term care is an industry that far outdoes soybeans in Northern Iowa now. And once the poor old souls have spent down all their money, we plug them into Medicaid, which in Myrtle can pay for years of caregiving and Depends and make a profit, too. The Station is also cheaply staffed and can keep people permanently employed thanks to Gentle Oaks, Myrtle's curse, and Medicaid. Sweet deal all around."

"I grind my own beans," Kenny teased. "Keep them in the freezer before that. Import them. They're top dollar, too."

"You sure you don't have a grand piano in your living room?" Charlie asked Harvey and wrapped the tomato and onion in the leaf lettuce, topped it with a ketchuped fry and pushed the rest away as she had the beer.

"Cross my heart. But, my dear, that throaty voice of yours is about to convince me to go out and purchase one shortly."

Kenny made shooshing noises, like he was steaming milk. "Even grate my own nutmeg nuts."

"Well, if it wasn't a natural death, you'd expect someone had just taken a pillow and held it over her head until she suffocated. Probably two someones. The bed was well-rumpled, which could mean either a struggle with death, with a murderer, or she was a restless sleeper. She was dressed in nothing but her diapers. Let me see, my writers—who are nearly as crazy as the inmates of Gentle Oaks—would probably deduce from those facts, and that her arms were lying crossed on her stomach, that another person was pinning her down across her middle to keep her from struggling with the person holding the pillow. That better be a damn good latté, Cowper."

It was marvelous—just what she needed. Hers came first, and soon Harvey, Edwina, and the proprietor were each having one, too.

But everyone, including her mother, seemed to have gone into some kind of shock. The marshal, who was having just a cup of plain coffee, sat writing down what she'd said, reading it back to her to be sure it was right.

"Oh, come on. That was all just conjecture. My guess is she just up and died on her own. And, Del—you have a cellular but not a Palm Pilot to document evidence?"

"You come up with all that just by looking at a dead body you can't touch? A person you don't know anything about?" Kenny pretended to be really impressed.

"So what do you suggest we do?" Harvey Rochester had turned ashen.

"I don't know. Don't let anybody wash any pillowcases? There might be some kind of bodily fluid coughed up in the struggle."

"Call the Oaks," Rochester ordered Marshal Brunsvold, and the two departed without finishing their coffees.

"Is this place weird or what?" Charlie asked her mother.

"You don't realize how convincing you can be, Charlie."

"Why a pillow?" Kenny chewed on a cold french fry.

"Well, something like a pillow then. Used to be you couldn't get much in the way of fingerprints off a pillow— now you might get the killer's DNA. I had a writer once who used cotton stuffed up the nose and down the throat of a victim, but that left shards or traces of cotton on the victim that the famous TV detective ID'd with cotton wads found at the perp's home. Hey, this is all fiction. The coroner will know what to do."

"He has to depend on the first cop to reach the crime scene to secure it, right?" Kenny winked.

"Marshal Del." Oh, boy.

And on that note, Uncle Elmo Staudt staggered in, a layer of snow on his cap and the shoulders of his coat. "Am I glad to see you gals. It's gettin' bad out there and I was worried you got lost."

Their host seated Uncle Elmo in his chair, presented him with a stein of his own and a promise of fries and a hamburger on the way and then seated himself beside Edwina. "So what's the news at the Sinclair?"

"Well, this front's moved in faster than they thought with

the ice already and now snow to cover it, so if you plow off the snow, you leave the slippery ice exposed. If you don't, nobody sees the ice under the snow and goes into the ditch. But the real story is about my sister dying up at the Oaks. Helen's really going to be hell to live with now. Talk is, it was murder and maybe my aunts, too. But know what I think now? Anybody was going to murder anybody around here, they'd of started with old Abigail."

"But she's not up at Gentle Oaks," Charlie pointed out. "Does this front mean we'll have trouble getting to Mason City tonight?"

"Hell, we'll have trouble getting back to the home place. Mason City airport's closed down. Minneapolis, too. Ain't anybody going nowhere until tomorrow at the earliest. Not that unusual for winter. Been mild a lot longer than anybody thought it would."

"Looks like you have no reason to avoid investigating the deaths at Gentle Oaks, doesn't it?" Kenny Cowper sounded smug, like he'd conjured up the storm for his own entertainment. "Soon as we have Elmo settled with his food, I know exactly where you should start, too."

CHAPTER 16

⬥

*I*F CHARLIE HAD thought the ambiance of Myrtle, Iowa, dark and gloomy in the wake of rain and sleet this morning, she didn't know dark and gloomy. They left Uncle Elmo describing the collapse of his barn to Ben the watchman and stepped out into so thick a snowfall the snow wasn't white.

"You got chains for that rental?" Kenny pointed to the lone morbid mound at the curb. "I'll check it before you try to take off." He looked like some kind of a god himself when he raised his arms to the totally invisible heavens and said, "God, I missed this in Florida. Got me a new snowmobile out back all ready to go."

If he was a god, he was a nutty one. All Charlie could think of was another night at the home place and missing the plane out in the morning. "I better call the office."

She rummaged through her purse, only to find her cellular missing. If she could get any lower, she didn't know how.

"We'll use the phone back at Viagra's." Edwina sounded low, too. "You probably left your cell out at the farm."

Kenny unlocked a door two or three down from Viagra's and ushered them into a darker, colder, danker place than outside, switching on some wall switches to display the Myrtle Museum.

"Used to be a drugstore," he explained the marble-topped soda-fountain bar and narrow, wire-legged stools of one display.

Edwina ran a finger through the dust. "Used to be a real soda fountain. I liked the black cows best. Sort of like a choc-

102

olate sundae with cashews on top, served in a tall Coke glass."

"Did you ever dress like that?" Charlie pointed to a red-lipped woman with a Coke bottle in one hand and hair tied up in a scarf with the knot on top.

"That was more my mother's era."

"Lots of generations of stuff here," Kenny said. "Only place in town we keep locked because of marauding collectors and the thieves who sell to them."

There was an old post-office display, wood-burning cookstoves, an ice box, quilts and clothing and carpentry and cooking implements. And a large upright tank sort of thing with tube coils, a spigot, and, perched on top like the Tin Man's hat, the largest funnel she'd ever seen. "Is that a still?"

"Nah, used to make molasses."

"That is a still. Where'd it come from?"

"Arly Truex's fruit cellar, actually." Kenny opened an old photo album on top of a glass display case that had come from Marlys Dittberner's grocery store on the corner. He lit a gas lantern, kept for the purpose apparently, so Charlie and Edwina could look into the past. Even on a sunny day with the place on fire, this old stone building would be dark.

"Cousin Helen's family had a still in their fruit cellar?"

"Lots of people collect antiques. End up giving them to museums."

On the first page of the album was a daguerreotype of poor Myrtle's tombstone, the space between her name and birth dates blacked out or a very precise piece of damage to the picture. "Was there originally a family name on that stone?"

"Beats me," Kenny said, turning the page. "It's all a mystery I don't remember hearing much about as a boy growing up here."

"Just hints and innuendos."

"Yeah, if it's important, it's not discussed. Gonna make your investigation tough, Charlie Greene."

I'm not investigating, you gorgeous jerk. "How come you

and I and my daughter and Harvey and Marlys all have the same color eyes?"

"We must have a common ancestor? A prolific one. Those eyes show up in about twenty percent of the population around here."

"Myrtle. I saw that painting above Abigail's fireplace. No bunch of old-guy farmers that long ago would have bothered to have a portrait painted of an ugly daughter they intended to enslave as a spinster caregiver. And why name the town after a poor soul like her? This legend doesn't wash, barkeep."

Kenny turned another page to reveal a formal and crowded family daguerreotype. Inked in underneath, in perfect flowing handwriting at odds with the stiff image, was the caption explaining—FATHER, MOTHER, AND THE SIX LIVING CHILDREN. It was sort of a black-and-brown picture, the eye colors indistinct. But on the opposing page was a small, single picture of a young woman in a tidy little hat tied under her chin, big expectant eyes that could have been dark, and hair that was obviously blond or gray or colorless. The flowery caption beneath that read MYRTLE.

"That's not the ugly Myrtle in Great-aunt Abigail's painting."

"Abigail fancied herself as an artist at one time."

"The Victorian penchant for revising history." Edwina looked up over Charlie at Kenny Cowper, the lantern on the display case hissing and flickering shadows across her face and the bare brick wall behind her. "I sure hope those people meant well, because they screwed up more history, science, society, medicine, government—you name it—with their pretend facts. And we accuse communists and dictators of doing that now."

"And don't forget families." Kenny had bent to look into Edwina's eyes, Charlie knew, because she could feel his breath in the hair on top of her head. She hated when men did that. "They screw up families, too. Whole little towns full of families."

104

"How did that still survive the purge?" Charlie wanted to know.

"Old Abigail doesn't get down to the museum anymore." He turned another page to another huge family caption here was THE STAUDTS. And on the opposing page were two little girls and a baby ANNABEL, GERTRUDE, AND ABIGAIL. Abigail was the baby. "Although she gets out and about more than she lets on. Ben walks her to church and up to visit at the Oaks in nice weather. Neighbors drive her in bad."

Charlie asked her mom why Libby's middle name was Abigail. Charlie had chosen the first and consented to Edwina's choice of the middle.

"I don't know whether I thought I was getting even with you for deciding to keep the baby or if I thought it would make her pure and chaste or a combination of the two. Or maybe the name was forever burned into my psyche."

Del Brunsvold stuck his head in the door, a cold eddy of wind and snowflakes swirling past him. Charlie's feet were so cold already she could barely feel them. "Got to get the Greenes up to the Oaks, Kenny. Can you get their rental off Main Street?"

"Oh, Jesus, I forgot. He's going to plow. We're talking massive destruction here." Kenny closed the album. "More later, ladies—sorry, women. When the marshal plows, even stray dogs, drunks, and Marlys Dittberner get off the streets."

Marshal Sweetie's Cherokee gunned, skidded, tossed snow to either side like a TV commercial for dud dudes. Charlie didn't even want to think about what he and that really big dump truck with the blade on the front did to anything hapless caught on Myrtle's streets in a blizzard. And a blizzard it was.

"Yell if you see a tree coming up too fast in the middle of the road—means we're not in the middle of the road."

"How can you even tell where we are?"

"We just crossed the tracks, so we're headed in the right

direction." Delwood was obviously elated—imagine getting high on the kind of snow that melts in the sun.

The coroner had not been able to make it to the Oaks today, partially, Del guessed, because of the roads, the accidents, and perhaps other suspicious deaths in Floyd County. Phone lines were down and cellular communication intermittent. So Harvey the boss decided the marshal should bring in the only investigator he had on hand at the moment and plow a path for food and staff to get to and from. And, Charlie suspected, keep the marshal as far away from the crime scene as possible. "There's the gate. Don't hit the wall."

The only good reason to go to Gentle Oaks Charlie could think of was that it was kept very warm and maybe she could thaw her feet out. Her boots were dress boots, not mukluks. And the longer she could stay away from the drafty home place, the better.

"Tree, tree!" Edwina shouted, and the marshal set the brakes so the Jeep just skidded into an oak trunk—so big none of the branches showed down out of the weather—instead of smashing into it. "Charlie, don't freak on us now."

"I'm okay. But how do we get back to the farm in all this?"

"Don't worry, we'll take you out there on our snowmobiles. It'll be a blast, a glorious blast." He gunned and rocked and backed and forwarded until they were presumably on the drive again.

"I can hardly wait."

Sure enough, some lights wavered ahead in the drifting snow that hammered them when they dashed from the red Cherokee to the porch of Gentle Oaks. You couldn't even see the branches of trees above here either, but Charlie could see them from memory, feel them. If you believed in the archaic hippy culture's "vibes," this place simply did not have good ones. Period.

Well, what do you expect? It's filled with dying people who don't die.

"Until recently."

"Until what recently?" Mr. Rochester met them at the door.

"She talks to herself," Edwina explained.

Harvey ordered the marshal to get on with his plowing and be back here in time to help transfer one shift of employees to homes here in town where the last shift was now resting and bring the resting shift in. "There'll be no going and coming except from here in town. We do, however, have a plethora of insanely eager volunteers with snowmobiles to help with the shuffling duties. But I must get staff to The Station to cook supper for these lost souls and transport it here, as well as breakfast in the morning. Going to be a long day and night. Meanwhile, ladies, step inside and please try not to murder our beloved and insufferable administrator."

The place really bustled now that no one could go home. The dining room was half filled with people playing music in one corner and people helping inmates cut out snowflakes in another. The staff kept looking up at the large TV, where the Munchkins danced around Judy Garland and Toto. Marlys Dittberner, supposedly well over a hundred years old, skipped around tables like a fifty-year-old, making Munchkin sounds, grabbed the dusty eyeglasses right off some lady's face, and danced out of the room singing, "We're off to see the wizard, the wonderful wizard of Oz, because, because, because—"

The imprisoned employees continued their duties but with waning cheerfulness, except for Darla Lempke, who led a chorus of wheelchair-bound zombies in a song that only she was singing—joyfully—like she was blind to her drooling, snoring, confused, mostly silent, and largely toothless choir.

Just beyond the dining room, which Harvey explained was the activity center between meals, they came to another wing of rooms where a woman's voice groaned and cried out over the blaring TV in her room with monotonous heartrending repetition, "It's so-o-o haarrrd to be alive . . . nowww."

"How do you keep from going crazy here?"

"Ahh, my dear, the world is crazy, but the answers to it

all may lie at Gentle Oaks," intoned the mover and shaker of Myrtle. "Now here is the crime scene again, perhaps not as pleasant as this morning, and here are all the pillowcases I saved from the laundry. Two thirds of them have some sort of fluid on them. What do I do? This isn't going to work, is it?"

"No."

"Perhaps if you got a better look at the deceased? I don't know when the coroner will get here. Meanwhile, we've had to move Ida Mae's roommate out. Can you help me, Ms. Greene? I know you are not a professional crime-scene investigator, but things deteriorate fast."

"I will deny anything you see me do or hear me say. But I'll look her over and then she should be outside in the deep freeze. You can take all credit or blame for whatever I tell you I notice in the next few minutes."

"Deal. Hurry."

"Okay. Hard to tell the time of death because this place is kept so warm."

"Drives the staff insane, but these frail people are always cold."

"Right. There is a definite odor of death here and some obvious rigor has set in, blood settled on the bottom of her considerable bottom—that's the bruising, some here on her stomach as well. I thought everybody lost weight here."

"She has. You wouldn't believe how huge she was in her past life."

Charlie lifted both of Ida Mae's eyelids, even the one that had not been completely lowered the last time she was in here. Since then, someone had taken care of it again. "Clouded corneas. I estimate she expired last night probably before midnight and while the full moon raged. I see no signs of entry or exit wounds or bruising on the neck that would indicate murder by stabbing, shooting, or choking. No outward signs of poisoning. The bedclothes have been straightened up since this morning—which could mean a demented inmate—"

"Resident. Or even a member of the staff might have re-arranged things. Cut to the chase. Are we talking staff, resident, visitor from the community? What? Who could do such a thing to such a frail population?"

"My vote is for the Grim Reaper. Next, it would be staff, other residents, or their relatives and friends. Can I go now? My feet are warm."

But Elsina Miller blocked the doorway and right behind her, Darla the bouncy social worker. Charlie's illegal examination had not been private after all.

CHAPTER 17

◆

*D*OLORES THE TOMCAT did not have the dark Myrtle eyes, and neither did Sherman Rochester of the suspicious socks. Somehow, Charlie couldn't see either one of them murdering the lingering dead. The two nutty Fatties were capable of anything and had relatively strong upper bodies but were confined to wheelchairs.

Charlie couldn't even believe she was thinking like this. If she were her old self before the accident, she'd be clawing her way out of here and back home somehow, or at least to Mason City, the only living airport for miles.

Oh, right, you'd steal somebody's snowmobile, plop your mother on the back and soar off on roads you don't know and couldn't see anyway. The coroner can't even get here in this weather and he's used to it.

Harvey, the actor businessman, was having an intermittent conversation with the Floyd County coroner on Del's cell phone, explaining what Charlie had said about the deteriorating victim as well as the crime scene. As the conversation came and went, Harvey would throw theatrical hysterics and Darla and Elsina would try to comfort him. Somewhere not too far off, Marlys laughed. It wasn't an aged cackle, more of a deep-throated, lewd laugh—but unmistakably Marlys Dittberner.

"He wants to talk to you."

"You've got to be kidding. I'm a professional literary agent. You've got RNs around here who know more about dead bodies than I do."

110

"He wants to talk to you and back at the crime scene and—" he turned to his admiring staff "—to you and me alone."

They were in the dining activities area and had to pass again the poor wretch who found it so hard to be alive these days. Harvey, still trying to keep contact on the cell, had a hold of Charlie's wrist and hurried her along. She looked back for Edwina, who was talking to one of the inmates, and happened to notice a very un-Christian narrowing of the administrator's eyes as they followed Harvey and Charlie's progress away from her.

Another suspect?

Greene, Elsina's not here at nights or on weekends.

Actually, in Ida Mae's room, the transmission was much better, still by no means good, but Harvey and Charlie followed the coroner's instructions as carefully as possible, checking and reporting each other's every move to the county official. Reporting odors, swelling from gas buildup, bruising, taking swabs from the poor woman's nose and throat and, yes, genitals, with sterile Q-Tips and putting them in bags they labeled as they went along, Harvey rushing to the door to order new supplies when needed. They wore surgical masks and rubber gloves.

"He orders an on-site autopsy, I'm outta here," Charlie warned.

It didn't come to that, but there were certain incisions to drain certain fluids, scooping certain samples from the diaper—and certain places on the corpse to describe intermittently by cellular again and again. Coroners are ghouls. Literary agents are not.

Ida Mae Staudt Truex was then buried in a hallowed limbo in the snow outside in a fenced area—just below the smoker porch—where sealed hazardous and infectious waste containers were kept. There was plenty of room for a body.

"Jesus Christ, what an experience," Rochester boomed to Charlie, the ones ordered to deep-freeze the corpse alone.

"No, dear Elsina—I am not born again, back off now. But, Ms. Greene, I'll wager your feet are cold again."

"Tell me this coroner from Floyd is a medical doctor," Charlie said.

"Actually, he's a mortician."

"Oh, shit."

"We got plenty of that."

"I know, Gladys. How are you?"

"He's one of my boyfriends." Gladys reached for Harvey's hand and missed.

"And the coroner's not from Floyd, just serves Floyd County," Harvey said. "The county seat is Charles City, and that's where he is. Floyd was supposed to be the county seat but the railroad chose to go through Charles City instead, so—"

"Is he good?" Charlie asked Gladys.

"Oh, you bet. Really good."

"Does he have a piano in his living room?"

"Three of 'em, maybe four." Gladys had gas and shared the fact with everyone in the hall.

" 'Warning: Liquid oxygen reservoir. Warning: No smoking. Do not place flammable materials in this closet. Please return all equipment to this closet after using and return the key to the nurses' station.' " A tall woman in a walker and mismatched pink sweatpants and sweatshirt stood in front of a closed door reading out loud the sign attached to it. Most of the residents were dressed that way, and most were in wheelchairs, many with oxygen tanks strapped on the back. At least she could walk. Her walker had a split green tennis ball over each back foot.

"Unfortunately, unless it's a case of stroke, speech seems to be one of the last things to go." Harvey Rochester dumped their disposable masks and gloves in a hazardous-waste container behind another locked door.

" 'Warning: Liquid oxygen reservoir. Warning: No smoking. Do not place flammable materials in this closet. Please return all equipment to this closet after using and return the key to the nurses' station.' "

"That's enough, Rose. Go play with Darla. Darla, come get this creature."

" 'Darla Lempke, Activities Director.' " Rose read the social worker's badge as they waited for a break in the wheelchair traffic.

"That's very good, Rose," Darla said. "Who am I again?"

"I don't know."

"Ciga-riga-rooo?"

"It's sooo haaard being alive nowww."

"Help me, please. Somebody help me."

"Charlie, you going to be okay?" Edwina asked and followed Charlie into the ladies' room.

"I want to go home and I don't mean the home place." Charlie scrubbed her hands and forearms and made a cold pack out of wet paper towels for her face. "I'm about a fraction of a hair away from a hissy-fit panic attack—full blown. I'm just not ready for this particular stage of life yet."

"I don't think most people ever are. And it's really getting out of hand now with so many lingering so much longer than their minds." Edwina wasn't as tall as Libby but she was taller than Charlie. She held Charlie and the wet towels against her shoulder and Charlie cried. A lot. And a long time.

"What if we have to stay here all night? It's snowing so hard it practically buried Ida Mae for us." They'd stuck a push broom into the snow—handle down, bristle side up—to mark the spot, and when she and her mom stepped out of the ladies now the broom stood totally coated in white, the bristle end less than a foot above the snow. And Dolores the tom sniffed at a human turd in the middle of the hall.

"Maybe we can stay at Helen's tonight. I don't see anybody getting us out to the farm in this. Don't lose it now. It'll be all right, honey."

"Got a match?"

Charlie ignored Sherman and his socks to stare at her

113

mother. "You know, I haven't seen you smoke since I met you in the Minneapolis airport." Charlie had never known her mother without a long brown cigarette and a cough. "When?"

"You smoke?" Sherman inquired.

"When I got home after your accident. Decided it wasn't worth it."

"Just like that? Can people do that? I mean, don't you have to go to therapy and everything? I thought it was like alcoholism and drugs and stuff."

"Got a cigarette?"

"Believe me, this trip is trying my resolve. If I can get through this, I can get through anything."

"Ciga-riga-roooo?"

Sherman and Flo were sure examples of how hard it must be. They didn't know who they were, but they knew they wanted a cigarette.

"Charlie, don't look at me like that. People can change at sixty. I'm still the mother you knew."

"Yeah, but no glasses, no cigarettes, you did your eyes, colored your hair, dated a younger man, you're squaring your shoulders and not stooping, had your teeth capped."

"Yeah, and I'm in a fitness-workout program at CU, almost free for faculty. We do weights, yoga, swimming, running, Pilates—"

"Mom, pretty soon I'm not even going to know you. Why are you doing all this at your age? I mean, I'm glad you quit smoking, but what's the point with all the rest?"

Before Edwina Greene could answer her daughter, a familiar mewling sounded from one of Sherman Rochester's socks.

———————————————————◆———————————————————

"Larry, can you hear me? I won't be back tomorrow. Edwina and I are snowed-in, in Iowa. What? All I'm getting is static—"

"—been trying to get you all day."

"Someone stole my cellular, just found it. I'll get back to you as soon as the storm clears. Could you check on Libby for me? Let her know what's happening?"

"What's happening?"

"Oh, Edwina and I are stranded in a nursing home full of really old maniacs. But don't tell Libby that, just tell her I'll try to call her tomorrow. I'll probably be a day or two late." The rest was static, but she had her contact with the outside world in her hand. It still worked. The real world, other people's nightmare, was Charlie's ballast and still out there. How the hell did old Sherman get her precious tether to reality? And why did he put it in his socks? It wasn't even silver.

Charlie looked through her purse to see if anything else was missing. Her Palm Pilot. "Harvey, could your grandfather have stolen my Palm Pilot, too?"

Rochester and Darla looked at each other and seemed agreed that it was unlikely.

"He usually just takes silverware," Darla said. "But if you hand him something, he's more likely to put it in his sock than his pocket. Gladys steals letters and magazines to slip to Rose, who will read aloud until someone goes nuts and takes them away from her. Rose steals signs off the walls. Marlys—"

"Marlys was standing next to you when you were telling off Elsina Miller this morning," Edwina said.

Marlys Dittberner roomed with Gladys, and both old women watched Harvey pull a suitcase out from under Marlys' bed. "That's mine. I'm going home today. It's all packed," Marlys told him.

"It certainly is." Harvey pulled out Charlie's Palm Pilot, flight schedule, and key case. The rest of Marlys' packing consisted of dentures, one bedroom slipper, and hearing aids with strings and clips to attach them to clothing so as not to lose them, but now all the strings and clips were tangled together. Plus a roll of toilet paper, pairs of dusty eyeglasses, several ballpoint pens, an empty clipboard, hats of various sizes, and an unopened box of Efferdent.

As it turned out, Cousin Helen couldn't take the Greenes in that night because her guest rooms and extra couches were filled with stranded help from Gentle Oaks. At least the nursing home wouldn't be understaffed during the storm if the snowmobiles could get them about.

The stranded administrator would have to sleep either in the lobby or her office—it was that bad an emergency. Charlie wondered about Harvey Rochester's big house—but no one offered beds there that she heard about. What, he had a huge family everyone forgot to mention?

So it came to pass that Charlie and Edwina and Uncle Elmo would spend the night upstairs at Viagra's. Well, it was an emergency and respectable women couldn't be seen there. Oh, boy.

CHAPTER 18

❖

*T*HAT NIGHT, CHARLIE had her first low-fat and low-sugar meal since she'd been in Iowa. Fresh salad greens with chopped carrots and whole sugar snap peas. Pasta with chopped basil, tomato, red and green bell peppers, green onions, parsley, garlic, and sprinkles of olive oil. Warm French bread, a good Chianti, a small chocolate truffle each. French-pressed coffee.

Uncle Elmo complained that this would have been meatloaf, mashed potatoes, cooked green beans, and apple cobbler night if Viagra's was open for business. He drank beer instead of wine and refused the coffee. "You should never have gone to Florida—twenty kinds of uncooked vegetables and not a shred of meat."

Charlie leaned back against a couch, replete. They'd eaten sitting on pillows on the floor around a square coffee table in front of a small wood stove, music playing softly on a CD somewhere behind a bookcase partition. "I thought it was magnificent, Kenny. Wonder what Elsina Miller's having tonight."

He chuckled. "Figured you two wouldn't hit it off. Wonder why. She's eating whatever's being served the rest up there. Del said nobody'd take her in."

"Oh, yeah. She'd have them up all night trying to convert 'em." Uncle Elmo lowered his upper plate to clean bits of raw veggie off his gums.

"Not even the woman preacher?"

"Oh, she don't live here. She's got two churches, one here,

117

one in Floyd. Lives in Floyd. Besides, our preacher's Methodist. That Elsina's Baptist. You got baking soda, Kenny? Have to soak these dentures in something. What about you, Edwina? Looks like you got false teeth, too."

"I'm fine, these don't come out. Charlie's contacts do, though."

"I've got baking soda and saline solution. I've got an apartment-size washer and dryer if anyone needs to wash out a few things, and some T-shirts for you to sleep in. If the electricity holds up. I'm surprised those wires haven't gone down, too."

"So everybody in town is taking in employees of Gentle Oaks in this emergency, except Harvey Rochester, who owns the nursing home and the biggest house in town?"

"Well, he can't, you see, little Charlie. Because most of those employees are females, and females find him irresistible and he could get in a whole lot of trouble even if he wasn't home. I expect you noticed his resemblance to that fella that was one of Elizabeth Taylor's husbands."

Charlie watched the laughter fight with the fondness in the barkeep's eyes and a real smile part lips that usually settled for a closed, sardonic grin. "God, I missed this in Florida."

"Get me another beer, Kenny. I'm trying to die. See, there was a school superintendent in the county not long ago caught stepping out with some of the high-school students. Stepping out to motels far from home. Lost his job and family, life ruined forever. Things have got to a point these days a man don't dare smile at somebody ain't his wife or mother."

"So how about you, Charlie Greene? Is it fun being a Hollywood literary agent?" Kenny set a beer down in front of Elmo.

"I love it," Charlie said. "It's hectic and stressful and exciting and gives me something to get up for every morning. It's my identity. What's your identity, Kenneth Cowper? All these books, your fab figure, your sensitivity to the horrors up at the Oaks—you just don't profile as a tiny-town barkeep somehow."

"Squirt." Edwina came suddenly alive. "Kenneth Cooper, right? *The Last of the Manly Hardy Boys.* I've been trying to remember what was so familiar about you besides the Myrtle eyes and you as a squirt. I loved *Dead Time in Disneyland.*"

Charlie had never heard of him or his books—she wouldn't if he wasn't a bestseller. Even then, bestsellers crank through the industry pretty fast—if it's not your author, never filmed, and Cooper's a pretty ordinary name compared to Cowper.

He watched her churn through all this, the closed grin on his face. "I've heard all about you."

"Tell me you're not writing a nursing-home book."

"Why not?"

"Totally too depressing for the market. What would your market be? Women? No way, they get to change the Depends. Men? It's not exactly football. They want to see blood and bruises, not excrement. There's no glory in excrement, Kenny."

"Charlie, Kenneth Cooper writes nonfiction," Edwina said. "To think I was calling Kenneth Cooper 'Squirt.' I'm getting old."

"Don't tell me." Charlie squinted so hard at their host his grin opened into a smile again. "*The Legend of Myrtle.*"

"I was thinking something more like *The Curse of Myrtle*, which, you realize, must include Gentle Oaks."

"You write books, Kenny?" Elmo too squinted at the hunk. "How do you have time to do that and run the pool hall and run yourself to a sweat and lift all them weights and stuff?"

"And have time to visit your relatives at the nursing home?" Charlie added.

"I do the ordering and the bookkeeping for Viagra's, have things pretty well computerized. Jack does the cooking. Lorna does the bartending, Jody and Lou the cleanup. I come down to the bar in the evenings to keep an eye on things, sometimes at noon. But since we close down by ten at the latest, I have lots of time to write and research, work out, and enjoy life, too. And don't worry, I have an agent."

"Who?"

"Jeth Larue."

"Isn't Jethro Larue the one who stole Georgette Millrose from you, Charlie?" Edwina asked.

Charlie'd had an inkling there were writers coming out of the woodwork everywhere, but Jesus—in Myrtle, Iowa?

When Kenny's father died and his mother left for Florida, taking Kenny and his sister with her, she leased this building and the business to Jack and Lorna. They were his secret weapon. "They couldn't make a go of it, so eventually in order to get rid of me, my mom sold me her holdings in Myrtle to get rid of them, too. Turned out a perfect deal for us both. I need to get away to do my work. Here, I can arrange my privacy and my socializing as I want."

Viagra's was actually beginning to make a profit. "Harvey's right about the cheap labor and low food costs compared to the rest of the world. You keep things the way people like them, you've got customers, steady customers who live forever."

With the Internet and e-mail, he could communicate with the outside world. Downstairs at Viagra's, he communicated with a rural and aging America. He also wrote articles he could sell to the outside world without having to live in it. "I don't know how long I'll stay, but right now I love it. Like you love Hollywood, Charlie Greene. Now, let's get your clothes to washing before the power lines come down with the weight of ice and snow."

After the home place, and during an ice-and-snowstorm brutal beyond imagining, upstairs at Viagra's was a paradise beyond imagining. Fed, warm, safe from Gentle Oaks, Charlie drifted off to the voices of her mother and the writer whispering somewhere among the bookcases while doing her laun-

dry, and to Uncle Elmo's snores. And she was even aware of
when she sank further into a sleep, deep as the snow piling
up outside, in Kenny's T-shirt, which, like his coat, came to
her knees.

———————————————✦———————————————

Charlie lay naked in the dirt and watched by candlelight as
Kenneth Cowper lowered himself on top of her with a hu-
morless grin. She was trying to remember why she should
want to fight him off. He was unbelievably beautiful. She must
have forgotten something. Her body ached like in a stupid
romance.

And then a scream, and right over the hunk's shoulder she
saw a door in the ceiling lift up, and a halo of light above it
revealed wooden steps. But above everything stood Great-
aunt Abigail Staudt, looking like a vengeful god with the halo
haloing her whole body and with a bloody package in her
arms.

"Harlot," she yelled and threw the package down on Charlie. Kenny was gone by now, of course. But there was an old,
yet polished, still next to the wooden steps, the Tin Man's
funnel hat still on top.

"Charlie?" Her mother's voice. "For godsake, Charlie,
you'll hurt yourself. What is it?"

"It's all bloody. Get it off me."

"It's a dream." Edwina. "She had one last night, too. Since
the accident—"

"No, it's a baby. It's dead. Get it off."

"Charlie?" Kenny Cowper. "Elmo, grab her feet."

"Relax, Charlie, and open your eyes. You can't see till you
open your eyes. Now take a deep breath and another. Relax.
You closed your eyes again, why?"

"Boy, she's strong for such a little thing." Uncle Elmo.
What was he doing down here?

"I don't want to see it. It's all dead and bloody. I can't
move. Kenny, I can't move."

"It's because I'm lying across your stomach, Uncle Elmo's got your feet, and Kenny has you by the shoulders. Charlie, you've got to wake up—don't sink back into that hell, whatever it is."

They forced her to stand and then to walk. The floor was wood and not dirt. It was daylight, and there was no door in the ceiling. "No baby."

"No blood. Keep walking," Edwina ordered on one side of her.

"Tell us about the dream," Uncle Elmo said on the other side. "That way, it won't come back."

Kenny stood in front of her, barefoot, in tight Levi's, no shirt—

"Oh, Jesus."

"Keep walking. Don't close your eyes."

—hair still wet from the shower, one half of his face still covered in shaving cream—and of course with her contacts out, he was clothed in a warm, fuzzy—

"Oh, boy."

"What?"

"I almost did it again. Can women do that?"

"Do what?"

"They can't. It's a male fantasy, dreamed up by Frank Sinatra's press agent. Read all about that in *Variety*."

"I better grind some coffee," Kenny said and turned his back on Charlie.

"Oh, no. Don't do that. Ohhh, oh, my God."

"I'm shoving her straight into the shower, Uncle Elmo. Could you bring her clothes from the dryer?"

"Yeah, that and Kenny's coffee ought to bring her around. You sure she's not on some kind of drugs, Edwina? That was one strange way of reacting there."

CHAPTER 19

✦

A SHOWER AND a shampoo, clean clothes to put on afterward. Kenny Cowper-Cooper even had a hair dryer and presented Charlie with a latté adorned with nutmeg sprinkles when she came out of the bathroom. Thank God he had his shirt on. Good thing her mother and Uncle Elmo were here, too. Charlie's main weakness with guy anatomy was the well-formed male back. Forget the buns. Just the back of the back.

"And I have for you," the barkeep announced, "an egg-delight hot dish that will warm your innards." His face was half-shadowed by beard because Charlie's shower had used up the rest of the hot water before the power lines failed and the water he was heating had to make coffee. "And hot rolls from the freezer and, Elmo, real live bacon."

The hot dish was one of those baked scrambled-egg-potato concoctions, with onions and garlic and cheese and more little veggie bits, that you cut in squares. Kenny had a gas stove to cook on and a wood stove to heat with, and even an old hand-crank coffee grinder from the museum.

The snow had stopped coming down and now blew into drifts instead to further entrap Charlie with the curse of Myrtle and maybe her own. She sure hoped the Sinclair carried feminine supplies as well as videos.

Kenny's nest reminded Charlie of several lofts she'd visited in the Village when she lived in Manhattan. The walls were exposed brick with old-fashioned radiators under the windows and metal pole supports where once there had been a load-bearing wall dividing rooms. All it lacked was the noise of a busy street outside, the elevator, the buzzer, and the security cameras.

Uncle Elmo went downstairs to smoke. Edwina insisted on cleaning up the kitchen. Kenny brought out the photo album they'd begun to look through at the museum before Charlie's nonexistent skills as a crime-scene investigator had been called up to the Oaks.

"You never did tell us what your dream was about except for the dead baby with blood on it," Kenny said as he opened the album on the coffee table.

"I was in the fruit cellar with a candle like poor Myrtle. Great-aunt Abigail opened the door and threw the bloody thing down on me." And, like a typical male, you disappeared. Every time she shows up, you're outta there.

Edwina came over from her side of the kitchen bookcases. "That woman used to give me nightmares, too. And my mother. And now my daughter. Tell you one thing, we'll never bring Libby here unless that old witch is dead. Maybe not even then."

"Libby's your granddaughter, I assume."

And of course Edwina had to show him a picture or two from her billfold.

Kenny's whistle went dry.

"Stay away from my daughter, Squirt," Charlie told him.

"Yes, ma'am. You got any pictures of Charlie when she was a baby?"

"Why would she have a picture of me as a baby when she's got a gorgeous babe for a granddaughter?"

"That's all you know about me, smartass." And Edwina pulled a small black-and-white photo in a protective plastic casing from somewhere deep in her wallet.

Kenny studied the photo and then turned a batch of thick pages in the album, turned them forward and back a few times. Finally he laid the coated photo down on a page. In Edwina's photo, a totally bald baby with enormous dark eyes appeared to float in the folded arms resting on a lap of someone mostly out of the frame.

But on the page, the identical baby—in an identical one-piece terrycloth version of a jumpsuit, with feet and snaps up the front—stared at Charlie from Marlys Dittberner's lap. Marlys wore a tight, sleeveless top, her pale hair disappearing down her back, straight-cut bangs covering her forehead—reminding Charlie of old pictures of the young Mary of Peter, Paul, and Mary fame. Even by this time, Marlys was too old to be showing upper arms gone loose-fleshed and wrinkly.

"I'm beginning to think there's more to the curse of Myrtle than living too long." The barkeep author turned back some pages to a baby looking much like the one that was supposed to be Charlie, but wearing a white dress with eyelets and booties on her feet, fat little legs showing beneath her skirt, the same big eyes staring up at Charlie—Libby's eyes. Marlys carried more weight here and wore her hair in a bun. She had thick shoulder pads and dark lipstick.

"You believe in curses?"

"I believe in people believing in curses. I believe in frantic mothers trying to keep their daughters straight in a world that approves of boys being boys so they can learn to be men. Frantic mothers pointing out what happened to the legendary Myrtle down through the generations. Because the tiny town of Myrtle had some large and unique problems, or at least thought it did, and had to lay the blame somewhere. If you consider yourself moral and upright but shit keeps happening—you have to find the devil causing it. Without alluding to it, of course."

"So what was Marlys Dittberner's role in all this?" Charlie asked.

"I don't think I know," Edwina said. She was sitting on the back of a couch, dishtowel still in hand. "But my mother sent me that picture of a baby available for adoption. Your father already had two nearly grown children by his first marriage and wasn't anxious for another. But he finally agreed to adoption."

Kenny had once overheard someone down in the bar pointing out to his elders the color of his eyes as part of the curse, obliquely of course, and he remembered it but hadn't understood it until years later in Florida. He'd confronted his mother and she'd slapped his face and then fallen into his arms crying instead of answering his question. "Seems my little sister was pregnant—she was fifteen. My mother thought by getting us out of Myrtle, she'd escaped the curse. I think the book I'm researching now and intend to write next began that day. That's while I was still at Florida State and had never published a thing. This is the sucker I was born to write."

"So dark-eyed folks are cursed to live too long or get pregnant as teens. Great Witch Abigail said those with black eyes should not spawn, and I'm a perfect example of why. But you will not get pregnant, Kenny."

"I didn't understand it until I came back here—what? nine, ten months ago—and filtered through some of the innuendo and the unspoken. We, Charlie, are cursed with being oversexed."

Tell me about it, Charlie thought.

"Tell me about it," Edwina said aloud.

"Mom—"

"Charlie, the entire community, tiny though it is, follows your career avidly. Because you have our eyes and you had a child out of wedlock. I didn't know about you, or don't remember if I did, until I moved back here to take over the family pool hall and found out they even knew about my sister's abortion. There are grandparents here who will not let their granddaughters visit them in Myrtle. Helen and Buz have two dark-eyed beauties in Lincoln, Nebraska, that they go visit but never invite. The whole thing is the power of myth, of legend, of things like curses, even in down-to-earth places like Myrtle, or maybe especially in places like this because of the guilt brought on by unrealistic expectations of what morality can accomplish. Farming communities know a lot about animal and plant nature, too. Sometimes it's hard to sync with God's plan according to the Puritans."

"You still haven't told me about Marlys."

He turned back some of the album's pages and there was "the house." It had been ornate and grand—obvious even in sepia—and nearly as big as Harvey Rochester's house, but older. The porch had curlicues everywhere. And the front lawn then had a semicircular drive where a little girl with what appeared to be white hair posed in a pony cart and held the pony's reins and looked directly at the camera. The caption read MARLYS STAUDT AT THE HOUSE.

"That's Marlys Dittberner? She was a Staudt before she was married? How old is she? I thought the home place was where the Staudts started."

"Wealthy farming families often had a house in town for the older generations to retire to so the next could do the farming. It's hard to find dates for things—her generation was born at home and women who didn't work weren't kept track of except in family bibles."

"She worked," Edwina pointed out. "She was running Dittberner's when I was a girl, and she was an old lady then, I swear."

"I haven't been able to find any records on her or bibles either," Kenny said, "but by what I have tracked down going on around her, she's got to be something over a hundred and five or six anyway."

"But she's still up and walking." Charlie leaned over the album.

"And the smartest person with no brain I've met this side of Capitol Hill," Kenny said.

"Del thinks she's my great-grandmother."

The unmistakable growls of Mr. Rochester registered below and ascended the stairs to Kenny's loft. He appeared without coat or hat but from mid-thigh down, he was coated with snow. He stood surveying them all, a grinning Uncle

127

Elmo behind him, and emoted, "Barkeep, sir. I am in need. Desperate need."

Charlie had the fleeting thought that if she tried to tell anyone at Congdon and Morse, Inc., on Wilshire in Beverly Hills, about Harvey Rochester—or anybody in this room, or in this tiny town, or in Gentle Oaks, or the Myrtle Cemetery even—she'd be laughed right out of the office.

"Tell me, Kenneth, that you can brew some of your demon coffee, with perhaps a dollop of brandy in it and spare a dry piece of toast for a poor and weary pilgrim in this infested place."

While the teakettle heated over the gas flame and more of the casserole and rolls were rewarmed and after the noise of the hand-crank coffee grinder, Harvey Rochester explained that dear Elsina Miller, beloved administrator of Gentle Oaks, had, against all odds, walked through the storm to Harvey's house and demanded shelter and food last night.

"I left her with cornflakes, preaching to a dozen Mexicans in a language they only barely understand and from a culture that reveres one woman only—the Virgin Mary, who in any language our Elsina is not. Well—she's likely a virgin." He paused for a moment at that thought, studying it, then blinked it away. "But Teresa and Miguel are there to keep them all in line. I, by God, had to escape."

"Why not to the Oaks?" Charlie asked.

"Listen to me, my child. I spent the night before at that bedlam for ancient psychopaths in the full of the moon. They were still howling last night pretty good, too. Then the power goes off. Then our resident gravedigger, plowman, and upholder of law and order is careening about the town in the humvee of dump trucks like a loose lunatic—I literally had to run for cover twice on the way here and he didn't even see me. I shouted profanities and he didn't hear. Let us hope he runs out of gas before he kills someone." He gentled down when coffee and the casserole on a tray appeared before him, with rewarmed dinner rolls, jam, and butter. "For you, sir, there is a place in heaven, I vow," he told his host.

"Edwina, why did you lie to me all these years about where I came from?"

"I didn't want you coming back here to find out about this place and the supposed curse. So I said I got you in Boulder."

"You are a scientist. You don't believe in curses."

"No, but like Kenny, I believe in the power of guilt and the uses to which it can be put. The traps it can lay. But this time, I didn't have the strength to face Myrtle alone."

"Mom, did your mother have these eyes? You said she was pregnant when she married."

"Yeah, she did," Elmo answered instead. "Edwina, do you realize that we are the only people in this room who don't have the Myrtle eyes?"

Not for the first time, but even more urgently now, Charlie was wondering what her own black-eyed daughter was up to while the cat was away.

CHAPTER 20

◆

S O WHY WAS I born in Marlys Dittberner's house? And why did she end up with the Staudt house in town instead of the guys in the family in this agrarian, male chauvinist, Taliban society?"

"You work in Hollywood and call this a chauvinist society?" Kenny brought her another cup of coffee—not a latté, just tasty and rich.

So she peed all day. So she'd get some Depends. Probably carried them at the Sinclair station.

A knocking sounded from somewhere below, "Uh, Kenny? It's Ben."

"Come on up, Ben. Saved you some breakfast and there's coffee in the pot."

Kenny presented the watchman with a steaming cup, a glass of orange juice, and returned to the gas stove to cook some more bacon.

"I didn't get bacon," Harvey complained.

"You're already the fat cat in town. Ben's our token homeless person." No wonder their host had made a whole casserole. It was fast disappearing.

"What do you mean, homeless? He gets a free bed in the back room of the Sinclair and his washing done by the mayor," Mr. Rochester pointed out.

"It's not free. I'm the town watchman."

"Doing what? Never mind."

"It's on the books," Kenny said over the bacon sizzle.

"Myrtle's got books?" Harvey Rochester stared at Ben and Elmo, who simply shrugged.

"Ben breakfasts at the Schoolhouse Café during the week, but it's probably not open today because of the snow, and he lunches here at noon, has his dinner in the kitchen at The Station in the evening while they're getting it ready for the Oaks. All part of his pay for being watchman, huh, Ben?"

Determined not to let them deter her with rural fables this time, Charlie insisted, "So why doesn't anybody answer my questions?"

"Because you ask too many at once and we forget what they are," Elmo said.

"Okay, so why was I born in Marlys Dittberner's house?"

"She was in the habit of taking in runaway girls. They usually run away in them days because they found themselves in the family way. Back then, a girl in that condition and without a husband tended to disappear. 'Whatever happened to pretty little Alice?' 'Oh, she went off to Ohio to live with her Aunt Helga, who's sick and needs someone around to help out.' And that's the last you'd ever hear of pretty little Alice. Just disappeared. Nobody wanted to talk about it."

"Like Myrtle." Charlie stood at a front window. She could see where Del had plowed a lane on Main Street.

"Most of them did go off to live with faraway relatives, have the baby, and some family would adopt it and the girl would be sent out to work until she could find a husband or earn her living. But I always wondered if some of 'em didn't end up getting whupped to death in the barn one night by a angry daddy and get buried on the farm. Nobody but the family would know any different—they'd just disappear. It was a terrible sin to get with child without a husband, brought down such shame on a family, and shotgun weddings weren't so common as some would have you believe. Things was different then."

"But some would go to Marlys' house and she'd take care of them and adopt the babies out? Why did she do that?"

Even through wind-swirled snow, Charlie could see the trench line in the vacant lot across the street where the cave-in had all but filled. Looked like it was heading for the pool hall. "That was true everywhere, not just in Myrtle or Floyd County or Iowa, Charlie." Mr. Rochester moved back away from the stove, fed and finally warmed. But he accepted another cup of coffee with a soothing dollop of brandy.

"Girls in my school days were still disappearing," Edwina said. "Guess I never thought much about it. But the whispers were if she moved and her family stayed, she was going to have a baby. She was soon forgotten. Once ruined, forever ruined then. How old is Marlys Dittberner, Harvey? You must have records on her at Gentle Oaks."

"Actually, damn few for someone who lived here all her life. And those records don't tie down how long that life was. She's outlived all her children and I've never talked to anyone with a mind left who knew her as a child. She was always a grown woman to all of them I questioned, and birth records were mostly stored in family Bibles then because no doctor attended and people pretended the messy birthing process was a joyous, antiseptic surprise from God. I can tell you though, having been given entrance to one of her dead children's records and memorabilia, that she was not originally a Dittberner but married an Auchmoody before that. So she married at least twice. What's that sound? Either it's Charlie's confounded cellular phone or our barkeep has taken in a feline."

Charlie was momentarily so soothed and warm and sheltered from this hostile environment that she didn't know where to look for her purse. No problem. Old cool Kenny handed her cell to her. He was getting as irritating as her mother but had the good sense not to touch her hand with his when the phone was exchanged.

It was a desperate Larry Mann. Her secretary and good friend and favorite date. First problem—the weather blonde on CNN had assured the nation that all residents of Minnesota and Northern Iowa were buried under tons of snow with power and communications out, and there must be hundreds if not thousands dead or in dire danger of being so because even National Guard helicopters could not get to them. "Charlie, I can't believe I'm talking to you. You're right in the middle of it. Are you freezing and hungry and thermally perishing? We're frantic here."

"Jesus, what's happened there? Is Libby in danger of—"

"No, we're frantic about you. It's mildly balmy here. Hilsten is threatening to parachute from a chopper or something to save you. Except no one's sure where you are. You went to Minneapolis and then to a Mason City? Where did you fly from there? Tell me quick before we lose contact again. Hurry."

"Settle down. I'm fed, warm, and sheltered as is the rest of Myrtle, Iowa, and even its one homeless person. We drove here from the Mason City airport. And please tell Mitch to stay in L.A.. He's one problem I don't need now." Charlie had inadvertently saved the superstar's life twice and he was heaven-bent on returning the favor. "Edwina and I are safe and sound, and I'll get home as soon as the weather and roads clear. Larry, give me a quick rundown on the state of the office while we've got contact."

"Shirley Birkett is freaking in Tampa. Said she'd quit and wanted to change her mind. Quit what? The agency?"

"No. She's got some screwy notion that writing novels is a job and not just work she's lucky to get. Let her stew till I get back."

"The Duesenburg contracts arrived this morning."

"How do they look?"

"They look like you're going to cross out three pages and consult the lawyers before the author signs. Oh, and Monroe's interview on *Celebrities Tonight* airs tonight. Have they ever done a writer before?"

"Norman Mailer I think I remember was on in the early days. Tape it for me, will you? Talked to Libby?"

"She's cool and made it to school today. Maggie and Mrs. Beesom had her for dinner last night and she's dining at the Esterhazies' tonight, so rest easy for a while on that one. She doesn't watch the news so she's not as worried about you as the rest of us. I'll leave a message on Ed Esterhazie's voice mail that you're okay and not to stir her up. Take care, boss."

"Who is this wonderful Larry person? You're positively misty-eyed," Harvey Rochester said just as Charlie decided to check her voice mail. "My jealousy consumeth all."

"One of my best friends."

"Her secretary," Edwina said. "He's drop-dead gorgeous."

"You have a secretary?" Ben the homeless person squinted in disbelief. He had long lashes and almost no eyebrows. He never took off his knitted cap, so you didn't know if he had hair.

"You got a man for a secretary?" Uncle Elmo raised his eyebrows. They were about an inch thick and stuck out in all directions.

There were three frantic messages from Mitch Hilsten that Charlie ignored. How do you tell a superstar to get a life?

"Your secretary is drop-dead gorgeous and he's just a friend?" Kenny didn't sound convinced.

"He's gay," Edwina explained. "That's what she loves about him."

"Three hundred thousand dollars! Congratulations, Charlie Greene, this is John Stone of United Pacific Bank and Trust of Southern California and you have been approved for a line of credit twice that amount! UPB and T of SC looks forward to doing business with you. Your personalized checks will be mailed to you immediately. You have twenty-four hours to call me at—"

"Jesus, now I'm getting telemarketers on my cellular."

"Never say that word around Elsina," Rochester intoned.

"Telemarketer?"

"Jesus."

"You love your secretary because he's gay?"

"Makes him safe," Edwina told Kenny.

"You wouldn't understand," Charlie told Kenny.

"What makes you think I'm not gay?" Kenny asked Charlie.

"Somehow, I just know. Positively."

"Positively?"

"Is it getting too hot in here, or is it just me?" Ben unbuttoned his shirt.

"Now stop that," said Edwina Greene, who'd had to give up hormone replacement therapy because of breast cancer.

"I think you need to quit feeding that stove," Uncle Elmo advised. "You mean gay as in joyful or gay as in—"

"Charlie Greene, I have a buyer for your condominium. Offer's the greatest. List with me soonest and discover the deal of a lifetime!"

"Charlie Greene, are you interested in exotic places, scenes, sex? Young, innocent prepubescent children innocently await your desire and tutoring. Nice, obedient—"

"Jesus."

"Don't say that word around—"

"I know." What I don't know is how these horrible people could get my cell number. I'm going to have to filter everything here, too. "Is there no place safe from telemarketing?"

"Gentle Oaks," Harvey answered. "We don't let them have phones at all. Insurance companies are always trying to sell them policies that will pay if they fall down. At horrific fees. They are feeble people who fall down all the time. Even those in wheelchairs decide to stand for no reason—they've forgotten they can't, you see. But they're in a twenty-four-hour nursing environment. What more could a policy do but send them to a nursing home where the government pays for it anyway? After all their money is used up, of course. And once it is, what reason do their bereft heirs have to pay for anything? We live in a strange world. I hate to be too insistent, but you don't suppose we could use your wonderful cellular device to converse with the coroner of Floyd County, do you?

135

I'm at your mercy, lady, and in deep dung up at Gentle Oaks, upon which an entire town and a good portion of Floyd County depend for a meager living."

"You need a new scriptwriter, Harvey."

But "twas not erelong" in Harvey language before Charlie was torn from the warm, erotic world of Viagra's to the hell-hole of Gentle Oaks in Marshal Delwood's humvee of a snow-plow.

CHAPTER 21

✦

"MARLYS IS AN unusual name," Charlie told Harvey Rochester as they fought the weather up the few steps from the drive to the porch of Gentle Oaks. "Seems like she wouldn't be that hard to trace in this small place—her past, I mean. I've only seen that name once before. There's a mystery writer—"

"Marlys is not that uncommon a name in Northern Iowa and Southern Minnesota. I know of two in Floyd alone, several in Nora Springs." Harvey brushed snow from his face and eyebrows and it blew right back in again, even under the porch overhang. You couldn't see any oaks at all, but you could sense them hovering over the building. Well, okay, Charlie could. "But Marlys Dittberner is a true enigma because she was married to an Auchmoody first."

"She was born a Staudt, then married twice. What's so enigma about that?"

"Kenneth showed you the album. There is some question about the veracity of that book, Charlie. Like our history, it has been fiddled with by those who wish to make it as they wish so strongly that they truly believe the changes they've fiddled." He pulled and pushed at the door to the lobby and Charlie lent what muscle she had. "Must be frozen shut. There's a buzzer here somewhere."

"Maybe it's locked from the inside."

"We do not lock people out of Gentle Oaks, child."

Charlie didn't see how the coroner could get here today if he couldn't yesterday. The blowing, drifting snow alternately hiding and exposing the ice underneath and causing whiteout conditions was worse than the blizzard that came before it. They were pounding on the doors, he cursing, she yelling, and taking turns punching the buzzer. This was serious here. The marshal and his humvee dump-truck plow had dropped them off and disappeared into the whiteout to destroy monster drifts so people could get places that wouldn't be open anyway. Charlie had been in some really strange places, but. . . . People from Southern California are not prepared for either Mother or people Nature in Iowa.

They were about pounded out and shouted hoarse and not bothering to hide their panic when two abominable snowmen snuck up behind them. The snow was so blowy and sticky and they were all dressed in so much padding, Charlie realized she too must look abominable. But Buz and Helen Bartusek got right in her face and wanted to know what was going on and Harvey explained their angst at not being permitted entrance to this "abode for the decrepit, weak, weary, and senile."

"They're not senile. They're confused," Helen shouted over the howling wind.

"Can you say Alzheimer's, Nurse Helen?" Mr. Rochester shouted back.

All four were in the process of rushing the door when Mary Lou Hogoboom opened it and they tumbled in nearly on top of her.

The Bartuseks had come by snowmobile. How else, stupid? The generator at the Oaks had pooped out according to Nurse Hogoboom, and they'd locked the doors to keep Marlys in and the cold out even though it was against the fire codes. Breakfast had arrived—cold cereal, frozen milk, and ice-sludged juice. No hot coffee, tea, or cocoa. Only remnants of the morning shift had arrived. The mood was not pleasant here. Mary Lou Hogoboom was about an inch from hysterics. "Pipes freeze and we can't flush the toilets—think about trying to breathe in this place."

Nurse Helen, daughter of the latest corpse, was well past hysterics. "You buried my mother out in the hazardous-waste area?"

"Just till the coroner gets here." Charlie put Kenny's knee-length jacket back on after littering the lobby with its snow coat. "She'll keep better that way."

Buz and Harvey tromped off to work on the generator. Helen turned on Charlie. "She'll keep? My mother will *keep?* She was murdered."

"Was she a vegetable, Helen? Were all the recently deceased vegetables?"

"Doesn't mean they weren't murdered. So what did you find out about the murderer?"

"My first guess is that their time had come and nature took its course. My second guess is that someone from the town or on the staff decided to put them out of their misery. My third is that one of the inmates is a little more clever than we think. Or it could be a combination of natural and assisted death. So now there have been six, right? And they've all been pretty well gone mentally. What else do they have in common?"

"They were all women. Hey, you're better at this than I thought." Helen took off her thick glasses to rid them of steam by rubbing them on her sweater. "And they were all born Staudts."

"Are there any more 'born Staudts' here?"

Cousin Helen blew her nose so hard into three consecutive tissues that her glasses steamed up again and she still had to breathe through her mouth. When she unsteamed her eyewear on her sweater again, her unprotected eyes walled like one of Edwina's used to. "My God, there's at least two I can think of."

"Now don't panic. It could easily be coincidence." One more dead "born Staudt" and I'm gonna forget the nature thing myself. "But there does appear to be a possible pattern here."

"I told Buz you'd been detecting a lot and would be better than old Delwood."

Actually, cuz, I get most of this from reading endless film scripts, manuscripts, teleplays, proposals, and treatments. Damn near every story has a murder in it these days. My deductions are totally unscientific and unreliable—but if it makes Cousin Helen feel better until the coroner arrives, what the hell?

Darla Lempke was there, but the administrator's office was dark. Elsina must still be converting the Mexicans. Darla had lost her bubbles. Sherman and Flo sat together at a table carefully cutting up construction-paper figures that Darla had made to show them as examples.

"You let these people have scissors?" Charlie couldn't believe it.

The activities director slumped in a chair. "I've worked two straight shifts without sleep and little food. I'm a social worker, not an aide. The residents run around half the night. I'm not supposed to work nights and weekends. I'm cold."

"Ciga-riga-rooo?" Flo tried to cut the sleeve of her sweatshirt.

Sherman squinted at the social worker. "Who are you, anyway?"

"I'm Darla. You know who I am."

"I don't know who I am. You smoke?"

Dolores the tom sat high atop a cabinet along the wall behind Sherman and Flo, alternately hissing and washing behind his ears. Even the cat had lost it in this place. Snow began to blow on the big TV screen next to him like it was blowing past outside the windows.

"Where are the aides?" Darla screeched at Mary Lou Hogoboom, who was rushing through the cafeteria to someplace else. "This place can't operate without the aides."

"You're always complaining that they're lazy and hiding somewhere when you have something for them to do." Harvey walked in still looking wet. "At least notice that the lights are on, dear child, and the heating system is gargling. It'll take a while to heat up the place, but the pipes haven't frozen yet."

"You fixed the generator." Charlie was hoping to hurry out like Mary Lou, not wanting to be drafted into service by Darla Lempke, no longer a cheerleader for the positive.

"No, it's deader than Ida Mae. Apparently the power lines are repaired for the Oaks at least. Health-care facilities are given first priority in emergencies. Hope it lasts. I sent poor Buz out into the storm to gather the snowmobile cowboys to round up the aides and the Mexicans, many of whom are one and the same, to relieve the situation here. Where's Nurse Helen?"

They had moved out of the cafeteria by now, leaving Darla with the problem of no cigarettes for Sherman and Flo, who both smelled strongly in the need of a change. Which reminded Charlie of her own impending problem. She wondered if, with all the female employees, there might be a stash of female sanitary products here. Plugs and pads, as Libby termed them.

"She rushed off to check out women who had been born Staudts, I think."

"Charlie, as soon as this storm is over and the roads are clear, I am going to Mason City and buy a grand piano—the grandest piano I can find." Mr. Rochester's eyebrows, thick but not hoary like Uncle Elmo's, were highly expressive in some way Charlie didn't want to deal with. Her feet were so cold she probably wouldn't even get a period this month.

"Do you play the piano?"

"No." The eyebrows rose and arched, and fortunately somebody screamed. He backed off when Helen came running down the hall. "Charlie, it's Doris Wyborny. You were right. Oh, dear Jesus. Oh, God."

Helen sort of collapsed toward them still on the run and Harvey caught the brunt of her. Charlie was beginning to feel edgy. She was either on the edge of a migraine, a panic attack, or the damn curse or, worse, all three at once.

Doris Wyborny lay on her back in her bed as had Ida Mae Staudt Truex. Her roommate lay in the next bed relentlessly pleading for help, relentlessly ignored because there wasn't any.

"Was Doris born a Staudt?"

Helen and Harvey looked at each other and shrugged.

"She was something like a hundred and four. I'm not sure what she was before she was married." Helen reached to pull the sheet up over Doris's face and Harvey grabbed her.

"Do not touch a thing. The coroner is on his way."

"Don't close her eyes or mouth, fold her hands—anything," Charlie agreed. "Did it get cold enough while the power was off to cause this death naturally, do you think? It's possible at this age, it was just her time, you know."

"I doubt it got that cold," Harvey said, then added ruefully, "She's been at the Oaks for twenty-two years. Something of an institution. Outlived her whole family, including the two kids."

"Twenty-two, how awful. Was she a vegetable?"

"Only the last five or six years."

"Help me, please help me. Somebody," Doris's roommate wailed.

Charlie had half an urge to grab a pillow and help the woman.

CHAPTER 22

*A*S TO OUR enigma, you should know that on record since Marlys entered Gentle Oaks eight years ago, she has been found trying to, nearly succeeding in, or threatening to bury herself alive on or in the grave of the town's namesake a number of times."

Harvey and Charlie sat in Elsina Miller's office still waiting for the coroner of Floyd County, who lived and had his business in Charles City because the railroad changed its mind and course after the county had been named.

Charlie had taken off her boots and wrapped Kenny Cowper's warm coat around cold feet. She'd also managed to swipe a handful of plugs from a lower drawer in the nurses' station and felt back from the edge a bit—as long as that door to the nut hatch stayed closed.

Harvey leafed through assorted papers in Doris Wyborny's file. Doris had been born a Streblow.

"Marlys is amazingly quick. She could sneak into a room and smother some half-conscious person pretty easily. She has the run of the place." Charlie had a gut feeling that the ancient and mobile Marlys Dittberner was the key to something. Charlie's gut, however, was more often wrong than not.

"Rose is very mobile, but if she set out to do something, she'd have forgotten what it was by the time she'd entered the room. Flo and my grandfather are slow, but they do wander in their quest for something to smoke."

"Helen may have secretly wished to put her own mother out of her misery, and her great-aunts, too. But what about

143

the others? We need to make up a list of the dead and look for comparisons. Kenny could come up and do it while visiting his grandma. So could the marshal, for that matter. Ben seems to have access everywhere. As you said, you don't lock people out of Gentle Oaks. Up until Doris, women totally out of it who were born Staudts have been the pattern."

"Don't look at me. Every time one dies, I lose the money coming from the government."

"But there is a waiting list, right? Those beds aren't empty long."

Mr. Rochester glowered and took another file out of the cabinet, tapped her on the head with it, and dropped it in her lap. "You are good at this, you know it?"

Charlie found him suspicious because, like Helen, he pretended Charlie knew what she was doing. And they were both desperate for her to investigate because they knew she had no professional training. Who better than an amateur if you're the perp? But Harvey didn't have Helen's motive. Didn't mean he didn't have one at all.

It was Marlys's file, and mostly empty—two sheets of paper filled out by a neighbor who had brought her here when the community could no longer put up with her antics.

"But she must have had some insurance papers and a Social Security number—I mean, if she ran a store, owned a house."

"There was a fire in the courthouse, back in the nineteen forties. A lot of the records are gone. People her age, you can't be sure records even existed. She never drove a car. She kept setting fire to her own house—one of the reasons the neighbors wanted her up here. To get her Medicaid payments started through the bureaucratic mill was somewhat of a hassle, but so was Doris Wyborny's and others'. Women didn't own property as a rule, or work for wages, when Marlys was young. If Marlys was young. They were just Mrs. Somebody."

"But she inherited from her husbands, surely. She ran the grocery store. She would one day be eligible for benefits."

"As the widow of Lester Dittberner. No wills or deeds or anything survived."

"Wouldn't she have had to have a Social Security number to pay her taxes on the store?"

"You know, you are good. Wonder what happened to it. Unless her son owned the store. He died here years before she came."

"How old is the Oaks?"

"About fifty years now. I inherited it from my great-uncle from Swaledale. It's been added on to and modernized a good bit. Uncle Herman had plans to build a series of long-term health-care centers in small towns around because expenses are low out in the tullies. But he found that so many of the children were leaving the Midwest, and their parents followed them when they began worrying about aging. But in Myrtle, the elderly seemed to have too many living parents to go off and leave. Some siblings might migrate, but not all could."

"So there are locals with relatives incarcerated here who are in and out all the time?"

"Actually, few visit after the first year or two. And their loved ones are residents, not prisoners. And this has turned out to be a long, long-term care facility."

"So it was Herman and Sherman Rochester?"

"There was a third brother—"

"I don't want to know. What happened to Herman?"

"He's in Room Forty-three."

The coroner arrived with a sheriff's deputy and the press. Myrtle was suddenly on the map. The situation could not have been worse if a slew of presidential candidates had invaded.

Neither Mr. Rochester nor Charlemagne Catherine realized that the wind had dropped and the air cleared of whiteout until helicopters sounded overhead. Which caused another whiteout as the blades stirred up the snow on the ground. Two copters had the good sense to land on the drive in front of the building, and one tried to land on the lawn ornaments in the center circle and thought better of it to set down back out on the road. But the cadre of approaching snowmobile heroes couldn't be blocked and began downloading Mexicans as fast as they could.

"In California, we call them Hispanics or Latinos," Charlie muttered, determined to commit some murder of her own if Mitch Hilsten, superstar, dared step down from one of those choppers.

"In Myrtle, they're Mexicans, and the only ones who live here are my housekeeper and groundsman, a married couple. Their relatives travel from Mason City each day to do the real dirty work on farms and here at the Oaks."

Buz brought Elsina Miller the administrator up to the doors with a big wink for Harvey. "Thank God that creature is out of my house, else I would never return to it. Remember, do not say the word 'Jesus' in her presence. She will go on for hours, days, and weeks. She is the bane of my existence."

"Why do you keep her on?"

"She's a wonderful missionary for Baptist donations for the needy elderly."

" 'Nuff said." Charlie backed away from all the commotion coming at them, but not before the missionary administrator noticed her standing beside Harvey Rochester through the glass doors leading from the porch.

Charlie grabbed her boots from the office and ran for the ladies' room in the hall inside the really smelly part of the institution. She just wasn't up to a photo op. Neither was Gentle Oaks.

Marlys Dittberner ran naked down the hall, mouth wide open in a scream—no teeth. This time, she lifted Charlie's whole purse by its shoulder strap on her way by, almost taking Charlie's shoulder with it. This time, Charlie had no mother to fly into the arms of and cry. There went all the plugs and this was not a good time for that. To hell with Marlys—Charlie raced to the nurses' station and stole another, then ran back to the ladies' room, and of course it was not empty.

"Out of my way, Sherman." She shoved the poor old guy into a stall and locked herself in another. She had brought only two pairs of pants and one was still out at the home place.

With at least some protection in place and in bad need of Tylenol, she stepped out of the stall to find Sherman Rochester leaning on his cane looking around, probably for something to stuff in his socks. So she led him to the door to the hall, hoping he would distract whatever attention was festering out there, and gave him a shove before going back to wash her hands and plan how to find Marlys and her purse and her sanity.

When she was composed enough to peer out again, it was to see a cast of strangers, a hookup, makeup, and script under discussion with a talking head, and handheld cams. The wheelchair folks caught up on the cables began to form a traffic jam between her and the naked Marlys. This was not all out of a Mason City newsroom.

Charlie dearly wanted to lock herself back in a stall and have a good cry. But she stepped out into the fray just as Rose began to read from a flyer. She read without intonation, pronounced the words clearly and slowly but as if she didn't understand their meaning. She did pause at periods and commas, and sometimes for no reason.

"Jesus loves everyone and all who come to Him are saved. Are you saved. He will help you. Jesus is the son of God, creator of the earth and the heavens and the universe. Jesus can forgive you your sins. Are you forgiven."

"Ciga-riga-rooo?"

"Excuse me, sir. You're running over the cables here. Could you back your chair off them?"

"Who the hell you think you are, you son of a bitch? Get outta my way."

"Jesus, what's that smell in here?"

"Smells like shit."

"We got plenty of that."

"Got a cigarette?"

"Jesus loves everyone and all who come to Him are saved. Are you saved."

"Help me. He-ll-lp me. Somebody, please. . . ."

CHAPTER 23

*D*OLORES-THE-FAT, ALREADY IN a snit, took an instant dislike to the press and upchucked a hairball on the soon-to-be-talking head's shoe. "God, what's that? Its stomach? Get that off me."

"Excuse me, ma'am, do you work here? We're having some trouble with the traffic—"

"No." Charlie shoved Fatty Truex's wheelchair into Fatty Staudt's knees to get herself through the pileup in front of the cameras and caused a vituperative altercation in the process.

"Somebody stuff a sock in those geezers' beaks. We're about to go live."

"Please, lady, could you tell our viewers a few facts about the series of murders occurring here?"

"No."

"Can you send us some of the staff to interview? These people aren't really suitable."

"Oh, really." Charlie escaped behind the jam of wheelchairs and walkers and the nurses' station and around the curve in the back wall just as the reverse countdown for showtime began. Only to come up against Cousin Helen.

The nurse's tears dripped onto a thick sweater with subdued colors and rows of angry racoons duking it out like her Fatty grandpas back at the newscast. She stood next to the door to the smoker, looking down into the hazardous-waste storage area enclosed in chain-link fencing and drifted snow. "I don't see a push broom."

"It's under one of the drifts. Helen, where is the staff? National news media with television cameras are blocked just inside the door to the hall here."

"All hiding. Afraid it's an INS raid. What if you can't find my mother?"

"She's not going anywhere, trust me. Can you go and take care of the television crew? And have you seen Marlys? She stole my purse."

"Everybody's looking for Marlys. What about my mother? It's all her fault anyway. Even you." She slid the glass door open and walked out into the cold of the smoker to grieve in peace.

Charlie held the door from closing. "What's whose fault, your mother's?" Before she could get an answer, three things in close succession distracted her. The tomcat tore up the hall one way, fur all puffed like he had a Doberman on his tail. The naked Marlys tore down it the other way, chased by her own demons, without Charlie's purse, and headed straight for the photo op of the decade.

And Harvey Rochester with two other men, all bundled up and snow-crusted to the knees, appeared at a slower pace behind her. The helicopter, forced to set down out in the road, had brought the coroner and deputy sheriff. They'd walked around to a back door to avoid the public exposure Marlys Dittberner was about to garner in spades.

The coroner, who was really a mortician, was also something of a surprise, as were nearly all the people Charlie had met since she'd come to Iowa. He was jolly, for one thing—which didn't seem proper in either a mortician or a coroner. In fact, he was more than jolly. He cracked up at every other thing Charlie said. He'd probably heard she'd been between the sheets with Mitch Hilsten, which would make even more ridiculous her pronouncements on Marlys' running naked into the limelight and Dolores hacking up a fur ball and the Fatties cursing and coming to blows for the cameras, as well as Rose reading deadpan and toneless immortal prose from one of the evangelical pamphlets from Elsina Miller's office in front of a national broadcast.

He stood over the expanding body of Doris Streblow Wyborny wiping laugh tears from his cheeks. "I always love to come to Myrtle. Okay, stand back, put up your masks—this is going to get messy."

He stuck a small knife into a ballooning Doris, and the deputy sheriff took off gagging as Doris deflated in an audible hiss. The coroner's name was Leland Mosher. He was short and considerably overweight, with great jowls and belly and receding hair, and an expression that made hardened old Charlie even want to cuddle him—kind of like a koala the size of a polar bear. You just knew there was soft fuzz on him somewhere.

"Leland, are you certain that was necessary?" Mr. Rochester asked in his deep Broadway diction. "We have been through a great deal here, you realize."

"Sorry. I just love working with the deputies. Expected your lovely detective here to be a little squeamish. Life should be more fun. Death sure isn't. Fun is where you find it. And in my profession—" He wore thick, dark-rimmed glasses, which he peered over now with a sigh that made Charlie laugh, too.

"My detective sees murder all the time," Harvey proclaimed in a comic, prissy "So there." "She works in Hollywood."

"Well, that explains a lot, doesn't it? Do you know Dick Van Dyke?"

The comic coroner kept heaving belly laughs—literally, you'd have to see it for yourself—while cutting into a poor dead woman and sniffing stuff everybody in Bulgaria could smell by now. The deputy walked back in only to grab his mouth and run back out, leaving the mortician convulsed.

Charlie and Harvey raised eyebrows over their masks and shrugged.

Meanwhile, Marshal Delwood was busy digging through the drifts in the hazardous-waste compound for Ida Mae Staudt Truex, under the watchful if teary eye of her daughter Helen Truex Bartusek, still up in the smoker.

The jolly-ghoul coroner asked Charlie to relate her impressions of what was going on here.

"I'd rather not. I really am not qualified."

"Would you rather be thrown to the network lions, Miss Greene? I'd like particularly to know if you see any similarities to the previous body you and Harvey here examined and took samples of for me."

"Well, they both were lying on their backs with a sheet and light blanket pulled up to their chins. Doris's eyes were wide open. Ida Mae's had one eye half closed. There was no blood. They both appear to be very heavy for their age, but it's hard to tell how much of that is bloating. Like I've been telling everybody, they could have died because it was time, because someone felt sorry for them, by help from some medicine, or a pillow held over their heads to suffocate them. Both had defecated, which is not unusual in death." Or anytime in this place. "If it was murder, it could have been done by anybody—the doors aren't locked."

"She's even suggested that I might be knocking off the residents to make more beds available for those on the waiting list, Leland. Can you believe that? I, Harvey Rochester?"

"Now, let her finish. Time for your theatrics later. Go on, Miss Charlie. Let's pretend we all know these are premeditated murders. They will be seven, a sizable number for this community."

"Until Doris here, there was a pattern. The victims were all women who had been born Staudts. What if somebody made a mistake? Thought she was born Staudt? Or what if this is all getting out of hand? I think that the deputy and the marshal should spend the night here."

Everyone but Doris stared at her. The coroner/mortician had sobered up.

"Now stop that," Charlie said.

"This has got to be the nuttiest place on the planet," Charlie complained to Kenny Cowper, cum Kenneth Cooper. "No wonder you're writing a book about it. It's too unbelievable for fiction, good thing you're doing it nonfiction. Everybody bugs me to find out what I think—Harvey, Cousin Helen, even the coroner, and then when I tell them, they make fun of me."

Marshal Del finally found Ida Mae, and she and Doris Wyborny were air-lifted with Coroner Leland to Charles City and the mortuary/funeral home, leaving a very morose deputy behind to protect the patients. You could hear the marshal's dump truck roaring around town, clearing the streets with a vengeance. He'd caught hell from Cousin Helen for not being careful enough while digging around for Ida Mae. Not like she felt anything.

"How do they make fun of you?" Kenny set a beer on the bar in front of Charlie.

Her mother sliced a thin slab of smoked cheese, put it on a cracker, and handed it to her. "You're looking kind of pale. Did you have lunch? You have to be careful now, you know."

"I haven't had anything since breakfast, and I still haven't found my purse. They make fun of me by looking dumbfounded when I answer their questions and say things like 'Wow, you're good at this,' when all I've said is the obvious. Know what I think? I think the whole town's in on this. Look, I'm crying in my beer."

And all of a sudden, she was laughing. So were Kenny and Ben and Edwina. Kenny was doing the cooking again, his staff laid off until people could get into town. Supposedly, they were to be treated to "the catch of the day." Smelled a lot like beef.

"What kind of line did you catch it on?" Edwina wanted to know. "A steel cable?"

"Where's Uncle Elmo?" Charlie looked around. "Don't tell me he drove our rental back to the home place." Her messed-up metabolism felt better already with a little cheese and beer in her.

"Hitched a ride on the county plow. Don't worry, Charlie. He knows the ropes out here." But Edwina looked worried as she cut her daughter another cheese slice. "Kenny and I were going through the album and a few other mementos from the museum—asking him all kinds of questions. We upset him. He's got his own ghosts to deal with. He doesn't need ours."

Charlie took another grateful swallow of beer, and energy chased the ditzy bubbles away. "So what's for dinner, barkeep?"

It was a three-inch-thick grilled sirloin, medium rare. There would be enough left over for hash tomorrow for the whole restaurant, big cow. Fresh veggies were gone, so they had frozen string beans with basil and garlic, and grilled hashbrowns from the freezer with rosemary and sage and grilled onion. The barkeep rhapsodized on each ingredient.

They all ate side by side on bar stools.

The marshal of Myrtle stopped by when they were halfway though the meal to claim his share.

"God, you can write books that actually sell and cook, too? Anything you can't do?" Charlie asked the barkeep.

"Not really."

"So, when do you serve your shift on night watch up at the Oaks?" Charlie asked Del.

"I heard about that being your idea. I spent all day and all night plowing and moving food and dirty dishes to and from that place, moving people, digging up Ida Mae—and you want me to work tonight, too? You're one cruel woman."

Kenny stretched comfortably. "I suggest we watch the evening news over a cup of my special coffee, kick back, and then go up to the Oaks to find Charlie's purse. She may well be leaving town tomorrow."

The marshal bent to look out a window at the darkening sky. "Anybody know how long a full moon stays full?"

CHAPTER 24

✛

*T*HE DAKOTAS, NORTHERN Iowa, and Minnesota are just beginning to dig out of a snow-and-ice storm, the likes of which have not been seen for a century."

"Lot worse in 'thirty-six and 'forty-seven. Had a lulu sometime in the sixties, too. And more since. He don't know nothing," Ben scoffed.

"In an era of climate upset due to global warming leading to dry winters even in the nation's upper mid-section, this region was unprepared for what happened."

"Hell, every street in Myrtle's plowed and sanded already," said the gravedigger. "Whadaya mean, unprepared?"

"The National Guard in three states was called out to rescue travelers stranded in cars, many of them overnight." Pictured—a guy in heavy camouflage brushing snow from a car window to peer inside. "There are no confirmed deaths as yet but many are missing and deaths are expected from this killer storm." Pictured—cars skidding off a freeway and into a ditch. "Farmers and livestock were particularly hard hit." Pictured—a farmhouse with the snow drifted up against one side to hide the first-floor windows, and aerial shots of snow with roofs and trees but not roads.

"There was, however, a bizarre story out of a tiny town in Iowa named Myrtle, which a reporter, Duane Webber, from our affiliate station PORK-TV, was able to reach by helicopter." Pictured—moving shots of the shadow of helicopter blades on snow.

"Duane, can you tell us what's happened there?"

"Yes, Dan, apparently there have been six suspicious deaths—the coroner of Floyd County has termed possible homicides—in this nursing home named Gentle Oaks in this tiny village of Myrtle, Iowa." Pictured—Duane on the porch of Gentle Oaks, his breath steaming, his demeanor serious but obviously distracted by events off-camera. Probably the Mexicans racing to avoid what they thought was the INS. "This home for the sick, elderly, and disabled has been virtually saved and provisioned during the power outage and blockage of the roads by valiant local men on snowmobiles." Pictured—Buz Bartusek helping Elsina Miller out of a snowbank, rows of snowmobilers grinning and waving in the background.

"But, Dan, inside these doors yet another, this the seventh, alleged murder has taken place during the storm, when no one could enter or leave, not even a murderer." Pictured—camera moving through doors into lobby. And then through the double doors into the "stench" zone.

"This isn't live," Charlie said. "It all happened hours ago. The rest has got to be outtakes. I know, I was there." And there she was all right.

"Which means, Dan, that the murderer must be someone from within. Allegedly." Pictured—Charlemagne Catherine Greene shoving Fatty Staudt's wheelchair into Fatty Truex's knees and, as both men rear their upper torsos in combat, racing off down the hall with the expression of someone intent on committing yet another murder. At least the sound had been an outtake. When the skeletal Fatties let loose, the obscenity quotient far outdid the stench quotient.

"I'd just got my period," Charlie whispered to her mother, who patted her hand.

Charlie hated it when Edwina did that. She knew it was supposed to be comforting but it seemed more like "that's okay, sweetie, I know you're weak. I'm your mom."

"Ben, you been seeing old Abigail through this?" the barkeep asked suddenly. "We all kind of depend on you to keep

157

watch—when we get busy with storms of the century and such."

"Oh, yeah, she's fine. Nasty, but fine. If she turned nice, I'd call in the doctors. Maybe the governor."

Without the odor and even with the dishabille, because the real working staff had not yet come on duty, the residents of Gentle Oaks did not appear as gruesome as they had to Charlie during the day. Of course Marlys must have been an outtake. But no, she was there, too.

They'd been unable to interview Harvey Rochester, who owned the home, because he was currently with the aforementioned coroner. Pictured—Rose reading from her pamphlet, Sherman poking his cane into the back of a vacant-looking woman in a sweatsuit and walker, and a head shot of an ethereal Marlys Dittberner floating by with white hair streaming as she passed behind Elsina Miller.

"But, Dan, we were able to talk to the administrator and spokesperson for Gentle Oaks." Pictured—the spokesperson looking benign, all-knowing, and unperturbed by the obvious jostling of those who were perturbed by being caught up in the cables and the crush and the added confusion outside their minds.

"What's she saying, Duane?"

"Well, Dan, there seems to be some problem with the mike."

"Yeah, right, Duane. We can hear *you* just fine," Charlie said and watched Elsina's lips moving between beatific smiles and repeating the word, "Jesus" joyously and often.

"She seems to think these deaths were God's will and not murder and that the deceased are happy with Jesus now."

Dan Rather was cracking up. "She's delivering a sermon."

"Right." Now the man from PORK-TV was being jostled.

"Thanks for that report, Duane," Dan said to PORK and then addressed the studio behind his own cameras. "Anybody talk to edit about this?" And then he looked out at the few people eating at the bar in Viagra's. "We'll get back to you on this late-breaking story when the coroner of Floyd County has weighed in. And thank you, Duane."

Brief cut to Duane, who, along with the camera, was shoved into the double doors behind them. "What the *bleep?*"

"We got plenty of that."

Dan Rather lost it.

"Keegan Monroe is your client?" Kenny said when *Celebrities Tonight* came on and Charlie wouldn't let him turn it off.

"My purse will keep a while longer. I just want to see him."

"Never heard of him," the marshal said.

"You heard of *Phantom of the Alpine Tunnel, Shadowscapes, Glory Boy?* He wrote the screenplays." The barkeep was impressed, anyway.

"Don't look like much. He gay, too?"

"No," said Charlie. "Just very rich. Now be still a moment."

Keegan was not an actor and didn't come off as well as Mitch Hilsten would have. He'd put on a lot of weight since he'd gotten out of prison last spring, but when he began talking about the new project, *Open and Shut*, he just came alive. He talked about his weight gain—a reaction to prison food once he was released—and how it fit into this project, which was really about making love with food.

"Oh, sick." Marshal Sweetie.

"Shut up, Del." Kenny.

"Like what? Bananas?" The watchman.

"I've got to get home," Charlie said. "I have a life, damn it."

"You all right, Edwina?" Kenny the host asked.

"Got any scotch, Squirt?"

The lights on inside had attracted a few die-hard customers now that the streets were plowed. So Kenny called Lorna to come tend the bar and Delwood drove him and Charlie up to the Oaks in the official Cherokee.

"Your mother's about at the end of her rope," Kenny told Charlie. "Too much history here."

"So's her daughter," Charlie replied, fighting cramps. "And I don't have any history here. I can't believe anyone would expect Edwina to give up her life to care for the Wicked Witch of the Midwest. Her family has lost all touch with reality."

"Men sacrifice their lives in war," the marshal said tentatively.

"For glory, right? And when they're too young to know better or defending their families from slaughter by other guys out for glory."

They were met in the lobby by Mr. Rochester himself. He looked awful.

"Did the INS come for all the Mexicans?" Charlie knew she felt more awful than he looked.

"We do not hire illegal aliens, forsooth. And we are once again fully staffed and running smoothly. No, the problem is—"

"I just want my purse."

"Miss Greene has gone testy on us," Kenny explained. "What's your problem, Harvey?"

"God," Marshal Del said. "Don't tell me you're looking for Marlys."

"No, it's Darla Lempke. We can't find her."

"Her grandpa probably picked her up in his titanic tractor with lugs."

"He came for her, she wasn't here. He called from home—she's not there. You were here today, Charlie. Can you remember the last time you saw her?"

They looked under Marlys' bed. No purse. No Darla. Marlys wasn't in her bed, nor was Gladys in hers.

"They wander. They do not sleep much. They are warm and fed and showered and Marlys has clothes," an aide who could speak English assured them. "Even though the moon's not so full, all here are restless still. Like they are called somewhere they don't know how to get to."

"So, Marlys is wandering around this place with clothes on?" Del's skepticism was lost on the Latino, who had no badge, whose smile was more weary than angelic, like that of the administrator who was actually in the stinky zone.

Elsina Miller came out of the ladies wiping her hands on a paper towel. Somewhere Dolores the cat moaned venom, but the rest of the place was surprisingly quiet. Only two room buzzers called for help and the only voiced request was the woman who considered it so hard to be alive now. No blaring televisions.

"God is in His heaven, Jesus is here with us, and all is well at Gentle Oaks. The residents all sleep comfortably in their beds."

"We just saw you on TV," Del said. "Your sermon sent Dan Rather into hysterics, but all sound was deleted. PORK panned you bad, babe."

"I think it's cool Jesus is here, but have you seen Marlys or Gladys? And have you ever been here at night with the moon just short of full?" Charlie was getting real anxious about her purse now and worried that somehow being more involved in the insanity here would lengthen her stay.

"Elsina's never been here at night at all. Tonight I think should be her baptism," Harvey said. "She, Darla, the families, and the doctors of course, are the only ones who have no clue about the realities of caring for ancient adults twenty-four hours. Seems to me it's time for management to taste reality. After all, Elsina, Jesus is here with you."

Kenny looked around, posed with his hands on his hips, and shook his head. "Listen, hear it? It's too quiet in here."

"They are all asleep in their rooms," the administrator insisted.

They were not all asleep in their rooms, but they were very quiet. Dolores the big tom with big hair stalked the halls of both wings, nervous, watching the shadows, hissing at the slightest sound.

"I haf never seen him act like that," said the tired aide. She wore a back brace. Charlie had read that the percentage of nursing-home staff with serious back injuries incurred on the job is higher than that of any other occupation. Adult babies are heavy.

There were plenty of shadows and many slight sounds. These poor souls wandered, those who could get out of bed. Some who couldn't sat on the edges of their beds and watched the shadows of those who could.

Charlie, Kenny, and Del stepped out onto the smoker porch, where they could see the moon. It still looked whole to Charlie and had a mist around it that made it seem even bigger. It was white tonight, mirroring the ground below.

The deputy sheriff joined them and lit up. He looked at the moon, too. "I used to work the kill in the packing plant in Mason City—but I've never seen anything like this place. That was just blood and guts and the terror of animals so thick it seeped through your skin and made you sick. This is terror so strong of folks so weak and bewildered it makes you even sicker. It's in the air here like it was at Armor's, only worse. Man, I can't explain it."

"I think you explained it very well," Charlie told him with a shiver.

"Everybody's a writer these days," Kenny griped. "That was beautiful."

"I'm no writer. I get this duty again, I'm no deputy." He took another deep and satisfied drag and started a continuous slow, thoughtful, determined nodding. "Tell you another thing—I've always been mildly religious. But I have another run-in with that Miller woman and I'm going to take up heavy drinking. Just to get even with Jesus."

They followed him inside—Charlie humbled somehow—

to find Elsina Miller and Mr. Rochester embracing, she screaming, he roaring.

And Rose reading, "Darla Lempke. Activities Director." Reading from the badge. Rose had found the badge.

Elsina had found Darla.

CHAPTER 25

◆

"CHARLEMAGNE CATHERINE, GET in here," Mr. Rochester roared. "Miss Miller, be still now. And where the hell is that damn deputy?" They stood in front of the door to a room Charlie had never seen inside.

It was lit by a bright light from above that reflected off-white, ceramic-tiled walls and floor. The only color in the room was the royal-blue waterproof cushion, seat and back on a shower chair, and Darla Lempke. The chair frame, formed of white poles, sat on casters over a drain in the floor between two waist-high walls, also covered in white tile, that jutted out into the middle of the room. A cabinet stood on one side of the low walls, a high-wheeled stool on the other, with Darla Lempke sort of wrapped around the wheels, her thick black hair splayed up against the white wall.

A shower curtain, pulled open now, divided this portion of the room from a sink and hair dryer and shelf with hair spray and shower caps, plus a commode stool into which the sheriff's deputy was busy upchucking whatever he'd managed to find to eat today. And in the interim, between the poor wretch's retching and Mr. Rochester's enraged intakes of breath, came Rose's starkly flat and unemotional eulogy, "Darla Lempke. Activities Director."

Harvey managed to disengage himself from his now merely whimpering administrator—rather reluctantly, Charlie thought. She, Kenny, and Del exchanged raised eyebrows at that but chose to ignore the implication. Now was not the time.

"Well, this sure blows my theory," Charlie said instead.

"Mine, too," said the marshal.

"And mine," echoed Kenny Cowper. "Guess it just goes to show, real life's not a murder mystery, huh?"

Charlie could not have agreed more, but she wasn't about to tell the hunk of Myrtle that. Like police and mystery readers and editors, she preferred patterns when dead bodies multiplied, especially in a short time in the same place. This would have been a perfect locked-place murder scene if anybody'd locked people out—so Duane from PORK was right. It had to be somebody from within, at least during the snowstorm.

Darla Lempke had a clear plastic hose with a shower nozzle on the end of it wrapped around her neck. The other end attached to the spigot on the wall where the water came out. This allowed somebody to sit on the stool on the other side of the tiled wall and keep reasonably dry while showering someone in the bath chair. Bathing helpless, way elderly, full-grown babies—Charlie hadn't even thought about how that was done. She'd hung up on the bowel movements instantly and not moved on very far.

Stupid Hollywood silliness, which Charlie was ever making fun of even while working it, seemed suddenly dear when confronted by a reality so awful and unalterable it didn't have to face edit. She could better understand why people looked for a reward in death for suffering in life, why the Hemlock Society and Dr. Kervorkian made good sense to others.

Unfortunately, that was all too early and too late for Darla the activities director at Gentle Oaks.

"Get on your cell phone," Kenny told Del. "Looks like the deputy's busy at the moment." He knelt down to get a better look at Darla in one easy movement. Nothing even cracked in his knees. "What do you think, Charlie?"

"Except for the hose around her neck, she doesn't look strangled somehow. But if she was suffocated like Del and I think the others were, would it look like strangulation? And she wasn't a vegetable and she wasn't a born Staudt. We can't move the hose to see if there are marks on her neck. And if you say I'm good at this, I'll—"

Kenny Cowper looked up at her very directly, matter-of-factly, "You'll what?"

"Tell my mother, Squirt," Charlie said, breaking that odd tension breeding when he was around. She really had to get out of here, real soon.

"I am aghast, unbelieving, tormented, shocked beyond credulity. Here lies a murdered innocent young woman and you can—what is going on with you two?"

Same thing brooding in your eyes, Harvey old boy. But Elsina? The three of them eyed each other with the dark Myrtle eyes.

Delwood broke the tension this time. "Charlie, coroner wants to talk to you."

"You were supposed to call the sheriff, you idiot," Mr. Rochester said.

"I did. They're together."

"Miss Charlie, describe for me what you see quickly. I'm already on my way. There's no doubt that she's dead?"

Charlie saw a crumpled form, eyes vacant and wide open, mouth partially open, tongue visible, but she couldn't tell if it was swollen or rolled up. There was no breath, no movement. There was no life in Darla Lempke.

"Good. Now, my dear, I want you to cover your hand with something clean and clothlike and very carefully move the shower hose away from the girl's throat. Try not to rub any clues off it. Feel for a pulse in her neck without the cloth on your hand."

"If you're on your way, can't you do it? I don't want to disturb the crime scene."

"You've been wonderfully patient so far," said the mortician. Charlie couldn't remember anyone ever saying that to her before. "Do as I ask and I'll explain later."

Charlie grabbed a clean white washcloth from a pile on a nearby shelf and did as he asked. "There's not even a red mark, let alone a bruise. It's not wrapped around that tight really. She doesn't look strangled, but I don't know what strangled looks like except in movies. There is no pulse in her neck."

"Excellent." Leland the jolly ghoul laughed. "Now, do you smell anything unusual in that room, or around the body?"

"Not really. This place is pretty much nothing but smells. The most pronounced one at the moment is vomit."

"The victim vomited? You didn't mention that."

"Not the victim, the deputy sheriff. In the stool."

Leland Mosher, mortician and coroner, giggled. "Miss Charlie, I want you to get him and the town marshal and our delightful Harvey out of there—is there anyone else nearby?"

"Kenny Cowper, the bartender. And all the resident lunatics in the halls."

"Are the lights on?"

"Yes."

"I want everyone out of the room, the hose as you left it, the light left on, and you to use your cloth-coated hand to lock the door behind you and them, and you to watch that they touch nothing upon leaving. Door moldings, nothing. You may flush the stool, however."

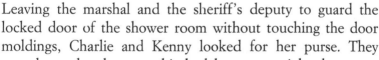

Leaving the marshal and the sheriff's deputy to guard the locked door of the shower room without touching the door moldings, Charlie and Kenny looked for her purse. They stayed together because this had become a right dangerous place. In the dim nightlights, they saw people without teeth and their mouths open who looked dead but, unlike Darla, were breathing. Without machines.

People sat up in bed listening and looking—but they didn't hear or see Kenny or Charlie because their hearing aids and glasses were on the bed table or because they were past finding any artificial device useful. But though they were very aware of danger, they'd forgotten how to use the buzzers next to their beds that would bring staff to their bedsides or forgotten that the buzzers had ever existed or how to mechanically manipulate them. But they hadn't forgotten how to fear. One man was so afraid he forgot his legs didn't work and he got out of bed as they walked in. Kenny lifted him off the floor and gently placed him back in bed, pulled up the covers and raised the side bar so he couldn't get up again. Must be awful to not be able to do anything for yourself, have lost any way to convey that awfulness, and perhaps, unlike a real infant, have shadowy memories or learned instincts telling you that you did know all this once.

"One of your people?" Charlie asked. She just hated big strong men who could be so gentle and kind. Guys didn't have to—that was women's work.

"No. Herman Rochester, the creator of Gentle Oaks."

"I have a hunch the key is to find Marlys and Gladys. They're kind of the brains of this outfit," Charlie said as they tiptoed out of Herman's room. Poor guy was whimpering. "And Sherman—he's pretty bright."

"Compared to whom?"

"Compared to florid Flo, his smoking buddy."

"Kenny, is that your voice?" a woman said from the next room. "Please come here."

"What's wrong, Grandma?" He went to her and Charlie followed.

Even in the dim light, she could tell Kenny's grandmother didn't have the Myrtle eyes. Hers were a faded blue. "I'm so afraid. Please take me home, Kenny."

"I can't, Grandma, you know that. You need nursing care, around the clock."

"Kenneth Cowper, I've never been sick a day in my life and you know it. Why do you hate me so to leave me in this awful place? I can take care of myself just like I always did. Help me sit up. I'm very thirsty. They don't even let me have water here."

"There's a full pitcher right here on your bedside table.

There's ice in it, and a straw to drink out of. Every time I come, it's here. You just forget. If you'd ring the buzzer, an aide would come and help you drink it."

"I don't need help drinking. What buzzer?"

He held the straw to her lips, showed her the buzzer hooked to her sheets.

"Where's your father? He'll help me."

"He's dead, Grandma. Been dead for twenty years."

"Why didn't you tell me?"

"I tell you every time I come here. You just forget."

"I never forget. You never come here. I need a cigarette."

"Tomorrow. Now, what were you afraid of?"

"I'm never afraid."

He kissed her cheek, covered her, and pulled her railing up, too. "Night, Grammy."

"Don't you wish you'd never come back to Myrtle? That was horrible," Charlie said when they were out in the hall again.

"It's life, Charlie. Don't take it personally."

"You sound like the ultimate businessman. And it's death, stupid."

"That's what I said."

This place was really larger than it looked from outside. Probably because the trees above it and the fields around it were so huge. There were in fact two nurses' stations, each unattended at the moment, and a scratching sound from behind the one on this wing.

"Could it be rats?" Kenny asked.

"Or another dying person suffocating alone."

The nurses' station was a long counter desk with chairs behind it and a glass shield in front of it from desktop to head-high if you were standing. Dolores, the portly Siamese tomcat with long hair, clawed the wall where Charlie at first assumed there was a scratching post, but it was his wrestling with something that made the faint rustling sound, something loose in the wall. He butted it with his head, then pulled at it with his teeth. Kenny reached down to yank a sweatshirt out of the hole that became a rubber cat door without it. Dolores looked up at Kenny and hissed before he plunged through it.

The gorgeous barkeep took the shirt to a light above the nurse's station just as a zombie in a hospital gown lurched past—so slowly Dolores could have taken a dump, gone to a movie, and come back in to have dinner by the time he finally rounded the curve to disappear, his bare, sagging ass flopping with every slow-motion step through the gap in his gown. This place reminded Charlie of an animated museum where the mummies walked with their wrappings coming loose.

Kenny Cowper nudged Charlie with the sweatshirt to show her the thick black lettering on the inside of the back of its neck; *Marlys D.*

They both turned to look at the cat door.

"She couldn't have," Charlie said. "Could she?"

"Maybe if she left her shirt behind."

They raced to an outside window that looked onto another raised loading dock and saw Mr. Dolores squatting there with tail raised high, in blissful contemplation of the heavens bright with moonlight. Moonlight that delineated small, human footprints in the snow next to him.

"She's headed for the graveyard again," Kenny said, pointing out the path of the footsteps leading off from the base of the loading dock.

"But that's not how you get there from here."

"It is as the crow flies. And Marlys, too."

"She flies? You mean like a witch?" The moon above seemed suddenly to double in size.

CHAPTER 26

✦

WE'LL BE BACK in minutes, soon, really fast, but there's an escapee who got out the cat door and left her shirt behind and could perish in the cold," Charlie told the deputy as Kenny held his fireplug coat for her to scramble into. "We have to take the marshal and his Jeep. If the coroner comes before we get back, tell him what happened."

"Let me get this straight," said the lawman. "First, you're going to go off and leave me alone here with these creepy-crawlers."

"You're the law. You'll be all right. And Harvey Rochester's here somewhere."

"Oh, yeah, that makes me feel real better." His irises looked suspiciously large, like Mr. Dolores's did when trying to get to the outhouse potty. "And second, you want me to tell the sheriff of Floyd County that one of these human critters escaped through a cat door?"

"That doesn't sound likely," Marshal Del agreed.

"And third, why would you keep anybody able to escape this place from doing it if they could? Even if she perished, it couldn't be worse than this. Not like she's safe in here. Why not let the poor thing die?"

"Because it's against the law," Charlie told the law with authority.

✦

"I can't believe this is the same woman who questioned saving Marlys in her derelict grocery store the other night," Kenny said as they raced to Del Brunsvold's Cherokee but paused to sniff the warm wind, listen to the icicles and trees dripping, before climbing in.

Yeah, Greene. Marlys Dittberner wants to escape the misery of derangement while she still knows what it is, and you would deny her that right.

I just don't want her doing it on my shift. When I'm back home, she can do whatever she wants. I don't want to take the responsibility.

In the Myrtle Cemetery, Kenny said, "You were thinking about your dealing with your mom someday when you watched me dealing with my grandmother back there, weren't you?"

"You're so good with those people. I just want to get out of there and pretend places like that don't exist."

"And you're in a rush to send poor old Marlys Dittberner back." Marshal Del turned on a heavy-duty flashlight that looked like it should come equipped with a snarling police dog. "I have to, I'm the law."

It was still cold to Charlie's "hot-water blood," but the humidity had to be two hundred. The wind blew snow off oak limbs in plops, icicles snapped and stabbed to the ground. In places, the earth lay bare of snow but filled with wet, or frozen dead leaves. In others, the drifts were taller than Charlie. It was an entirely different landscape than it had been on her first day here to bury Great-aunt Gertie. What, four days ago? Felt more like a couple weeks.

"The secret me hopes we never find her. But the other me worries for her out here without even her shirt." She probably saved my life by taking care of my birth mother so Edwina and Howard could adopt me. I can't let her die. Yet I can't let her suffer anymore. I can't go on like this.

The marshal's flashlight was more a distraction than a help. Moonlight on snow, without the heavy leaf cover, made for shadow limbs across drifts and gravestones but not dark moon shade. Branches with bare twigs looked more like claws, where once the leaves had made fingers before they fell to clutch at clothes and hair.

"Somebody go look at Myrtle's grave," Charlie said. While I deal with my issues.

Del and his maximum flashlight wandered off. Kenny asked softly, "What if we find her, Charlie?"

"Hope she's dead already? And if not, take her back alive?" Why should I make the decision, big guy? "I mean, you know her." And I've got some extreme cramps here. She'd swiped a couple more plugs at the nurses' station but this could get serious. "Kenny, do you know who my birth mother is?"

"Your mother and Elmo and I discovered something about your family this afternoon with the book from the museum. I think Edwina should tell you about it."

"Is that why she ordered a Scotch after dinner?"

"Hey, you guys, come here," Del Brunsvold's voice came across the snow and graves without even an echo of the boyish grin.

"Is she dead?" Charlie asked hopefully.

"She's gone. But she was here. I think we've found our murderer."

Myrtle's stone rose out of a drift, but still tipped forward to shadow the writing in the snow. Marlys had been trying to dig her way in again but there was far too much of that snow. It looked as if she'd dug with her hands like a dog might with his front paws. She'd tried several places. So old, she must have been so cold and so tired. But finally she'd picked up a stick and made letters in the snow. Scraggly letters, overlarge and incomplete because of snowmelt. *"Charl—g—home or die—You—next"* was readable only because of the size of the letters and Del's powerful flashlight.

"If Marlys could think, remember, plan, and write this clearly, she's probably the only resident at Gentle Oaks who could be the murderer," Charlie told the men. "And it really looks like an inside job. I don't want to think this, guys.

Which still doesn't mean she wasn't trying to help people out of their misery."

"She comes and she goes." The marshal switched the light to the small footsteps leading off down the wind-cleared parts of the road into the cemetery. She'd left before they arrived. They followed the prints far enough to see that she was headed for town. At least she was wearing shoes.

The haunting sound of a dog howling at the moon, which seemed to get bigger as the night wore on, made them run for the red Jeep Cherokee. The marshal gunned it toward Main Street and Orlyn Sievertsen's doghouse, all the while watching for Marlys, fallen from exhaustion and cold at the side of the road.

"I don't see Marlys Dittberner killing anybody," Kenny Cowper said. "I don't really know her that well, but she's one disturbed puppy. She has so many problems and fears—why would she focus on anybody long enough to kill them? And particularly Charlie, who just got here? And why warn somebody if you're going to kill them?"

"Ken, I spent more time looking for Marlys since I became Marshal, I can believe anything. She takes up damn near half my time and the taxpayers' money."

"I may have just got here, but I was apparently born here. She's crazy," Charlie offered. "Crazy people can be very clever people." I don't want it to be her, either.

Viagra's seemed to be doing more business. Charlie noticed a CNN news van parked at the curb in front of it and two pickups. "If I was born in the Dittberner house, which was the old Staudt house, where was Edwina born, do you think?"

"I figure, like most of us, you were both born in the hospital in Charles City," Del said.

"Where did Edwina grow up, live with her parents? What house?"

Del backed the Cherokee to the town's main intersection where Main Street crossed the street that crossed the bridge, passed the Sinclair and the Dittberner house, before heading for the railroad track. At the intersection, the ruin of the Dittberner grocery store stared across at the ruin of another building. This one was made of that odd brown stucco you saw a lot of around Myrtle. In fact, there were twin buildings, both in the same shape. They, like Marlys's grocery, reminded Charlie of ghost towns in the West, sagging window sashes like bags under sad eyes, crumbling thresholds like trembling lower lips.

You read too much fiction, Greene.

I know, but dead buildings are so heartbreaking. "At least we bury dead people."

She was in the backseat, the guys up front since this was a serious mission here, and the Jeep stayed parked in the middle of the street in front of the twin buildings. The guys turned to peer at her, Del around the headrest and Kenny over his.

"Okay, I talk to myself. Don't ask. My mom grew up in one of these?"

"These were stores in the business district with nice apartments above, both owned by Edwina's grandparents on her mother's side. Edwina and her parents lived in the apartment above this second building, the in-laws above the first," Del said. There had been a series of thriving businesses then and those shops were rented as barbershops, meat markets, electrical stores. A whole series of businesses came and went over the years before the commercial centers moved to strip malls along major highways out of other towns, national chains in or near larger population centers.

"Bargain stores."

"Nobody loves bargains more than your German, Scandinavian, European peasant breeds," Kenny said. "Could be my next project after the Myrtle book."

"What did you do, win a lottery? Jethro Larue and the industry aren't going a to let you diversify that much, even in nonfiction. Secret to success in publishing is to write the same thing over and over. I'm here to tell you it works."

"Yeah, this was swank living, those apartments. They had stairs going up the outside of the buildings with railings and covered lattices and arched grape arbors at the top. Screened back porches so you could sit out and see over to the river, get the morning sun. And your mom's grandparents were always cooking cabbage stew with potatoes and onions and ham and carrots in it, and apple cinnamon strudel. The smell would waft all over town because they were cooking up so high. There're stories about these old buildings that go on forever."

"You're not that much older than I am, Brunsvold. I don't remember any of that and I used to live on Main Street."

"I just remember hearing about it, Ken, the stories, you know. And another story is that the first real donuts in town were made by Edwina's grandmother. Bet they really smelled good. Now we're down to those powdered plastic things at the Sinclair, Wonder bread or whatever. Imagine all those wonderful aromas wafting from those vacant, roofless buildings once, over a town half again this size."

"There's somebody in one of those buildings right now." Kenny said and opened the door on his side. "Do you suppose it's Myrtle?"

Charlie and Del tumbled out the other side and stopped to look at each other.

"He must have meant Marlys, not Myrtle," Del reassured Charlie and drew his mega flashlight.

"Just don't call her 'honey', okay?" Charlie could swear she smelled the donuts and the onions and carrots and ham. Why would anybody cook cabbage? There were still vine tendrils attached to the side of the second buildings. "Well, what family were these maternal grandparents of my mom's?"

"They were Auchmoodys."

"And Marlys married an Auchmoody. And Kenny told me once that we Auchmoodys knew how to wear a pair of jeans. Because of the color of my eyes?"

"Myrtle's mother was an Auchmoody. So was Kenny's grandfather."

"And so was Edwina's mother. But I'm adopted. Yet I came from this area. What am I missing?"

"Damned if I know. Those Myrtle eyes have spread everywhere by now, definitely all over the county, probably the country. I heard there were Auchmoodys in Texas during the Civil War. You know, these buildings still smell like sauerkraut? One night a week at The Station, they serve spareribs and sauerkraut. A real big draw. Serve it over mashed potatoes and swimming in juice. Oh, my."

Charlie and the marshal stood between the two buildings, where the wind had cleared out the snow but for one humongous drift. Charlie wondered if the marshal too was in no hurry to rescue Marlys, who took up half his time and the taxpayers' money. Not like she could be tried and jailed if she were the murderer. You just had to respect her determination to die and escape the Oaks.

The top of that one drift was as high as the second-floor landing on the inner building, and Kenny stepped out of the hole that once had been its door, carrying a bodylike load. "Del, I need help."

It wasn't Marlys this time.

CHAPTER 27

DELWOOD BRUNSVOLD STARTED to race up the steep footprint-pocked drift, but instead, brought it down with him, bringing Kenny and his burden, too.

"Edwina? What the hell were you doing up there?"

"Charlie, have a little compassion here. Christ, she's your mom. She was probably looking for her childhood memories and her roots," Kenny said, untangling himself from the marshal, the snow, and Charlie's mom.

"Looking for Marlys. Ben and I thought we saw her and we were out here trying to avoid the ubiquitous press and—"

"You weren't smelling sauerkraut and onions and carrots and donuts? Reliving your childhood?"

"Charlie, where do you get this stuff?" Edwina slid out of her enormous coat from the home place and rubbed an ankle. "Trust me, nothing smells worse than sauerkraut and no smell lasts longer, unless it's cooked cabbage."

She and Ben had climbed the drift and Edwina had fallen through a rotted floorboard just far enough to get stuck up to her thigh. Ben had kept going. "There really is a floor up there, and some of the walls and part of the roof. And I swear I saw Marlys Dittberner, naked from the waist up."

"Must of been creepy with the moonlight and the memories and all."

"Not as creepy as CNN at Viagra's."

That's one of the few things Charlie had often appreciated about her mother. She wasn't sentimental.

178

"Where's Ben?"

"I didn't see him," Kenny said. "Or Marlys either. Let's see if you can stand on that ankle."

Edwina winced, the ankle was tender. Kenny and the marshal decided to hobble her over to the Jeep and have Charlie and Del take her to the Oaks for a nurse to check it out, since they had to report to the coroner and sheriff anyway. Kenny would check out the CNN invasion at the pool hall and look for Ben and Marlys.

When they arrived with the injured Edwina, Gentle Oaks was once again in the midst of chaos. The sheriff and the coroner had not been able to contact the marshal, who had inadvertently put his cellular on voice mail. There had been yet another death at Gentle Oaks and Elsina Miller was upset because the loved ones of families, her aging angels, beloved of Jesus, had been disturbed in their blessed sleep by pagans.

Charlie didn't see any pagans but the place had that strange, sour odor left over from dinner still. Edwina identified it as cooked cabbage. Charlie had thought cabbage was eaten raw—like in coleslaw or fish tacos.

"Always seemed to me it grew stronger rather than dissipating."

"Why do they cook cabbage?" What Charlie had wanted to say was, Did you find out something horrible about my birth mom? Something that would make you hate me like Great-aunt Abigail does? I don't think I could handle it if you did. But I'd pretend to.

"Beats me. Old people like things cooked, mushy. Probably cook lettuce, for all I know. Actually, it doesn't taste bad—cabbage cooked with a little milk and butter, salt and pepper. But the smell gets into your clothes and hair, and the furniture even."

Harvey was getting ruddy from hypertension or dipping into the meds—as well he might. National newscast exposure about murder at Gentle Oaks would certainly have an effect on filling up the sudden explosion of empty beds. "The economy of Myrtle, and even Floyd County, could be at stake."

It seemed that Doris Wyborny's roommate would never again beseech all who came near to help her. Which blew the theory that Marlys Dittberner was responsible for the sudden rash of deaths. She had not returned, and the alarm went off only when people with ankle bracelets went out. Then again, Charlie didn't remember seeing one on Marlys. And she could escape again through the cat door anyway. But Edwina and Ben had seen her on Main Street.

Charlie sort of hoped Kenny had time to get the CNN crew too drunk at Viagra's to get here, and time to find Marlys and Ben, too. "You know, the Grim Reaper has been long overdue at Gentle Oaks. Maybe he's just catching up."

"I'm afraid not with Wilma Overgaard, Miss Charlie," the jolly coroner said. He always wore a white shirt and a tie. According to the wrinkles, he changed the shirt once a week. Even his jowls were good-natured, jiggling regardless of whether he was laughing or not.

The sheriff was small, slender, and about half bald. Sheriff Drucker squinted, blinked, and pursed his lips at the coroner's every statement like he was processing information. "Same M. O., but this one was botched. Badly. There's a murderer loose in this place. No doubt about it. Think it's time to call in Mildred?"

That got everything on Leland the mortician jiggling. "Oh, let's do. Time we have some levity around here, right, Harvey? It's getting depressing."

They'd gathered in the dining/activities room, Nurse Hogoboom inspecting Edwina's ankle, Harvey pacing dramatically, hands behind his back. Deep thoughts going on behind knitted brow? Charlie could only hope he was figuring out who was playing Grim Reaper at Gentle Oaks, so that everyone would quit looking at her like she should have this all figured out by now and so there'd be no reason for her and Edwina not to catch the first plane out of here.

"I will not allow that creature in this facility." Elsina Miller

180

glared at Harvey Rochester. "Mildred Heisinger is evil. A daughter of Satan and a charlatan." Her flowered dress had wilted. She was on the verge of tears. Administrators and generals are not meant for the front lines. How did Harvey manage all this?

"No, she's a psychic," the sheriff said. "Nice lady, too."

"Assisted living," Harvey said, like ancient actors would say *Eureka!* "That's the new thing now, you know. Long-term health-care facilities offer a service nobody wants, everyone dreads it. But assisted living is in your own space and there are merely people close by to help you when needed. Closest thing to being in your own home or that of a family member, but this way, you don't have to upset their lives. Or independent-living apartments with home health-care aides who come in to keep you in your home/apartment. It's the wave of the future. Everybody would want that service. Elderly. Exhausted caregivers."

Sherman Rochester, his grandfather, wandered by with socks clanking, poking at nothing but air with his cane instead of using it for balance. His socks, a hospital gown, and droopy diapers were all he wore. He still had hair, still asked the air in the hall in front of him for a smoke. Everybody noticed Sherman but his grandson. The coroner didn't even giggle. Just blinked.

"Is there anybody here who can live on their own, even that much?" Charlie asked. "With no mind and no memory? Your grandfather could care less if you as a caregiver were exhausted. He doesn't know who you are or who he is either. All he knows is he wants a cigarette."

"But we could separate the two wings, Charlemagne Catherine, put a nice central dining room in the less dependent wing. Spruce it up. I don't know why I didn't think of this before. I'm a genius."

Was everybody thinking what Charlie was? The coroner, Sheriff Drucker, Mary Lou Hogoboom, and Edwina watched Harvey thoughtfully. The sheriff's deputy and Marshal Del appeared sleepy but unconcerned, Elsina simply at the end of her rope. Was this assisted- and or independent-living thing a good way to keep the nursing home viable? Would it mean getting rid of a bunch of human vegetables first? Was Harvey the murderer here?

No wonder law enforcement settled on the most likely suspect and set out to prove his or her guilt. Real life was too up for grabs—just when you think you've figured it out. . . .

Wilma Overgaard sprawled half out of her bed and so did her bedding, as if she'd put up a struggle. Charlie had never seen her anything but flat out and immobile, but then, she had probably only glimpsed her twice. "I'm trying to remember if I heard her when I was here earlier tonight, or if her vocal agony was so persistent the other times I've been here. Is she the same one who thinks it's so hard now to be alive?"

"No one suffers in agony here. How dare you even imply God would allow such a thing," the administrator said from the doorway. "You should be glad for her. She has gone to the Lord."

"I am glad for her. I'm glad for all of them but Darla Lempke. I'm a little concerned as to where this all will end." Wilma Overgaard hadn't been dead nearly as long as the others, except for Darla. Both of them were fairly fresh kills. Someone had gone on a rampage tonight. Accelerated things. Why? Or was it a copy cat running with the momentum of excitement? Who among the inmates had that kind of mind or mobility? Besides Dolores the tomcat? Who among the staff was in the building to facilitate all the deaths? Or would they have to be, since getting in was easy? How many in the community would be relieved to see some of these people put out of their misery?

"Are we sure Marlys didn't slip back into the building when no one was looking? She manages to slip out regularly." Charlie didn't wish the poor woman to be the murderer here. But she hated to give up on her instincts, too.

Wilma Overgaard had either struggled against her attacker

or her body had been mussed up after her death or—what was that idea niggling so far back in Charlie's head, so weak but persistent? What was it about the mussing that was similar to the other dead bedridden? God, it was so close and so frustrating. Well, she'd better call it up soon, before this whole institution was wiped out.

Or was the Rampant Reaper really doing all involved a kindness?

The national press, the staggering number of already helpless victims murdered, had either convinced the sheriff of Floyd County to call in state and federal officials or had convinced state and federal officials to convince him. Whatever, a passel of investigators descended on poor Gentle Oaks, this time without helicopters or press fanfare, but the Mexicans disappeared anyway. The administrator's office was commandeered, and to Charlie's relief, real forensic types roamed the building. Unfortunately, so did the residents, particularly since most of the butt-wipers had fled.

At one point, Charlie and Harvey sat in a corner of the dining/activities room, both gray with fatigue, propping their chins in their hands, elbows on a table. Harvey said, "God, what I wouldn't give for one of Kenneth's killer coffees about now."

"Me, too. But you know what I don't get about you? How, as an ex-Broadway actor, you can really enjoy what you're doing here. I mean, after Broadway, how much empathy can you have with people who drool and leave turds behind when they walk down the hall? Who don't know who they are? I admit I haven't been here long, but I don't see scores of grateful relatives clamoring for an encore. Is it just the money? How can there be that much?"

"Well, insurance doesn't pay that much, but the government shells out once the family fortunes are spent down or the heirs' lawyers have figured out ways to get around that little problem. Most of the people in here came before the new laws and were able to gift any money they had to their heirs, so we're largely Medicaid here. But, lovely Charlemagne, after practically starving for so long in the arts and now actually earning a living, having money for investments—it's a challenge and a turn-on I would never have believed either."

Harvey was called off to the administrator's office for interrogation, and Nurse Hogoboom and Elsina Miller allowed out to the dining room. A twit who had no idea what was happening and was too young to have interest in the national news was sent to question Charlie and she fell asleep on him more than once.

The last time he woke her was with an expletive, and behind Charlie, Gladys said, "We got plenty of that."

The woman had her wrapped leg down and the shoulder strap of a familiar purse hanging from beneath a lacy nightgown.

"I didn't know Gladys could get herself up and out of bed and into her wheelchair," Charlie told Elsina, who drooped at another table.

"Neither did Miss Miller," Mary Lou Hogoboom interjected. "Old Gladys can get herself on and off everything but the freaking pot."

Charlie took another look at old Gladys, who stared back triumphant and sly. Or maybe in her weariness, Charlie imagined that.

She'd promised herself earlier to spend what she hoped would be her last night in Iowa out at the home place, well away from the erotic complications at Viagra's. But in the wee hours, she fell into Kenny Cowper's bed beside her mother, too exhausted by murder to worry about anything so mundane as an oversexed hunk who had the same color eyes she did.

This was not the first time Charlie Greene had been way wrong.

CHAPTER 28

———◆———

WHEN CHARLIE AWOKE, the bookcase-divided apartment sounded empty but for a dripping faucet. She lay there in the big bed—well, Kenny was a big guy.

We will *not* think of that.

Right. Wonder how Edwina's ankle is.

Charlie's mom had left the not-so-Gentle Oaks long before Charlie last night. Someone must have driven her. Maybe Kenny had come for her.

The ankle was swollen only slightly and Nurse Hogoboom had found some crutches that would suit Edwina. "Lots of people come in here on crutches but they're soon in walkers, then in wheelchairs, then comas. We kinda recycle the crutches around town."

Charlie wondered where Edwina and her crutches had gone.

That sly look on Gladys' face last night had really startled her. Then again, Gladys could keep track of the number of fictitious boyfriends to needle Charlie about. The old woman might be strong and mobile and clever enough to plan and carry out the demise of some of the weaker inmates at the Oaks. Fighting that purse away from her in the wee hours had been an eye-opener. But Darla Lempke was young, strong, agile, and quick. Yet the coroner/mortician thought Darla too was smothered.

Charlie hated nonfiction, real-life mysteries. But she couldn't resist mulling puzzles. They just nagged at her.

Harvey wanted to revamp to a ritzier asylum. He'd have

to get rid of half the vegetables to do that, and cordon off the cognizant old, so that the assisted and/or "independent" folks wouldn't be reminded of what was coming next. He was making a good start.

Cousin Helen might wish to get rid of a lot of "born Staudts" so she and Buz could go visit the dark-eyed grandchildren who couldn't visit here—and enjoy what life they had, in the warmth of Arizona before Gentle Oaks.

And the two skeletal Fatties were certainly mobile and strong enough to chase pretty young aides down the hall and figure out how to propel wheelchairs into fighting positions. Rose could remember enough to read. And then there was poor, clever, unbelievable Marlys Dittberner, perhaps the oldest person Charlie had ever encountered. She could have slipped into Gentle Oaks, committed a few murders, and slipped out again. But why did she keep trying to burrow herself into the grave of the town's namesake?

And Kenny-of-the-hormones had spent a lot of bucks on this place. Would he inherit some money if his grandma died? Would it be more convincing if a bunch of other Jack Kervorkian needies died first? The problem with puzzles was that there were always too many pieces with edges that didn't fit. In this one, Darla Lempke stood out like a cut-up piece of a camel swimming in an ocean scene.

The answer is in the way the bedclothes were messed up on Wilma Overgaard, the latest victim, or maybe the latest winner.

Oh, shut up. You know less about puzzles, crime scenes, and mysteries than I do. Which is saying a lot.

Charlie still lay there, still groggy, when footsteps sounded on the outside stairs.

Footsteps sounded on the stairs—Jesus, it's good you're an agent and not an author.

"Oh, bugger off."

Up at the Oaks early this morning, the doofus who got Gladys going with his reference to excrement was so startled when Gladys smiled without her dentures and wheeled up to invite him to be her boyfriend that he followed it with "Jesus," which of course set off Administrator Elsina on getting born again. Charlie wondered what became of him after she, Mary Lou Hogoboom, and Gladys fled the scene.

"Whadya mean, 'bugger off'? I live 'ere, Sheila." Kenny's head and part of his torso appeared over a bookcase. He pulled off a sweatshirt and used it to wipe the sweat off his forehead.

"Don't turn around. Wait." Charlie covered her head with the pillow. "Now turn around." She kept covered until she heard the shower running. She had to get out of this town.

When Charlie had taken her turn in the shower, coffee fragrance saturated the air of the place. "So where's Edwina? Did you ever find Marlys?"

"You realize you're hyperventilating?"

"Like you did after following me up the drive to the Oaks the second time I saw you? I hate romances. Besides, I'm inhaling coffee air."

"This has nothing to do with romance."

"I know." Her neck hurt just looking up at him.

"Drink your coffee and we'll walk to the Schoolhouse Café for breakfast. Where we'll be safer."

They stood out on his rickety back porch overlooking his snowmobile and the Sinclair. The air was cool, not cold. Fresh, not rush hour. They drank strong coffee and breathed deeply, didn't talk and didn't touch. Sufficiently caffeinated, they strolled around puddles, patches of ice, frozen mud, gooey mud, up to the Schoolhouse Café and ordered wicked omelets and orange juice. They got toast and potatoes, too. If Charlie had felt stared at the last time she was here, she felt scrutinized this time. At least the trees and sky looked friendlier now.

"I don't know where your mother is, but the Lumina was gone when I got back from my run, so she feels good enough to drive anyway. I hope she's out seeing to old Elmo. He got a little strange on us yesterday. Far as I know, Marlys has not turned up."

"I hope she doesn't. I hope she's out of her misery. Oh, God, there goes the sun again. I'd hang myself from a clothes hook in a closet if I lived in this climate."

"Actually, it's great for moody writing."

"You write moody nonfiction?"

"When it suits."

"Hey, Kenny? You seen Ben?" the wait person asked. The entire staff consisted of one waitress and one cook. "Didn't show up for breakfast this morning."

"No, but he was looking for Marlys last night with the rest of us. You checked the Sinclair?"

"Mayor says his bed wasn't slept in."

"Maybe Ben and Marlys ran off to get married." That brought laughter from everyone in the room.

The omelets were the special—eggs, ham, onions, green pepper, and cheddar cheese, for godsake. "I'm going to have to start lifting your weights."

"So what's this about my not turning around?" Kenny lowered his voice.

"I don't want to talk about it."

"Can Mitch Hilsten turn around without getting in trouble?"

"So what's with Ben? He lived here a long time or just wandered in one day?"

"I don't want to talk about it. You got a problem with buns?"

"Okay, backs. Satisfied? Now, about Ben—"

"What, like shoulder muscles? Sculpture?"

"No, from the waist up. And, yes, Mitch has a great back." But not as great as yours.

"Would you believe that's one I've never heard of? Okay, okay—" he put his palms up against the tough Hollywood-agent squint "—let's do Ben." But he grinned and chuckled over her preposterous weakness. At intervals, anyway.

It seems that Ben, the town watchman, was the illegitimate son of one of the dark-eyed girls who got pregnant, and an adoptive home was never found for him. He was sort of passed around among families. "Didn't have the mentality for school, so he dropped out early, but he was a good worker and earned his keep at various farms around, and then at the grain elevator for years. One day he got under a chute that dumped a load of oats on him. Buried for long enough that he wasn't good for much anymore. So he started wandering the town, reporting what he saw to anyone who would listen."

"Hence the town watchman."

"Right. Never got violent or nasty. Just watched things. And the Sinclair was the only place around with a lot of cash on hand at all times, so the mayor, who runs it with her husband, gave him a bed there, put in a shower. That was before Viagra's and The Station became viable businesses."

"So who was his birth mother? Was she a Staudt?"

"I don't know, Charlie. Marlys always kept the identities of the girls as secret as she could in a small town. Are you anxious to find out who your birth mother is?"

"You know, I don't think I am now. My life is so full, I just don't want to deal with it. What if she wants to extort money or horn in on my life with Libby or, God forbid, wants me to sell her screenplay?"

As they walked back to Main Street by another route so Charlie could see what little of the town she hadn't already, Kenny asked, "What have you got against romances? Women are supposed to love them."

"Yeah, we're supposed to love football, too, if you listen to the right promoter."

"That's not an answer."

"They make women out as needy people who have to have a man to survive."

"I understand that—I don't read them—but I understand that they outsell anything else and those days they portray gutsy women who demand a lot."

"But who will never be whole without Mr. Right. Hey, I work in Hollywood, I know the female dependency myth. That's what plays there. That's all that plays there. How about you, big guy? Need Cinderella to make your life complete, do you?"

"No, but then I like football."

"You'll be ready for Cinderella when you're a geezer and can find a blithe and dewy one."

"Is that why Mitch Hilsten became engaged to Deena Gotmor? And are you why they split up?"

"Actually, Mitch and Deena were starring together in *Paranoia Will Destroy Ya* and somebody's press agent decided it would make great press when the film opened if an engagement were announced. She was already humping Godfrey Arthur of the Gluecks anyway."

"That's why you're so cynical. A woman working Hollywood, and of course a teen pregnancy before that."

"That just now occurred to you? Hello? And let us add my welcome to Myrtle, Iowa."

CHAPTER 29

❖

*T*HEY PASSED THE Catholic Church, so small and so sad. Holes in the roof, boarded windows instead of stained glass. Crows peering down from exposed rafters like pigeons from the ruin of a barn that had shattered suddenly at the home place.

"You're using me for your book, aren't you?" Charlie said to the poor church, but really to the man beside her.

"How'd you know?" he asked the crows on top of the building or the sky or God or the universe, but really Charlie Greene.

"I know writers, God help me. They're driven. They never stop working and they feel free to use whatever and whoever comes across their vision."

The Solemn Lutheran Church wasn't far from the Catholic Church and was in similar condition except that its windows weren't covered at all. "Solemn? This is a joke, right?" Charlie asked.

"Lutherans tend to be Scandinavian and are given to somber moods."

"Looks like the Methodists won."

"They had the backing of old Abigail and her money."

"If she's got that kind of money, why can't she hire some Mexicans to take care of her like Harvey does? Until she's ready for the Oaks."

"Not a chance Edwina's going to move back home, is there?"

"She has a home and a career, friends, books to write,

191

lectures to give. Would you give that up for the family witch? This isn't home to her. She's lived in Boulder almost three times as long as she ever lived here. She isn't planning on retiring soon and when she does, she's considering Prescott."

"But this is where she was born, her parents are buried, where you were born—"

"And thank God, she's not sentimental. I don't know why she came back this time, really. These people are all remote history to her."

"There is a plot for her next to her parents out at the cemetery. But I suppose she'll be buried next to her husband."

"My dad's buried in Green Mountain Cemetery in Boulder, but Edwina has asked to have her ashes scattered over a special place in the Canyonlands of Utah, where her favorite rats and bats rule the night."

"At least she's sentimental over rats and bats."

"Make no mistake, Kenny Cowper, Edwina Greene will move back here only over my dead body."

They blinked at each other. She laughed, he chuckled.

"Man, is that an opener or what?"

"Yeah, had I but known, I'd sure as hell never said that."

"Don't forget, Marlys Dittberner predicted you would be next." His eyebrows raised to perfect arches.

"Maybe Edwina drove to the Mason City airport instead of the home place. Roads will be plowed, planes flying. Maybe we've already got tickets."

They stopped in front of the gray Victorian. The sun came out, briefly lighting it and the snow around it, but couldn't cheer it up much. "God, *Psycho* meets *Fargo*."

"Right. There's more wonderful material here than a writer could use in a lifetime. This place is a gold mine. And I'm the only writer in town."

"So what did you do before you became a famous writer?"

"I was a reporter for the *Miami Herald* for a few years.

Writers were seeping out of the cracks in the sidewalks. Myrtle's all mine."

"You either made good in a law suit, a divorce settlement, an inheritance, won the jackpot—if you'd made that good with your writing, even I would have heard of you."

"Your mother has read a couple of my books."

"Living and business expenses may be low here, but the remodel on that apartment of yours cost bucks. Wait, I know—you've got a Sugar Mommy."

"God, you Hollywood career types are vindictive. Okay, my sister and I share an inheritance from my mother's parents, left in trusts from the sale of farms, all set up before they committed suicide."

"Rather than end up vegetables in Gentle Oaks."

"Who knows? The trustees put the money in the stock market when we were small. While we grew, it grew."

"It didn't go to your mother first?"

"It was split three ways between us. My grandparents did not like my father, figured he'd blow her fortune trying to keep the pool hall alive in a dying town. And he would have. But by the time she could have collected her share, he'd managed to get in the way of a combine."

"And you want to return to your roots? Forget *Fargo*. More like *Psycho* meets *The Addams Family*."

"I know you think you're just talking Hollywood, Charlie, but you are really saying what I've already said. Listen to yourself. Read my lips. There is material here."

"But that's all reruns, or in syndication or cable stuff now."

"Remember, I'm doing fact, not fiction. How many baby boomers are dreading futures in nursing homes for themselves because they're dealing with parents already incarcerated? They can't deny the reality of aging, much as they want to. There's a certain sick fascination in the inevitable. You want to read about it to find evidence it won't happen to you. You'll just go to sleep one night in your own bed in your own home and not wake up. Do you have any idea of the growth industry in Iowa and much of the Midwest? It's medicine, hospitals, nursing homes, especially those run by tax-exempt churches. They and drug companies are cleaning up, along with lawyers who know how to work the system. Forget Family Farms and crop subsidies, corn and soybeans. Iowa's getting fat on Medicare and Medicaid."

"And Myrtle, Iowa, is an example so extreme, it's news." The last thing Charlie wanted was more ties to this place, but this hunk could pitch. She fished in her purse for a business card and handed it to him. "I know old Jethro Larue can pull wedgies in New York that I can't from Beverly Hills, but should he ever let you down, I wouldn't refuse to look at a proposal on this one."

This is really scary, Greene. We're almost doing business in the backwater of a backwater.

"That's the problem. Old Jethro is old enough to find the topic fearsome, loathsome, and nonmarketable."

"But you said baby boomers would get into this."

"He's way past baby boomer, Charlie. He's too close to the age of incarceration. This is not the topic for most people over seventy-five."

"Jeth Larue's over seventy-five?"

"Pretty damn close. And remember, a lot of older women who read, who are also most of the people who read, are going to be living at home independently longer than guys, who die earlier and watch more football than read anyway. And these women are still responsible for grandmoms and great-grandmoms in nursing homes. Charlie, we're talking demographics here. Larue's mother is still alive."

"You aren't making sense. He must have to visit her in a nursing home."

"He's got three sisters still living, so he doesn't have to confront that reality."

"I don't want to confront it either. Do you?"

"Only while I'm writing this book about it. And, Charlie Greene, my personal financial stability should have nothing to do with New York publishers not thinking I'm starving."

Too bad Shirley Birkett, the next Danielle Steel, was married and pregnant. Charlie could have fixed her up with Kenneth Cooper. They could have shared suspicions.

"Know what else? Harvey told me very few doctors will even visit a nursing home. They can't handle it."

"They have to, nursing homes are full of sick people. You're making this up."

"Law says family doctors have to visit four times a year. Harvey says they whirl through like dust devils, prescribe medications over the phone with the nurses the rest of the time. Things get serious, they send out a helicopter from Mason City, take them into the hospital where specialists, who don't visit nursing homes at all, fix them up and send them back to vegetate longer in awful ways the specialists never have to witness."

"Medicaid's not going to pay for a helicopter."

"Somebody's paying for it. Harvey's making out like a pig at a trough."

Abigail Staudt stepped out on her porch. "Just what is it you two want, standing there like that for so long?"

"Admiring your house, Aunt Abigail."

"Don't you call me aunt, hussy. Just get out of this town and take that good-for-nothing mother with you."

"She's been watching us a long time from a corner of her front window," Kenny said as they walked off.

There were no sidewalks, so they sloshed through the slush of the streets. Charlie's poor fashionable boots started leaking. "Do you want Edwina living back here?"

"I guess not, now that I've gotten to know her a little. She just seemed like the perfect answer to an imperfect problem there for a while."

"Like Myrtle seemed to her family."

"Everybody around here remembered your mother as the ugly duckling. Ugly ducklings are not supposed to have lives.

She's actually aged pretty well. So has my mom. But she's had some work done."

I'm not touching that sucker, Charlie thought, but said, "Is this stuff adobe or stucco or what?"

They stood in front of the ruin of a two-story house with that same brown coating that she'd seen often here and which coated the store buildings her mother's family had lived in on Main Street.

"I think it's some kind of colored cement. Lots of buildings were built with it or coated over, probably in the twenties or thirties. It was touted to never rot or need painting and originally a light tan in color, but it got dirty with the decades, which hadn't been predicted."

"You've been doing your homework."

"I have an interest beyond my book. I have roots here. As do you."

"Nobody feels rooted to a place they've never seen or hardly even heard of. So, you are using me as a possible outlet if your agent won't accept the Myrtle book because the reality and immediacy of nursing homes would upset him at his age, because you are delving into the intricacies of loyalty, family secrets and genes, and the lingering power of female guilt in a once agrarian society."

And because we both apparently belong to a horny strain of the same ancestry. Time for a reality check, big guy.

"Do you happen to know if the mayor carries tampons or whatever at the Sinclair?"

CHAPTER 30

WHEN CHARLIE MADE her purchase, the mayor and her dog were extra somber. Ben had not shown up, nor Marlys either. Even Orlyn Sievertsen's Lab and Saint Bernard hadn't seen her. "So how's old Elmo?"

"Something happened to Uncle Elmo?"

"You haven't heard? Marshal Delwood's been looking all over for you two. Elmo tried to kill himself out at the Staudt place—botched it. From what I hear, it's the Oaks for the poor guy."

On their way to Kenny's car, Charlie said, "Did you hear the dread in the mayor's voice when she said poor Uncle Elmo was headed for the Oaks? What I don't understand is why anyone stays in this town once they notice the first gray hair, eye bag, or wrinkle."

"Being dead might not be so great either, you know. And not everybody's a deserter in this army, Charlie. Some people feel sympathy, responsibility, for the suffering, aging members of the community."

"I hate that word."

"Aging?"

"Community. One more reason to steal my time and energy. Always something."

He drove her out to the Staudt farm in his Range Rover, forced to rough it by the warming weather and the county snowplows, slightly pissed that he couldn't have ferried her into the rural wild on his brand-new snowmobile. He kept the Rover in an off-ally garage behind the beauty/barber shop that was a converted house at the other end of Main Street. The shop was open two and a half days a week, which took care of the local population, so renting out the garage helped a lot. "Looks like you won't be flying out today."

When they reached the home place, the helicopter was just taking off for Mason City. And Edwina was destroyed.

"They'll resuscitate him to be a vegetable for twenty years, and he smoked and drank and ate so hard. It's not fair," Charlie said. She, Kenny, Edwina, and Cousin Helen watched Elmo disappear into the forever-frigging clouds of this place. "At least you must not get skin cancer around here."

"Oh, yeah, you gotta slather yourself with sunscreen, wear long pants, sleeves, slacks, and floppy broad-brimmed hats. Best thing is to stay inside. But that doesn't weed your garden. Plant your crops."

"Do you do all that slathering?"

"Why bother? We live forever around here, the way it is."

"I don't suppose you had time to buy plane tickets." Charlie leaned over to look in Edwina's face. Her mom sat on the bottom step of the back porch. The home place seemed desolate without the barn, the glint of sun on ice.

"We can't leave now, Charlie." Edwina looked like a battered wife, with blotches for bruises.

"I can."

"I need you. I think I'm responsible for what my uncle just did."

"Mom, he's been trying to kill himself for years and it had nothing to do with you." Charlie took another look at her mother and got a cramp that took her breath away. "I hate family."

"Me, too." Edwina tried a wobbly smile, acknowledging Charlie's capitulation.

"God, so do I." Helen Bartusek pulled a tissue from the cuff of her sweatshirt to wipe her ever-dripping nose.

"I don't," Kenny Cowper said.

The women looked at him as one. Nobody felt up to saying the equivalent of "well, duh."

Elmo Staudt had returned to the home place on the county snowplow, crawled into the cab of his half-buried truck with a cigar and two bottles of whiskey, and when sufficiently plowed, he took out a brand-new razor and got one wrist cut some but scraped good before he had a stroke.

Kenny was staring at the open door of the truck. Even from the porch, you could see the flashy red of blood on what lingered of the snow where the county plow driver had pulled him out. "It should have worked. He had all night to bleed to death. There should have been time. Must have clotted on him while he was unconscious."

The county plow person had been uneasy about something Elmo Staudt had said. Like "Thanks for the ride and good-bye forever," or similar words—and had stopped by this morning to check on him. He'd used Elmo's phone to call for help and, having been trained as a paramedic, did the wrong things to allow Uncle Elmo to make his own ultimate decision. In all fairness, the suicidal man had done much to undo himself. His blood ran thick and slow. Wouldn't you know? All the rich desserts and eggs and cheese and sausage had done their thing, but without clogging his heart. Clogged his brain instead.

Charlie went upstairs to finally change clothes and pack for herself and her mother and to weep for Elmo Staudt in private. It was a great relief to change into cotton socks and athletic shoes and fresh everything else.

When she came out onto the porch with the bags, Cousin Helen said, "You can't leave. Someone has to look after the house. I told you there's no place to stay around here anyway, and your mother and I have to go to Mason City and Elmo."

"Well, I'm staying at a hotel in Mason City or at your place tonight, cousin dear. Next time you call in evil relatives, consider accommodations and ramifications."

"Well, you can stay with Kenny while Edwina and I—"

199

Both Kenny and Charlie were shaking their heads at her.

"She just doesn't get it," Kenny said.

"I'd rather stay with Buz."

"I could stay home until my shift, and you and Edwina could go to Elmo."

"No, sweetie, manipulation isn't like that. Like poor Elmo's going to know who's out in the waiting room or not."

"What if he dies in the night?"

"We celebrate," Charlie answered. "At Viagra's."

Charlie and Edwina Greene ended up spending the night at the Comfort Inn in Mason City. They visited Mercy Hospital to check on Elmo Staudt. Mason City wasn't a city, it wasn't even a big town, but the hospital complex was enormous. Elmo Staudt was not expected to recover, so he'd been sent to a nursing home.

"I'm sorry, there was nothing we could do for him here," said a female at the front desk who knew all this by typing his name into a computer database. "He'll have excellent care there and should any sign of his coming out of the coma occur, the staff at Gentle Oaks in Myrtle will contact us immediately. We can have him back in no time."

Next, they drove out to the airport and purchased tickets for the day after tomorrow. On the way back, they stopped at an Appleby's for huge chicken Caesar salads, garlic bread, and Chianti.

"I'm not kidding about day after tomorrow being it, Mom," Charlie said over coffee. It wasn't as good as Viagra's but it was rich and strong. "I've had it with Iowa."

"Is it Iowa or Kenny Cowper?"

"That, too. And don't forget I have a daughter with the Myrtle eyes all alone back home."

"Great-aunt Abigail has blue eyes, Charlie."

"What's that got to do with the price of asparagus in China?" as her boss, Richard Morse, would have said, or something similarly out of frame.

"Let's not talk about it now, okay? It's so nice to be away from there. Let's enjoy tonight."

They showered and fell asleep trying to watch the news and read about it in the paper at the same time. In the morning, the TV and lights were still on. Charlie woke to grain futures and the price of gasoline and the governor's office calling for a full investigation of the nine suspicious deaths in the nursing home in tiny Myrtle, Iowa. The person behind the computer behind the front desk at the hospital here hadn't mentioned that little fact yesterday.

She didn't realize her mother's bed was empty until Edwina shouldered in with a tray of complimentary bagels, coffee, and juice. Charlie announced that she had no intention of spending another night in Myrtle ever again and would keep her room to ensure she caught the plane to Minneapolis tomorrow. "But I will go there with you today after I've made a few million phone calls."

"Charlie, be reasonable."

"I have been. Now it's time to get back to the real world." To forestall any pleas for pity, she muted the TV and called Libby, woke her up forgetting there was a two-hour difference in the time zones. While her daughter explained just how much she appreciated this fact, a color-enhanced commercial showed a machine on TV spraying some chemical mixture on rows of plants. Charlie had the feeling it wasn't Miracle Grow. Libby was not a morning person.

While Charlie ignored her mother's smirk and dialed the office to leave a message on Ruby Dillan's voice mail that she would absolutely positively be flying back to blessed California tomorrow, a strange assortment of letters and numbers zipped along the bottom of the screen. Ruby Dillan was the office manager at the agency, and the zipping letters and numbers attempted to inform Charlie of such things as the price of corn, wheat, soybeans, soybean oil, and soybean meal—of feeder cattle, hogs lean, and pork bellies. It was like a stock-exchange ticker tape, but it was out of Chicago. Iowa was a foreign country.

To further drive home her point, Charlie left a similar message on Larry's machine, her stomach starting to eat itself again at the thought of another trip to Myrtle. Just before she awoke this morning, she'd dreamed that she and Marlys Dittberner held a pillow over Uncle Elmo Staudt's face until he stopped breathing.

They were met with a new sound at Gentle Oaks—*La Traviata* or something operatic, sung at full volume from a deep voice that couldn't hold the pitch and ended each measure or whatever with a squeak or a rasp. More than one of the empty beds had been filled. The mind behind the voice was as garbled as the tune and the lyrics. Charlie's tone deafness made most music painful, but this was excruciating.

"God, I hate it when we get singers," Cousin Helen said.

His name was Eugene and he was a devil on wheels in a wheelchair, pulling himself along on the walk bars in the hallway at terrifying speed, driven by a music only he appreciated.

"Yeah," Mary Lou Hogoboom agreed. "He can't comaout soon enough for me." She grabbed poor Rose and her walker with the green tennis balls out of the way of the musical maniac just in time.

Eugene had once been a professor of music at the University of Iowa.

Charlie didn't want to be there when he met up with the scrawny Fatties. Retired farmers she could see, but a "professor?"

"The best brains go down the hardest," Helen reassured them.

"Ahhaa eeeiahhhh," Eugene sang/squeaked. Fat Dolores tore off in the other direction. The family of this songster had to hate his music a lot to allow him to be sent to a nursing home that had just suffered nine suspicious deaths.

"It's sooo hard to be alive nowww."

"Everybody keep me away from all pillows," Charlie said.

Uncle Elmo Staudt had settled in fast—mouth open, teeth out.

Charlie turned on her heel, "I'm outta here."

"Wait." Edwina pulled her back around by one elbow. "At least touch him, say good-bye—something."

"Mom, why are you putting me through all this? I've had enough. If you want to rot in this funky family stuff, be my guest, but—"

"Charlie, baby, he's your grandfather."

CHAPTER 31

✦

*E*VERYBODY BUT ELMO Staudt stared at Charlie's mom, even Rose, who'd followed them to escape the professor.

"He can't be her grandfather," Helen said finally. "The poor man never married. He—you mean . . . not Elmo, no way." But now they were all looking at Uncle Elmo.

"Well, he thinks so. Or he did." Edwina was strung so tight she jerked when the opera recommenced out in the hall.

"Mom, you gonna make it?" Elmo needed a shave. He looked kind of waxy. At least he probably didn't know where he was. His stomach seemed smaller to Charlie, his breathing steady but shallow. "What made him think he's my grandfather?"

Apparently when they broke up Marlys' possessions before shipping her off here, they'd sent quite a bit to the museum. She'd burned a lot of her papers but kept pictures of herself and the girls and babes she'd cared for. Some were pasted in the album they'd looked up in Kenny's apartment. "You saw the one of Marlys holding you. Well, back farther there was a whole envelope of loose photos pasted onto a page. Kenny and Elmo and I looked through them and Elmo was pointing out the girls he had known. All had disappeared. And then he came to one that just turned him inside out. Her name was Isobel."

"Aaaeeesposo, whadaleda emyoo!" Eugene wailed. "Waa dozeedough, wannapena zeedough!"

"Somebody get me a pillow," Charlie said.

One of the Mexican aides ran past the open door to the hall one way and soon another ran the other way.

"She worked as an au pair for a large family on a nearby farm, but also went to the country school then, the same school as Elmo went to."

Abigail Staudt and her sisters, all spinster teachers, had started an informal scholarship fund to get promising girls into the teaching profession, and Isobel had earned one. When she left town, Elmo thought it was to prepare for the two-year teaching certificate from the teacher's college at Cedar Falls. Apparently she'd dropped out of the world to have a fatherless baby instead. Elmo was convinced he was the father.

"Nowwww what the bloody hell?" Mr. Rochester roared out in the hall.

"It's quite all right, Harvey dear," said a smooth, serene voice that was not Elsina Miller's. Must be an actor, too—real people don't talk that way. "I'm quite accustomed to chaos."

Charlie watched Uncle Elmo's eyelids quiver. Oh, God, don't wake up and know where you are. But she said, "Isobel could have slept with other guys."

"Promiscuity didn't use to be so promiscuous," Cousin Helen explained with a sniff that was as much judgment as allergy.

Sheriff Drucker walked past Elmo's door, his arms full of Dolores, who looked ready to climb his head. "Settle down, Harvey. Let Mildred do her work."

"Laa feee madombo ohohohohohoh!"

"It's sooo hard being alive nowww."

"I suppose I should go out there," Nurse Hogoboom said with a sigh. "Everything's even crazier than it used to be. If I didn't need the money, I'd quit."

"You smoke?" Sherman Rochester.

"Oohhh, who is that ghastly gentleman?" The female voice in the hall lost some of its severity.

"That's his Granddaddy." Myrtle's Marshal Del.

"I am sorry, Harvey, I didn't realize."

"Just do your psychic thing, Mildred. Oh, Christ, what's this? Nurse, aide, somebody, get out here this minute." Harvey.

"Beginning to wonder how bad I need the money," Mary Lou Hogoboom muttered.

Cousin Helen didn't move either.

"Don't they wear Depends?" Mildred asked.

"Of course they wear Depends. They just know how to get around everything man can invent."

"Where are the Mexicans?" Helen whispered as if under siege.

"Disappeared, I guess," Mary Lou answered. "Wonder who all is here."

"You'd think they'd know the difference between the sheriff and the feds."

The sheriff's deputy wandered past the door.

"We all look alike to them," Mary Lou said.

"Is this man dead?" Mildred asked.

"No, Mildred, he's in a coma."

"Why isn't he in bed instead of a wheelchair?"

"Because it's daytime and beds give him bedsores. Now will you please—"

Charlie watched the short vignettes pass the door to the hall: the two nurses considering options, Uncle Elmo beginning to twitch all over, Edwina staring into space and inward at the same time. And Rose, who picked up a pillow from the empty bed next to Elmo's. She looked at it for the longest time and then, carrying it on top of her walker handles, brought the pillow to Charlie.

Oh, boy.

"You know where the Mexicans hide?" Helen asked Mary Lou.

"If I did, I wouldn't tell you. I'm a Democrat."

Elmo's eyebrows and ear hair and nose hair even quivered now.

"You see, Charlie, Isobel was your grandmother and—"

"Why? Because your uncle got laid? Mom, you're losing it. We gotta get you out of here fast. This place is unhealthy."

"Well, it's a nursing home," Cousin Helen whispered. "My God, what are you doing with that pillow?"

Mildred, the psychic, passed by in the hall and backed up to look into the room, nearly stepping on the toes of a young man with a Palm Pilot. Her publicist?

Mildred and the Palm Pilot guy entered Elmo's room, the psychic all in lacy pink, literally floating on prissy pink wedgies. Her hair had been dyed for so many years that it was pink and lacy, too.

Elmo groaned. Oh, Jesus. Charlie didn't think he was her grandfather, but she owed him something for his obvious affection for her mother—which, around here, was a lot to ask.

"Chastity was the only way to beat the curse of Myrtle," Edwina said for no reason, belatedly coming out of her trance.

Mildred was really heavy. She reminded Charlie of the psychics on TV. So how could she float?

"Hush," said the psychic in pink. "I must listen and feel. Hand me the cat, Sheriff."

Drucker brought the overweight Siamese longhair in from the hall and placed it in her arms. Dolores appeared to cling to her. Charlie would have bolted.

"It's all right, kitty, there, there. This creature is terrified of something."

"This is a terrifying place," Charlie said aloud by mistake.

"Much sickness and death here, yes—"

"This is a nursing home," Helen reminded them all again.

"A health-care center," Harvey boomed. "When will anyone stop with the nursing-home thing?"

"It's the place nobody wants to end up in," Charlie offered.

"Many, many injured and ill people come to health-care

centers to recover and return home to lead happy lives," Mr. Rochester said, not so serenely.

"Not anybody here," Mary Lou Hogoboom said. "Not since I been here. And Medicare pays for two weeks if you stay in the hospital long enough."

"Laaa, deeriato, pissssa ria deooooh oh-oh-oh-oh, delaymia de arrrhhh—"

"Come on, Edwina. I think our grandfather just choked off the opera." Cousin Helen grabbed Edwina's elbow.

"Mom, you stay right here. You haven't even looked at Fatty Staudt since you got to Myrtle. You can't get involved in this. We are leaving tomorrow, remember?"

But Charlie found herself suddenly alone in the room with Elmo, Dolores, and the psychic. She was revving up to join the deserters when Elmo said quite clearly, "Mildred?"

Viagra's was back in business with Kenny's secret weapons, one cooking and the other manning the bar and serving tables, too. There were even a couple of guys playing pool. The talk was of how wonderful the snow had been for snowmobiling and how bad it had been for the crops not yet harvested, and the murders at Gentle Oaks. Except at Charlie's table, where the talk was of Mildred Heisinger the psychic.

Harvey and Del regaled a smirking Kenny Cowper with the latest excitement at the town's biggest business. Kenny had gone upstairs for an apple he split with Charlie to go with her split pea Soup of the Day, the healthiest thing offered.

"All the Mexicans vanished. Mary Lou just up and quit and poor old Elmo kept calling to Mildred," Del said around a cheeseburger. "And she said, 'I forgive you, Elmo dear,' and turned as pink as her hair. And old Elmo just up and died with Charlie standing there holding a pillow."

"Charlie?" Kenny's eyebrows arched and he leaned back in the booth. "You didn't—"

"No. I wanted to. But I think he died without knowing

where he was. So he won after all. Do you suppose he and Mildred had dallied, too? I mean, besides Isobel? He must have been quite the young Staudt in his day. Wonder why he didn't marry and produce the male heir that Edwina's father didn't. And I wonder why Edwina has paid no attention to old Fatty up at the Oaks. She talks about him fondly cutting up watermelons at family reunions out at the home place and then says he's not that same person." Edwina had stayed up at the Oaks. "My mother should be rejoicing, not grieving, for her favorite relative. He had a right to not have to be a vegetable."

"Charlemagne, you believe in euthanasia? How can you live with yourself?" Harvey Rochester was obviously "taken aback."

Kenny lost his smirk. "So, Del, what did Mildred do when he died?"

"Shed a few tears."

"That woman can cry on cue and we all know that. But Nurse Hogoboom defecting without notice is inexcusable. We have to have one RN per shift. They work twelve-hour shifts and are expensive. I have one RN returning from vacation— but this is not the way it's done—without notice."

"Don't you use LPNs or whatever they're called now?"

"No, they can't give meds. RNs and aides are all we need, really."

"So when is Darla Lempke's funeral?"

"I have no idea, Kenneth. Whenever Coroner Mosher releases the body, I expect."

"Man, I'm going to have a bunch of digging to do, huh? But Ken, you should of seen the fireworks when old Elsina woke up from her nap in her office and discovered Mildred was in the place. You ought to get a movie out of that, Charlie."

"I don't make movies, Delwood. I'm just an agent."

One of Kenny's secret weapons brought the special coffee he'd promised if they were good and told him all the news.

"Kenny, Marlys is always missing, but me and the mayor are really getting worried about Ben. He still hasn't shown up anywhere."

"What do you think, Del? Should we notify Sheriff Drucker of yet another possible murder in Myrtle? At least there's one dead who died on his own terns." Kenny stood and raised his cup of special coffee and said above the not-very-much hubbub in the place, "Here's to Elmo Staudt, who managed to die after less than an hour at Gentle Oaks."

A cheer went up from everyone at Viagra's but Harvey Rochester.

❖

CHAPTER 32

*L*OVELY, FAT, AND ancient Mildred necromanced, or whatever those creatures do, over poor Elmo's body while no one attempted to revive him." Harvey wiped his brow with his napkin and Charlie wondered if he, like she, wondered how much more grease came off on his face than sweat on the napkin. "I kept pleading for someone to do something, but unholy hell exploded in the hall, which I'm sure our Mary Lou could have handled had she not turned turncoat."

"They got this professor with Alzheimer's in today and he's singing at the top of his lungs and the bottom of his mind. He taught at Iowa U, but his family's from Fertile. Enabnits. I mean, the man is driving the nuts nuts."

"They are not nuts, but merely confused, as you, Marshal, have been since birth. Surely you are not all listening to this jackal?" Harvey's blood pressure was blotching his face. "I mean, he's Delwood and a Brunsvold, for godsake."

"But the other morning upstairs, you called them 'ancient psychopaths' and Gentle Oaks 'bedlam' when the moon was full. Why, your grandfather is one of the sanest of the crazies there," Charlie said. "Would you take him home to live with you because he's merely confused? You even have servants, one a woman and both a minority yet. The people at that place are more than confused."

"Yeah, Charlie's confused," the proprietor pointed out, "but she's not ready for the Oaks."

"And did the Mexicans come out of hiding or did somebody stumble across their hiding place?" Charlie asked. "You got an underground railway from Mexico, Harvey?"

"I think they split up and have their own hidey-holes," the marshal said. "Probably under towels or sheets or something."

The pea soup, apple, and milk were just right for whatever ailed her and, unlike her mom, Charlie took strength in Elmo's passing. "Okay, not passing. Death. Uncle Elmo died dead. Sorry, Harvey, but after a half hour in Gentle Oaks, that sounds like Oz, man, nirvana, paradise. Even if it's just a big nothing. I couldn't be happier for him."

"So what did the poor confused Fatties do to the singing professor?" Kenny asked. "Come on, you guys, earn your coffee. And you've got to admit, Charlie, those two appear to be having a pretty good time of it."

"They told him in the vilest of terms to 'shut his yap.' Called him every unspeakable epithet invented before nineteen fifty. And when he continued his caterwauling, they simply dumped him out of his chair," Harvey said.

"And me and the sheriff's deputy standing right there," Del added. "Happened so fast, it was over before we could stop it. Just got their chairs on each side of him and lifted up his wheels till he slid out on the floor. Looked like a wiener squeezed from a bun. Beautiful timing for people so confused."

Kenny Cowper stared at Charlie. "You thinking what I'm thinking?"

"Yeah. Just because you can't go potty by yourself or walk, doesn't mean you can't plan and execute murder. Being outrageous and obnoxious doesn't necessarily translate into the inability to reason."

"There's this myth that murderers are smart for some reason. Committing murder is the dumbest thing you can do. Have our Del here after you, you're not careful."

"And old Elsina wakes up from her nap—great napper that lady," Del continued, flipping off the barkeep.

"She's not napping in her office, she's doing business or

praying," Harvey came to his administrator's defense—interesting ambivalence here. "You act as if the most profitable business in all Myrtle and possibly Floyd County is a comedy of errors."

"Well, then, she snores a lot when she's on her knees. Everybody says so. And Jesus tells her Mildred the godless heathen is in the building, threatening her beloved children. I mean, we had eight, ten murders recently, and a lot of them since the Greenes arrived. Don't take it personal, but Sheriff Drucker says one or both of you is a catalyst. And Mildred agreed."

"Oh, thanks, Mildred. I don't know about Edwina, but this catalyst sleeps in Mason City tonight and gets on a plane first thing in the morning. Just thinking about it makes me feel better."

"You're not staying around for all the funerals? You must be related to half the dead, especially Elmo." Harvey looked hurt. "I even ordered a piano."

"Oh, you did not. And 'especially Elmo' won't know the difference."

"How can you be sure what Elmo knows?" Kenny put his hands behind his head and leaned back in the booth to show off his biceps. He wore a white T-shirt with a great green Budweiser alligator on it. "You haven't been dead yet. And don't you want to solve the murders?"

"Besides, Jesus will hate you for it," Harvey added. "And tonight's ribs and kraut at The Station."

"Do they get ribs and kraut at the Oaks?"

"Absolutely. Most popular meal of the week. We have to take the pork off the rib bones and grind it and the gristle up for the toothless, but I was going to give you and your mother a free dinner at The Station."

"Aren't you worried about Marlys? You're not human. Is it because you're bionic?" the marshal asked.

"Charlie's bionic?" Kenny and Harvey said together.

"Yeah, she got new parts after that accident."

"Which parts?" Kenny wanted to know. He put his biceps down and the alligator undulated. It had a Budweiser lizard hanging out of its mouth.

"Charlemagne," Mr. Rochester said patiently, "if it's fear that is driving you away so soon, Mildred the psychic is patently a fake. You are worldly enough to know that, if our administrator is not. Her prophecy concerning you is about as useful or accurate as Depends is in keeping the denizens of the Oaks from fouling everything with which they come in contact. Their revenge against the living and healthy. But gentlemen of the law are quite taken with psychics these days and the local constabulary is proud of the fact we have one of our own."

Mildred the psychic had wandered Gentle Oaks, Mr. Dolores in her arms, which meant she was a lot stronger than her disintegrating hair, her wandering taking her to the most desperate of Elsina's beloved, in spite of Elsina's dire warnings. The psychic was unerring. Fakes usually are. And she and Dolores had come back down the hall and stopped at the next most deprived bunch—including Kenny's grandmother.

Harvey had asked her why she was carrying the damn cat around the building. "That creature weighs a ton."

"Because cats have such power. And this is the most powerful feline I've come in contact with."

"I can believe that," Harvey said. "You know his fur balls stain concrete?"

"Their senses are so acute," Mildred had said. "They not only divine the thoughts, fears, and feelings of these poor souls who cannot speak for themselves, but can pass on the vibrations of these emotions and, in a garbled language, relay the meaning to those of us who are sensitive."

"She moved from the rooms or wheelchairs of the most vegetative first, carrying the cat, both looking real spooky," Del told Kenny. "And then onto those who still talk or think in their way, and the confused nuts who move or walk, too. And when she got to old Mrs. Bublitz, who told her and the

214

ceiling how hard it was to be alive now, the cat moaned and Mildred the sensitive had a revelation. 'This woman is in such pain and distress, she prays for death.' Duh."

"And when she'd carried the animal hither and yon and hither once more, she finally stopped in front of Charlemagne here and returned the beast to his rightful place on the floor, where he promptly relieved himself on the carpet, such was his sensitivity," Harvey added.

"And her whole pink-lace front was a mass of cat hair and snags and loose lace threads," Charlie offered, to pay for her coffee.

"And Charlie asked her if there was a message in all the sensitivity and fear bouncing off the walls there—and Mildred said, 'I'm afraid there is, poor dear. The consensus seems to be that you are next.'"

"Just like Marlys wrote in the snow on Myrtle's grave." Kenny squinted with mock importance. "And you still don't believe in the wisdom of the demented or in the curse of Myrtle?"

The tough agent from Hollywood leveled him a look to match the gravel in her voice. "You got pea soup on your alligator, Cowper."

Over the unkind remarks concerning how hard-nosed California women were, Charlie heard a welcome reprieve from her purse and scowled at her companions as she answered the call from the real world. It was Larry and he said the words all agents and writers love to hear. "Charlie? I hope you're sitting down."

"Out of the blue," Charlie told the startled men at the table after her conversation and followed it by a victory whoop she'd learned from her daughter the cheerleader, "from whence all good things flow."

"That doesn't even rhyme," Myrtle's lawman, gravedigger, plow person said with obvious disappointment.

"I wish I could make a woman that happy," Harvey said wistfully.

"Kenny, if you take Visa, I'm buying whatever's on tap for everybody at this table and your secret weapons, too."

Charlie dialed Shelley MacArthur and woke him up. He worked security all night and wrote and tried to get some sleep in the daylight hours. "Shelley? I hope you're sitting down."

"Charlie, I'm flat on my back in bed, as you know. Tell me this call is what I think it is. I'm getting too old for joking around, babe. Tell me you sold my historical and not as a children's book so I don't have to take out all the good stuff."

Charlie told him what he wanted to hear: "And not just to Pitman's, but to Constellation. I'm out of town, I'll get home tomorrow. Don't do anything till you hear from me and we've signed. Looks like a deal we can't refuse. I'm so proud of you and happy for you. I knew this idea would fly."

They were both crying when she hung up and raised a huge stein of whatever was on tap to the guys at the table and said, "I don't have a screenwriter or book author, male or female, who doesn't have a beloved historical in a drawer that I can't sell. They're not 'in' right now. I never thought in a million years Shelley would sell that project, but he's going to make some real money for once. And me, too."

"But you just told him you knew his idea would fly," the marshal said.

"That's agent talk." Kenny crossed his arms over the alligator and the lizard.

"Here's to sheer dumb luck, a proposal on the right desk at the right moment, and to Harry Potter." She raised her stein.

"It's a children's book?"

"No, but it's really imaginative, been turned down by every publisher in town twice. It's unique. Which is hard to sell these days because you can't compare it to anything that's been a success. Just like Harry Potter was turned down everywhere, which proves that the current wisdom is fallible. I can't say any more but I feel like dancing on the table—on air. To hell with curses and dementia and Depends. I have a life, a future, sanity. And tomorrow I'll be home."

"Don't forget," Kenny said. The Budweiser lizard had a Budweiser frog hanging out of its mouth. "You are next."

CHAPTER 33

✦

*I*ARE NEXT. I are next for the deal of a lifetime. I are joyous," Charlie rhapsodized, rubbing it in as she, Kenny, and Del cruised up to Cousin Helen Bartusek's house in the official red Cherokee. The day had continued to warm and melt and they had the windows down. The streets were rivulets where they weren't mud. "What's that smell?"

"Spareribs and sauerkraut," Del said, inhaling a sigh. "Cooked slow most of the day. That aroma draws people from as far as Mason City."

"Smells like everybody at Gentle Oaks died at once with all the windows open. I will sleep in Mason City tonight and fly out of Iowa from there in the morning."

"So you keep telling us." Kenny sounded bored. "Did you know Mason City is River City of *Music Man* fame?"

"You're kidding. I didn't see a river." The show was currently enjoying a new life on Broadway.

"You were probably only looking for a bed and the airport. Meredith Wilson was raised there. He's even buried there. So, have you thought over my Myrtle proposal?"

"Jeeze, how many propositions you guys got going?" Marshal Sweetie asked.

Charlie explained patiently to them both that she kept her professional and personal lives separate. "And I told you I'd look at it, Kenneth."

"What about Mitch Hilsten?"

"He has never been a client, nor will he ever be. I handle writers, not actors. And our relationship is highly overrated."

"Lucky guy. So, I have a decision to make?"

"Actually, no." Nothing like menstrual cramps to put you back in control of your life. "What do you suppose Mildred was forgiving Uncle Elmo for?" She changed the subject. "Think he was her lover, too? He has blue eyes."

"Heard stories he was quite the Romeo in his day," the marshal said.

"I heard the same thing about you, Brunsvold."

"Really?" Del turned off the engine. They all stared at Buz and Helen's house.

Edwina had called from the Bartuseks' asking Charlie to come up. Kenny and Del were on their way to search for Ben and Marlys. "I wonder how fast I'll lose my high once I get inside."

"I haven't been inside since Arly and Ida Mae Truex owned the place. Sat down with Buz and Helen at The Station to eat, keep a bottle of single malt at my bar for Buz. Picked up some expensive habits in Arizona, as he tells it."

"It's Helen. She doesn't approve of the pool hall, for women anyway. Wonder why she'd let me in her house? Buz drinks?"

"Drink or two—then supper on nights when she's working at the Oaks. He's particularly fond of Jack's fried chicken."

"He's retired, huh? From what?" Charlie was reluctant to leave them for Cousin Helen.

"He drove things—trucks, hauled grain and hogs to market, gasoline—even drove a bread truck," Del said. "That man could drive anything in any kind of weather."

"Drove the combine that ran over my dad. Too bad he retired before Elmo started looking for a way out." Kenny left the backseat to open her door, looked way down at her, and grinned.

"Your dad was trying to escape the Oaks, too?"

"That's what everybody says, but who knows? It sure wasn't Buz's fault. A barkeep has little business being out in the way of a combine. Dad didn't even hunt. Hey, that's only part of the reason I have problems with people deciding to check out early on their own. And, Charlie Greene, I really think you should try the ribs and kraut at The Station tonight. Del and I'll get you back to Mason if your mom needs the Lumina longer than you do."

" 'Del and I'—now we volunteer to help the only law for miles to do a duty he could do alone? Why is that, Cowper?"

"I don't trust her alone with you, Brunsvold. Or alone with me either."

The marshal sighed long and heartfelt. "Sure is different than in old Elmo's day, huh?"

"Looks like a pretty nice house for a truck driver and a nurse with four children."

"It was Ida Mae and Arly's house. They sort of inherited it because Helen was the only one who stuck it out here. She had two brothers who took off after graduating from college. One's retired in Oregon now and the other in Connecticut. They never come back."

"What happened to Arly?"

"He was real deaf," Delwood said. "Walked in front of a freight one night at the crossing by The Station, actually died from a blow on the head from the crossing-signal arm, got run over anyway. Yeah, story goes ol' Arly greased the tracks for half a mile."

"He was on his way to the pool hall, according to legend. Maybe that's why Helen hates the place so." Kenny slid in beside the marshal and they drove off to look for Marlys. And Ben, too.

The Bartuseks' house was two-story wood in a pale yellow with white trim, glassed-in front porches on both stories, cleaned-out flower beds rimming house and front walk. A birdbath with a heater in it, ornate concrete urns awaiting next spring's blossoms. Tidy, cared for, no chipped paint or drooping eves here. Piles of raked leaves showing through melting snow. The air was chilly but not cold, full of moisture for the dry linings of throat and nose, and it smelled so fresh—not empty, but filled with soaked earth and tree bark and leaves. No exhaust fumes or sea salt. The sun came out filtered by moisture haze but dispelled the gray gloom, and so did two cats from a clever cat door in the porch's siding instead of in the storm-screen people door. They both resembled Dolores the tom but had shorter fur, thinner bodies, and the markings of a tiger cat mixed with the Siamese. They came down the walk to greet Charlie as if she'd never been between the sheets with Mitch Hilsten or drank beer at the pool hall. They purred, rubbed against her legs, butted her ankles with their heads. Why didn't Libby's damn cat at home ever treat her like this?

Buz opened the porch door before she and the welcoming cats reached it. His big smile sort of lit up her day, his big stomach showing his fondness for Jack's fried chicken. The cats accompanied her in and sent a tiny dachshund off the porch and into the house by simply blinking at it. The porch also had screens and wicker furniture and carpeting and many of the plants they would transport back outside in summer. And inside, more yellow carried out the theme, bringing a hint of sun into the house.

It was the sort of a place, if you could bear the thought of being old enough to retire, you'd consider soft and snug, soothing for tired bones and aching head, sore joints, and a craving for tranquility. Comfortable furniture, abundant reading lamps, bright, light, secure, soft, mellow, roomy—yet cozy, perfect for commercials for retirement-oriented products like medications, diet energy drinks, herbal longevity scams, long-term-care insurance—safe shelter for your parents or investments. Most of Charlie's writers made their living off a significant other and some managed on ad writing. It took only a few hot talents to make her career.

If you could get a decent production staff and film crew to come to Myrtle, Iowa, this would be nirvana for all those set to reap the market in the baby-boomer geriatric boom on the horizon.

Charlie, here you are, with your money, in a tiny town in which a helpless bunch of your blood relatives have been murdered—and you are looking at the marketing aspects of this house? "You are sick."

Edwina, in the process of mincing across yellow-gold carpet without her crutches, stopped short and grabbed the flowery yellow couch.

"Oh, I didn't mean you, Mom. I meant me. Talking to myself again."

"So, what was it you were sick about, girl?" Buz flopped down in the ubiquitous Lazy Boy. There were two, both in a pale sage-green that set off all the yellow. The accents in the room were creamy white—lampshades, throw pillows, knitted afghans, figurines—along with two forest-green table lamps.

"I was just thinking what a great place this would be for a commercial shoot as a reason to save money for a retirement paradise. The colors are perfect, butter melting to cream melting to lemon—the gold and the green accents. The whole place screams comfort and tranquility."

Cousin Helen blinked at Charlie and melted, too. She toured the room turning on all the lamps and light switches. "I did my own decorating. Buz kept saying all this yellow would make us go blind—but he likes it now I've got it all together. It's like the sun's out even when it's not."

"Problem is, nobody wants sun to watch David Letterman." The dachshund on Buz's lap growled warning to the unimpressed cats circling the sage-green Lazy Boy.

"Oh, you can't stay up that late anyway." Helen threw a pillow at him and insisted on showing her guest the rest of the first floor. But not the second, Charlie figured, because it was all bedrooms she and her mother had not been invited to sleep in. Back in the living room, where she was still practicing putting weight on her injured ankle, Edwina told Charlie she'd been asked here because "I wanted to talk you out of leaving tomorrow. There's going to be a memorial service

Saturday and Helen and Buz have offered us a room and it would mean so much to me, Charlie. We'd have our own bathroom. There'd be a shower."

"For all those who've died recently at Gentle Oaks," Helen added. "Murdered and not."

"And there's ribs and kraut at The Station tonight," Buz said as if that should be a surprise.

"Hey, no problem. You can keep the Lumina even. Kenny and Del have offered to take me to the Comfort Inn tonight. I'll get a cab to the airport. I have to get back to work, if you don't."

"Charlie, tomorrow is Friday. It'll take you all day to get back and then it's the weekend. What difference will a day or two make?"

"One, do you have a clue to how much we've blown on canceling our flights already? Two, a weekend is a good time to be home when you have a teenage daughter, and anyone remotely connected to this little village who couldn't pick up on that fact is ready for Gentle Oaks. Three, due to modern technology, I can catch up on a lot of office work with e-mail, fax, and phone from my home so that four, I land at the office on Monday running. Five, I don't get outta here, I'm Loony Tunes."

Charlie's mother, the Bartuseks, the dachshund, and two cats squinted at her for seconds, everybody but the cats pausing to blink. Then Buz said, "They got taxicabs in Mason City?"

Charlie was mentally squinting at Cousin Helen and thinking, boy, I'd kill off a whole bunch of Staudt relatives, too, if my only future meant losing the chance to enjoy a comfortable retirement, hold onto what life I could salvage to enjoy home and Buz and gardening, to visit children and grandchildren, have a few winter months in Arizona. After working in the hellish environment of Gentle Oaks. . . .

Buz checked his watch. "Harvey will be looking for us. Cocktails, don't ya know?"

"It's only four o'clock."

"Yeah, well, folks don't stay out late in Myrtle and everybody's going to The Station for kraut and ribs, and Harvey, he has some things at his house he thought you might like to see."

Did Helen drink cocktails? Did these sudden invitations to homes where Charlie had not been invited before mean some kind of trap? She'd go along with the Rochester manse for the sake of Jane Erye. But she was outta here tonight.

CHAPTER 34

HARVEY ROCHESTER LOOKED and sounded more like Richard Burton the more he drank. What he drank were martinis with a lemon slice rather than a twist—prechilled Tanqueray and frosted glasses. They were really good, and Edwina and Charlie signaled caution to each other by an expression Charlie remembered but couldn't say how. Everyone but Cousin Helen had one and she actually accepted a beer. Maybe she was slumming. Then again, this wasn't a pool hall. Sniff, sniff.

There were tiny, fried-crisp veggie wraps with salsa, corn chips with a bean dip to die for. Again that warning look between the Greenes, sort of a family thing, a wide eye and then a hard blink. Funny that Charlie should remember it, wondered when it started. Probably in her childhood. Did she and Libby do that?

After a short tour, they were entertained in the living room, what Harvey called "the parlor." The rooms were spacious and separated with pocket doors that could be opened to nearly make the whole first floor one room with a hall and staircase in the center. Parlor, formal dining room, kitchen, and office/study took up the first floor, with what had been a pantry donated for a bathroom, with all the museum-piece facilities still there or recreated—like the toilet tank hung high on the wall with long chains dangling below. Upstairs there were two modern bathrooms, several bedrooms, and a sleeping porch.

Other than a game room, the finished basement belonged to the Lopezes.

In the parlor, Charlie munched a crunchy veggie wrap and looked out the curved bay window, noting with relief that there was no grand piano. In a place of honor and lighted with a picture lamp hung a painting of the Myrtle Staudt of legend, or so her host claimed. This Myrtle was not ugly like the one at Great-aunt Abigail's.

"So who's version is the real Myrtle?" Charlie asked her host, but both were watching Cousin Helen try to drink a Corona through the lime wedge stuck in the bottle's mouth.

"This one, of course. It's a family treasure and heirloom. And I'm going to put the grand piano over in that corner." He pointed to exactly the spot it had been in Charlie's dream, in relation to the bowed window. A love seat and chair sat there now.

"I still can't believe that horrible family would have bothered to have her portrait painted—and she's not even ugly in this one. And she has blue eyes. The legend-of-Myrtle story isn't working for me."

"Abigail Staudt, my lovely Charlie, is our Parson Weems, who, you may recall, made up morality tales to teach future generations the right path according to his particular take on it—using totally fictional material about real historical figures—myths, if you will, like George Washington and the cherry tree, Abe Lincoln and a railroad tie or something. Victorian ladies, which Abigail and her formidable sisters were even when the rest of the world was modernizing—and this is not unusual in parts of the Midwest, where change is generally suspect—were particularly adept at using this method to right the wrongs of the forefathers . . . and I forgot where I was going with this. Here, give me that." Mr. Rochester grabbed the bottle from Helen's hand, squeezed the lime into the neck, and handed it back to her.

"I don't have a clue where you were going either. Your Myrtle is not gorgeous by today's standards, but she's not bad.

Abigail's Myrtle is plug ugly. Myrtle's sisters must have been knockouts if she was the sacrifice."

"Myrtle had no sisters. She was the only sacrifice available. She and five brothers lived to adulthood."

"Still doesn't answer why you and I and Kenny and Marlys and my daughter have black eyes, does it?"

But they were watching Cousin Helen peer into her empty Corona bottle. Harvey motioned Miguel with a lift of his impressive Broadway brows and another bottle appeared in Helen's hand just before their host removed the lime wedge altogether and after Miguel had lifted the empty from her grasp.

"The Auchmoodys?" Charlie looked back at the portrait and finished her drink. Damn, that gin was good. She even accepted a small plate of corn chips and bean dip from Teresa, setting her glass on the table under the good-looking Myrtle.

Mr. Rochester smiled, dramatically of course, and held out his glass to Miguel. But it was Helen Bartusek who answered. "The damn Cowpers. Can't you see anything?"

Unlike Cousin Helen's house, this one was dark due to the beautiful wood of the paneled walls and pocket doors and floors. An enormous Persian-like carpet graced the center of this room, but even the floor-to-ceiling windows of the porches and the curved bay couldn't brighten it.

"So who do you suspect now of killing all those folks up at the Oaks? And I don't want to hear any more about the Grim Reaper. You must have discovered something or suspected someone," Helen said.

"Actually, I've suspected everyone. At first, I couldn't understand why anyone would want to pick on such helpless people. And the longer I'm here, I'm not sure why everyone wouldn't. They live forever at the Oaks. There goes any inheritance for their families. Harvey here sees a need for assisted and independent living to meet the modern needs of those who can't live alone but don't want to mingle with the vegetables. And the women in the town—and county, for all

I know—are trading in their jobs to care for the elderly at home day and night or in nursing homes, where they at least have shifts off and it isn't necessarily their relatives. You, Helen, in a fictional mystery, would be a prime suspect because you've got a lot to lose."

"Fiction, Nurse Helen, is a made-up story," Harvey condescended without being asked. "As opposed to nonfiction, which is made-up news—fact, if you will. Both attempting to convince you of a reality for a price, neither without the addition of a great deal of imagination."

Buz and Charlie's mother sat on a couch and appeared to be cracking up over the cocktail conversation under the portrait.

"I don't understand what you mean by Harvey's motive here." Helen finished off her second beer.

"Well, he wants to upgrade half a nursing home full of vegetables to assisted living—and it's the vegetables who are dying, which should certainly make his job easier. Except for Darla, who could be a shill to throw us off, or who could have discovered who the murderer was and had to be eliminated. You, Helen, are under a heavy burden of eldercare at a time in life when there should be an opportunity for you to enjoy your home and husband and travel before you are both too old. And your grandfathers are wacky enough to do anything. And strong enough, too. And Kenny Cowper might feel really bad for these lingering folks and sneak up after the pool hall closes, quietly suffocate the veggies. But Darla doesn't fit that theory either, unless Marlys and Gladys and the Fatties have secretly witnessed the murders and decided to take care of her for the fun of it or because they find her 'activities' aggravating and silly. There's little enough dignity left in their lives."

"You realize how ridiculous all this sounds?" Mr. Rochester looked impressed again. Or was it guilt?

"Murder so often does." The young Myrtle with the blue eyes gazed down on them with a faint curiosity. "She looks uncomfortably human for someone dead for so many generations." Charlie took a sip of her drink and contemplated the girl with Libby Greene's platinum-blond hair. Myrtle's was coiled on top of her head. "Why would you pay to have a portrait painted of a daughter doomed to servitude, and why aren't her eyes black?"

"Legend has it that her paramour commissioned the painting in defiance of her family. The painting has hung in this house since before my mother was born."

"Is your mother up at the Oaks?"

"My mother ran off to France with a distant cousin and enjoyed the blessed vagaries of Paris for years before succumbing to a stroke and dying in her sleep. I was able to visit her and Cousin Arnold many times as a young adult."

"If she'd had her stroke here, would she have suffered for decades at Gentle Oaks?"

"We make great use of antidepressants and anxiety medications at the Gentle Oaks Health Care Center. Our residents do not suffer."

"Do the Fatties get any of that medication? They don't ever seem calm."

"As much as we can get a doctor to prescribe. Think for a moment of what they'd be like without it."

"So the black eyes are Cowper, the platinum-blond Staudt. How about my hair?"

"Auchmoody," everyone in the room but the Lopezes and Charlie said at once, as if they thought she'd never ask.

"So my birth parents were probably local."

Myrtle was not as drop-dead gorgeous as Libby, but there was a certain resemblance. Charlie felt weary, and a quick memory picture of the room at the Comfort Inn beckoned. It was no five-star hotel but it was hers for the night, and she'd be on the plane bright and early.

Buz and Edwina chatted quietly now. Helen stood next to Charlie, tears on her cheeks. "I can't take any more. I want

229

to go to Tucson for six months and come back here for the rest."

"I appreciate your problem, Helen. Can't you just quit going to the Oaks, now that Uncle Elmo and your mother are gone? Quit your job and stay away from the place."

"Everybody'd talk about me."

"Was Uncle Elmo really my grandfather and Marlys my great-grandmother?"

"No, but I know who your grandmother was. And I don't know who got her in trouble. Could have been somebody from out of town. And I know who your great-grandmother was. You don't want to know. You won't like it."

Charlie didn't care. She would have lunch at the Minneapolis airport—there was a long layover. She wanted to try a Lefsatilla. She'd clear up a lot of business by cell phone during the layover. She'd be home for dinner, sleep in her own bed, have a wonderful, normal weekend in the real world. She better call Libby and tell her.

"I just can't take any more," Helen repeated and had to set her bottle of beer on the table to fish a tissue from the wrist band of her sweater and blow her nose. Her bottle was full again. That's when Charlie realized so was her glass. She'd meant to have one martini but could remember already emptying one. How many had she had? She'd been warned to take it easy on alcohol until her headaches and blackouts and the return of her accident were completely gone. And her blood-sugar thing. She did feel awful good. Which could be awful bad.

CHAPTER 35

———————◆———————

CHARLIE WENT ALONG to The Station for kraut and ribs for three reasons. One, she was tipsy. Two, she needed food. And three, Kenny and Del would take her to the Comfort Inn in Mason City. But she'd have to find them first and not until she got her chemicals straightened out with food.

There was a table reserved for The Station's owner and his guests in the nice if smoky section. Edwina felt so good after the martinis that she left her crutches in the car. The place smelled so bad it turned Charlie's stomach, which was turning on its own and needed no help. And she was so buzzy Harvey offered to fill a plate for her.

"Just half full, please." Least he could do after getting her drunk in her condition.

"Anything from the bar?" the hostess of the whiskey voice asked.

"Just coffee, please." Her cell went off and she stepped outside to answer it, weaving hardly at all. "Shirley Birkett is more than just the next Danielle Steel. She's far more quirky," she said in response to a plea from Larry, who'd been contacted in her absence to fill in some West Coast press on Shirley's first book.

"Charlie, are you looped? 'Quirky' is pretty lame these days."

"Just for lady mystery writers. If you can think of anything better, be my guest." Damn, gorgeous kid. She returned to the table to find Cousin Helen with another beer.

"I tell you, Buz, I'm not taking any more."

"Sounds reasonable." He set a plate of food in front of her and another in front of Edwina and went off, chuckling, to fill one for himself.

Charlie's plate came with a side dish of scarlet Jell-O with incarcerated banana slices. The green beans, cooked to mushy, floated in a sea of juice, as did the mashed potatoes and this pile of stuff on top—some of which was meat falling off bones, and the rest, she assumed, the foul-smelling sauerkraut of legend. This did not resemble the sauerkraut she'd seen on bratwursts. How anything could taste so good and smell so bad, Charlie wouldn't be able to explain if she lived as long as Marlys Dittberner. But she cleaned her plate, even spooning up the juices. Weird times call for weird behavior patterns. She'd be okay when she flew out of Iowa tomorrow. Salty, meaty, satisfying, rich—and the potatoes served as a sort of ballast. The Jell-O she skipped.

"What do you think I should do, Buz?"

"Whatever you decide, I'm behind it a hundred percent."

"I think I should quit my job, and right after the memorial service, we should load the dog and the cats in the motor home and head for Tucson before another storm comes in. Stay until spring."

"Sounds good. Maybe stop in Omaha and see the kids on the way."

"You travel with two cats and a dog?" Charlie asked.

"Oh, yeah. They're family," Helen said, as if that should be sending a message to Charlie.

"We got Lazy Boys in the motor home, too. Can't go anywhere without them neither. Sweet deal."

"Isn't that awfully expensive?" Charlie parroted the birdlike maiden aunts who'd come to her first dinner at the home place in the huge Buick a week ago tomorrow night. Especially for a nurse and retired truck driver.

"Buz and Helen were fortunate enough to have been gifted great amounts of money from Ida Mae and the Staudt sisters before the new rules about spending down one's assets before going on Medicaid went into force," Harvey said ruefully.

"All that cash and the house Gentle Oaks didn't get before having to hook up to the public tit. Lots of us were lucky that way, Charlie. Not so for our kids, but there are ways to see they get something after all this keeping people alive long after they want it. Helen, here, appears to finally have gotten the message how the rest of us feel about the Oaks," Buz said. "But it's hard for a nurse to see through the god-doctor business and thinking how she's told to think. I'm proud she's finally seen the light."

"You have any people up at the Oaks, Buz?" Charlie asked, thinking, oh, swell, another suspect. Good thing I'm outta here.

"Oh, yeah. Too depressing to go see 'em. None of 'em know me by now, anyway."

About that time, Charlie noticed that the two empty chairs across from her were filled with the studs from Myrtle. And they'd been there long enough to have filled their plates and half-emptied them. "Did you find Marlys?"

"Nope," one of them said.

"Charlie? You looped?" the other asked and leaned across the table.

Dolores reached over to refill Charlie's coffee cup, rubbing between Marshal Sweetie and the barkeeper's biceps in the process.

"Remember, you promised to take me to Mason City tonight. You coming or not, Mom?"

"I'm staying, Charlie. I think you should, too."

"There's a long layover in Minneapolis," Harvey said.

"I checked at the airport. Fewer planes fly on Saturday and Sunday and they're booked. We'd be stuck for the weekend. Can we leave right after you're finished?" she asked the studs.

"There goes my pie again," the marshal said. "That's one mean woman."

"Don't forget your announcement." Kenny smiled fondly at Charlie for no reason. If he was seen around Gentle Oaks, no one would question that he wasn't visiting his "Grammy." He could smother an inmate or two and be gone before anyone found them. Maybe Darla discovered this and that's why she had to go.

"Oh, yeah." Del stood and beat on his water glass with his fork. "Hey, listen up, everybody. Got me a question." The glass was plastic and got him nowhere, so he tried one of the Bartuseks' empty beer bottles and that didn't get him anywhere, so Kenny made a heart-startling whistle and the place quieted, all eyes turned on their table. "I just want you to know we're missing Marlys of course, and this time Ben, the town watchman, too. Anybody seen either one today, or last night even?"

There was some mumbling and head shaking, lots of shoulder shrugging, before people turned back to their food and conversation. The hostess stepped over from the cash register, still blowing smoke. "Can't promise, but I thought I saw Ben skulking around old Abigail's this morning. Hadn't had my coffee yet, so I can't be sure, but I didn't think anything about it. He's always fetching and carrying for her, so it's not like he shouldn't have been there or anything."

Edwina turned to Helen. "Thought you and Buz got her groceries and stuff in Mason City."

"We do, but Ben takes them over to her. She drives me nuts. Can't please her. She doesn't even say thank you. And you get to go off to Colorado and have a life. Well, we're going off to Arizona and have a winter, anyway."

"You can't leave now, Helen." Harvey looked to be hanging a few sheets in the wind himself. "RNs don't grow on trees and I have to replace Mary Lou already. Besides, there will be a murder investigation and you will be one of the suspects and so will I, according to our detective here."

"Well, I can leave town." His detective managed to get out of her chair without stumbling. "You ready, guys?"

But the guys and the red Cherokee didn't head for the stone bridge and out of town. Del overruled her protests. "Just got to stop at old Abigail's first. See if she's seen Ben or Marlys."

Kenny went to the door with him and they stayed inside so long, Charlie grew impatient. If they were hatching a ruse to keep her from that plane in the morning, they were in for a surprise and a half. She was still feeling her gin when she walked up the sidewalk to that front door. That evil front door. And she thought that was just the gin talking.

"You, too?" Great-aunt Abigail opened it before Charlie could knock and led her into the parlor. "Might just as well join us."

Said the spider to the fly.

"Oh, shut up." Charlie didn't even bother to apologize for talking aloud to herself.

Marlys Dittberner stood under the portrait of the ugly Myrtle. Long, streaming hair, grinning old face. She was missing at least her top dentures and wearing a period dress from some movie like *Titanic*.

"I warned you," Marlys said. "And you wouldn't listen."

"Her kind never do," Great-aunt Abigail said behind Charlie. "You know what to do, Ben."

Charlie looked around for the town watchman but caught only the closing of the pocket door on someone. "Where're Kenny and Del?"

"They're gone." Marlys did a little hopping dance.

"I knew the moment I laid eyes on you that you would ruin everything." Abigail Staudt wore her snowy collar again. "And now you must pay the price."

"The marshal's Jeep is sitting right out there at the curb. You're a totally crazy old—" But then, through the bay window, Charlie saw the red Cherokee drive off down the street. Had the Myrtle studs betrayed her? Nah, they were just teasing. They were really into teasing, those two.

We don't feel very good. Have you noticed?

"I noticed." There's something about the inevitable dashing of all your hopes and dreams that can make you sick. "I am going to leave here, catch that plane, see my kid, have my life back."

"You won't be catching your plane, Charlemagne Catherine Greene," Abigail said with bitter satisfaction. Her little half-glasses hung on a cord around her neck and she put them up on her nose only to stare at Charlie over them. "Ever. The curse will end with you. This was all your fault from the beginning."

"That's what Cousin Helen implied. I barely even heard of Myrtle. Never been here, except I guess at birth. I won't carry on the guilt. It's so totally out of the frame." In real life, Judy Garland would have poured a pail of water on Greataunt Witch and melted her.

The ugly Myrtle smiled above Marlys Dittberner. She didn't have her teeth in either. There was a muffled pounding going on inside Charlie's head, and one going on outside it, too. The pounding outside her head had far-off shouting in it. "Where are we going?"

"We're off to see the wizard," Marlys sang off-key. The furniture was sort of dancing.

"Out the back door," the wicked witch answered. "Ben, you there?" It was almost dark outside. And getting cold.

"The wonderful Wizard of Oz."

"Why? I feel sorta sick."

"Because, because, because, because, because . . . of all the wonderful things he does."

"Did you know Edwina married a Jew?" the wicked witch asked.

"Did you know Charlie is Isobel's granddaughter?" Marlys Dittberner laughed like it was already the full of the moon again. "A direct descendant of Myrtle herself. Like you."

"That is as insane as you are, you nasty old bat."

236

"I should know. I birthed all three of 'em. Because, because, because—"

Charlie lost her sauerkraut and ribs on the yellow brick road.

❖

CHAPTER 36

CHARLIE WAS DRENCHED in cold sweat when the semi jumped the median barrier and came toward the Toyota and Darla waved at her from the Oliver with lugs and she skidded the Lumina into the ditch on the ice. Charlie's guts ached. The air smelled wet and chilled, of trees and dead leaves instead of exhaust, smelled like Iowa, not California. Which made sense because it was Ben the watchman pulling her from the red Jeep, the antique Marlys dancing ahead in her silly antique dress, Abigail Staudt already on the porch of Gentle Oaks.

"I have a plane to catch," Charlie told Elsina Miller, who slipped out the door and held it closed. "I'm off to see the wizard."

"What are you doing here?" Great-aunt Abigail asked the administrator. "It's after five."

"They wouldn't let me go to my car. Help me. Is the marshal here? The founder, Herman Rochester, has been murdered."

"Because, because, because, because," Marlys Dittberner sang, then curtsied and shoved Elsina away from the door. "Because of the wonderful things he does."

Elsina bolted as residents began to push their way out, but they stopped and jammed the entrance when they saw Abigail.

"Ben, stop her," the wicked witch ordered and Ben let go of Charlie, who grabbed for a white pillar and missed. She went down watching a flurry of flowered skirt and knee-highs and Elsina ripping off the watchman's knitted cap.

Charlie started woozing out again but not before she noticed the lumps on Ben's bald scalp and heard Abigail bark orders to the crowd clogging the doorway. Someone could apparently focus the inmates, for a while at least.

When Charlie focused herself next, it was to blackness and the sound of moaning she thought at first to be her own and then, "My Lord Jesus, being buried alive is the most horrible fate I could ever imagine . . . and with this wretched creature. What have I done to deserve such a fate as this?"

"Buried alive? Hello?" The wretched creature fought her foggy brain to remember how they'd come from the porch at Gentle Oaks to the darkness, fought her eyelids open to meet only more darkness. Buried alive was getting serious here. "Elsina? Did you say Herman Rochester's been murdered?"

Elsina wept and sniffed and bawled, the sound like her voice oddly muffled.

The total dark did smell a lot like dirt. Moldy dirt. But there wasn't any weight of it on Charlie's face or chest. Her back rested on something bumpy and hard. She didn't hear any shoveling. There seemed to be enough air but the blackness was heavy. "Sweetie, stop that. What exactly is happening here?"

"I hate it when women call me 'Sweetie.' "

"You know, I do too. But I don't feel dirt on my face. Are we in a coffin?"

"I am smothering from something on my face. I can't see—"

"I can't either." Charlie vaguely remembered losing her dinner, but the martinis seemed to have been absorbed. She was on the downside of tiddly. She sat up and reached above her head. No grave ceiling. "But I can sit up. I can breathe. And we both can talk and hear. Are we in a crypt or a cave?"

Elsina was on her left. Charlie groped to find a textured cloth, a blanket maybe, with a moving form beneath. She pulled it away and her elbow hit no earthen wall. "Can you breathe better now?"

This moldy dark was so dark it seemed lighter when she closed her eyes. Claustrophobia suggested she would soon have difficulty breathing. Cool air brushing past her face told Charlie this was not so. That air felt and smelled damp but not wet. Water dripped into a puddle not far off she thought. But total darkness made distance even of sound hard to judge for some reason. "I thought Jesus wanted you to be good to the wretched."

"Of course He does. He's just trying me. What do you know about Jesus?"

"Not much. Maybe we are already dead and this is a holding cell between heaven and hell."

"That's Catholic nonsense."

"If you found yourself in purgatory, you'd just deny it?"

"I wouldn't find myself there because there is no such thing."

"Wow, faith is a powerful thing."

"That's the first intelligent statement I've heard you say, Charlie Greene."

A stealthy rustling sounded farther off than the drip and made Charlie's skin prickle in odd places, her breathing go shallow. Rats? Bats? Snakes? Spiders? Demons? "Maybe we're in hell. It's not as cold as I thought it would be under ground."

"That's it. We're underground."

"Underground where? Frankly, I don't like you either. But it's wonderful to have somebody to talk to right now. I had a dream not long ago that I was underground in Myrtle's fruit-cellar grave. So what happened? I was sort of out of it."

"You were drunken."

"That, too. This is a lot like being blind, I bet."

Elsina decided she'd been blind to come to Iowa and took off on a tale of woe not particularly germane to the situation. Charlie was just glad for another's voice. The administrator had fallen in love with Floyd County and especially Myrtle, after living in sinful Minneapolis, because of its simple life-

240

style, so Christian and caring as to have a facility like Gentle Oaks that tended to its elderly with such compassion they lived happily way beyond expectation. Charlie, having left Boulder for D.C., Manhattan, and L.A., tried hard to imagine that.

"When the sun shines, I could see Jesus in the sky, arms outstretched over this rich and fertile place. Now I'm buried and can't see Him."

"Why don't we see if we can move toward where that draft is coming from?" Charlie sensed one of them wasn't exactly tracking. "Maybe we can see Jesus from there. Bring the blanket."

"Why should I follow you? You curse and fornicate, drink alcohol."

"Okay, I'll follow you." Charlie tried standing up. She'd feel better moving away from the rustlings but now that they'd stopped she wasn't sure too sure which direction that would be.

"And Mr. Rochester, with all his flaws, showed such promise."

"You ever read *Jane Eyre?*"

"Is it a spiritual work?"

"By today's standards, it could almost be. I know—we're both dead. Just dreaming this whole conversation."

"If we were dead, our conversation would be with Jesus. He will guide us."

But Charlie found herself in the lead. You can't stand up and walk around in a grave. "Harvey Rochester drinks quite a bit. And utters profanities. He does not come across as religious."

"Once he gives himself to Jesus he will be a new man in body, mind, and spirit." The more times Elsina said, "Jesus," the stronger she became.

"Myrtle is not a particularly godly place. It has a horrific history of unwed teens and the jerks who left them with child and settled down to inherit the farm. Marlys practically made a business of taking them in and adopting out the babies born in sin."

Charlie was beginning to see strange things in the darkness, like a huge red spider frantically jiggling and writhing, dangling just ahead. One good blink and it was gone. Titanium plate or no, the wobblies and nausea of an impending migraine began to manifest. She'd been warned against stress until she had fully recovered from her accident. Why did doctors assume patients could avoid stress at will? There were pills for this in her purse. Where was her purse? Good old Marlys probably had the answer to that.

"Were you conscious when we were put down here? Do you know who did this to us?"

"They have become like children again, God's children." Elsina Miller's voice came froggy out of the dark. "They don't know what they do. They are innocents being led by the devil."

"Who?" Charlie felt her balance tilting and reached out to find something solid. Finally. It felt like wood.

"The beloved of God who are sheltered at Gentle Oaks until He is ready for them."

"The inmates. So who's the devil?"

"All televisions must be removed from Gentle Oaks. They are committing acts they don't understand."

"Like what? Murder?"

"You're no detective. You're not even very bright. People listen to you only because of your wicked reputation and your figure."

"Hey, no argument there. You think the beloved inmates are killing each other because they see violence on TV and are copying it? You know, that makes more sense than any theory I've been able to come up with." Charlie was under the sucking black earth of Iowa and hanging for dear life onto something made of wood that had gradients. Like steps. "Oh, my God, Elsina, we're in Myrtle's fruit cellar. Great-Aunt Abigail will throw bloody dead babies on us."

And sure enough the door in the floor above the stairs opened slowly with a regular Hollywood creaking and the spreading of blinding light. Charlie couldn't find voice to scream and there was no more sauerkraut left to throw up.

"What the bloody hell? So this is where the Mexicans hide when they think the INS is invading. My uncle never told me about this. It's not on the building's plans. How did you find it?" Harvey Rochester stood above them.

The only answer came from behind him, the call of the lonely *Ciga-riga-rooo?* bird and the low, warning moan of Dolores the tomcat.

"Mr. Rochester, please help me."

"Miss Miller? What in damnation are you doing down there?"

"Because, because, because—because of all the wonderful things she does."

Harvey Rochester tumbled down the wooden steps instead of a bloody baby—just before the lights went out in the ceiling of Myrtle's grave. Now it was even darker, a possibility she would have thought impossible only moments ago.

"Oh, damn. I think I broke my finger. Elsina, where are you, woman? Oh, sorry, did I hurt you, darling? What is all this about?"

Charlie heard the sound of her groaning and him trying to move safely in the invisible pitch. She just felt better for more company, but "darling?"

"It's about revenge, Mr. Rochester. The devil has taken over our work."

"Which devil?"

"Hey, Harvey," Charlie said. "Great to have you aboard. We were beginning to feel picked on down here. Do you happen to know where down here is?"

"Charlemagne Catherine? You, too? Who the devil has done this?"

"I told you about the devil. And this is not the first time," the administrator said. "I'm sorry about your uncle. The Lord had a reason He has not revealed to us." Elsina had called Harvey's house and the Lopezes had called Harvey at The Station.

"I thought you said he was murdered, and if he was a vegetable anyway—" Charlie shrugged a shrug no one could see. It was like living a radio drama, all sound and no pictures. She could visualize the speakers but other than the steps, it was just the three of them in an unfurnished emptiness.

"You know who committed the foul deed, Miss Miller?"

"Yes, I'm sorry, Mr. Rochester. The Lord moves in strange ways."

"You actually saw it happen? You're a witness? This isn't a setup? Thank the Lord for me, too," Charlie said and took back every unkind thought she might ever have had about Baptists. There was nothing she cherished more than having someone else solve a murder. Even her headache threatened to evaporate.

CHAPTER 37

✦

*I*T WAS MY grandfather," Harvey Rochester said from the bottom of his soles. His sigh came lower still through the dank.

"How did you know?" Elsina moaned again.

"Old Sherman hated Herman."

"Now stop that." Charlie struggled to bring sanity to an insane situation. "We are in serious trouble here, you guys."

"He hated his brother. Old Sherman had lost so much memory I assumed he would not recognize Herman should my grandfather wander into his room in search of a smoke. I should have known better. But in all fairness, Sherman didn't know Sherman, so how could he know Herman? Still, I can but blame myself, Miss Miller."

"Nonsense, Mr. Rochester. What more could you have done for either of them?"

"Hey, Harvey and Elsina, could we get back to basics here before—" Jesus, was that the sound of heavy breathing? "Where exactly are we? I mean, how did you get here?" Hell, how did I get here?

After a barely proper pause—who was Charlie to judge proper?—the owner of Gentle Oaks answered, "We appear to be in a cellar under the Oaks. Like a fruit cellar."

"Like in *The Wizard of Oz*," the administrator added.

"Why is that old movie so prevalent around here?"

"It's the only tape we still own. The mayor charges largesse for the rental of her tapes at the Sinclair. And it is one of the few of which Miss Miller approves. And the residents don't give a damn what they watch. In fact, they don't seem to watch at all. More like something to pacify the staff. Background noise for the empty-headed."

"Marlys must watch it, she's always singing it."

"Thank God it's not written down somewhere for Rose to read." Harvey had stormed into the Oaks demanding to know who had murdered his uncle and the whereabouts of his administrator. Gladys led him to a storeroom that had once been a kitchen, now used to store extra furniture or items needing repair. Gladys pointed at the rubber matting in the center of the floor and told him Miss Miller was in the cellar where she belonged.

"One never knows with Gladys when whimsy and mischief have degraded to lunacy, but other residents began to gather round and I thought it best to raise the matting and prove to all that the Oaks had no cellar." Instead, he found a door flat in the floor and a metal ring to pull it up. When he did, someone pushed him from behind. "And here I am. How did you get here?"

"Miss Greene was drunken and has no idea."

"Thanks to dear Harvey's martinis and kraut. The acid reflux is awesome, let me tell you. I was at Abigail Staudt's house and then I was here. And Ben and Marlys were there. And then I was out front at the Oaks, and then I was here."

Someone had thrown a blanket over Elsina's head and forcibly led her out of Herman Rochester's room after she'd witnessed his murder. "And I made my escape only to be confronted by Abigail Staudt and her henchman Ben, who forced me down here to try to communicate with a drunken fornicator."

"Why were you in Herman's room?" the fornicator wanted to know.

"Because they wouldn't let me go home, let me leave. They played with me, led me deeper into Gentle Oaks than I'd ever been. But I would have escaped if you hadn't been on the porch instead of the marshal. They wouldn't let me in my office to get my car keys." She began to cry again.

Mr. Rochester "there, there'd." Even Charlie felt for her. "Must have been scary." What were these two doing in the dark that made such suspicious sounds?

"There, there. . . . Don't worry, Charlie, I'm still going to buy that grand piano. The best there is."

"Use the money to rent some new videos from the mayor instead. Elsina, who else was there when Sherman did in his brother?"

"He said, 'Rose, bring the pillow.' And then he held it over Herman Rochester's face until the founder died. The room was full of the beloved children of Jesus, some of them holding the founder down."

"The residents?"

"Some I didn't even know could get themselves up and into walkers or wheelchairs. There was no staff anywhere."

The cellar, or whatever it was, stayed very quiet until Charlie and Harvey whispered in unison, "Oh, Jesus."

"They are innocents, misled by Satan."

"Why," Charlie asked no one in particular, "do I have the feeling he had some help and don't we know who now?"

Charlie had seen two nursing-home scripts that actually made it to TV with the same premise, both atrocious. And there'd been a manuscript in a similar vein, unpublished. And obviously a lot more she'd never encountered. It was not uncommon for writers to be overwhelmed by unforseen life problems at certain stages in their lives and feel compelled to explore them. Which didn't make the whole mess here at Gentle Oaks Health Care Center less awful to contemplate. Still, something niggled. Besides the sauerkraut-alcohol afterburn.

"So where was the staff all this time? The Mexicans? They don't seem to be down here with us. I don't think Rose and Sherman could have pillowed all of them."

"We're illegally short-staffed tonight," Harvey said. "I

thought you, Kenneth, and Delwood were on your way to Mason City and the Holiday Inn."

"They stopped at Abigail's to check out what had happened to Ben and Marlys. Ben and Marlys were there—but when I walked in, Kenny and Del weren't."

"Well, good. Marlys isn't missing at this moment at least. She's the bane of my existence, and the marshal's and Miss Miller's, I daresay."

"She's outlived her usefulness, self-worth, desire to exist," Charlie said. Hadn't Miss Miller been the bane of his existence just a few days ago? "Who can blame her behavior? Who would want to be her?"

"That is for Jesus to decide. Thank God, people like you don't have a say in these things."

"How could the residents know of this hole and I not know? I own it."

"Most of the inmates were probably around Myrtle when Gentle Oaks was built." Charlie felt for the wood of the stairs. In the thick darkness, she had no sense of direction. "Why can't we just march up those stairs, push the door in the ceiling open and go find a phone? We could do that by feel, couldn't we?" She had a plane to catch, felt considerably more together now, and had no idea how long that improvement would last. "What was here before Gentle Oaks?"

"Somewhere on the grounds was the original Staudt homestead."

"Why did I know you were going to say that?" Charlie couldn't find the stairs.

"It was burned to the ground many years ago and left to plowed fields long before it was Gentle Oaks."

"So we're in the cellar where Myrtle was murdered. Where the curse began."

"That was so long ago no wooden stairs would have survived."

"Somebody built new stairs since."

"There's no such thing as curses. That is superstitious nonsense."

"I bet Marlys knew of this hole at one time. Elsina, how can the incarcerated above us be children of God unless they're born-again types? Most of them are or were probably Methodist, Lutheran, or Catholic. If anything."

"We are all children of God. We just have to find our way back to Him."

"The lunatics upstairs can't find the potty. But they can kill each other."

"Each will be judged by a just God."

"Well, you have to admit she's glib," Harvey said out of the black.

You two are going to get along splendidly, once she remakes you in His image. If we ever get out of here. "So why were Great-aunt Abigail Staudt, Ben the watchman, and Marlys Dittberner at Abigail's house and not Kenny and the marshal, when the Cherokee we arrived here in was at the curb? And if this is where the Mexicans hide when the law descends and is mistaken for the INS, why aren't they down here with us?"

"Good question. Questions, actually, as usual. Californians speak in tongues, Miss Miller, I'm sorry to say."

"Having lived in Minneapolis, nothing surprises me."

"There seems to be a source of air coming in here. Did fruit cellars have ventilation?"

"Usually little chimney apparatuses, covered to keep out rain—still, definitely ventilation holes. But we are under the Oaks. I can't imagine from whence the draft is coming either, but I'm grateful for it. What? Listen, voices approach."

"We have to get up there and save those old people from the other old people," Charlie said, not real sure why. Or why they all flailed around and didn't hit any dirt walls or ancient fruit jars—barrels of long-dead apples or potatoes. Dead babies. Whatever. "I don't hear any voices." But she heard footsteps. And she walked into someone.

249

Someone who had been eating sauerkraut, too, who shouted right in her face, "Who goes there?"

"Harvey? Is that you, forsooth? Where are we? Del? Harvey's here. Del? Damn, that guy could get lost in his own closet."

The marshal and the barkeep, lured to the coal cellar under Abigail's gray Victorian in search of Ben and Marlys, found themselves locked in instead. They'd come across a wooden barricade in the dirt wall, forced it open to discover a tunnel, and since they couldn't force the cellar door into the house, and the old coal chute to the backyard had been boarded over, they hoped to find a way out on the other end of the tunnel. "Problem is, there's more than one connecting tunnel. Without a flashlight, we just got deeper and deeper in trouble and then I heard voices. Sweetest sound I ever heard. I've been bent over practically double for so long my back's killing me. But this has to be another basement, not more tunnel. I can stand up."

"We're under the Oaks, Charlie, Elsina, and I, and now you."

"A real underground railway, do you think?" Charlie asked.

"I'd bet something more recent than that, but something the old-timers up above us would have known about."

"A fruit cellar for burying unwed moms?" Charlie tried again and this time walked into the stairs instead of Harvey Rochester.

"Bootleggers?" Harvey said.

"I can remember playing with Buz and Helen's boys in their grandparents' backyard and getting into the fruit cellar there. It had a blocked-off wooden door at the back of it we were told to leave alone," Kenny said.

So of course the boys found a way to open it and with flashlights, found a tunnel that led to another wooden door. They couldn't open it but discovered later that it opened into somebody else's fruit cellar. When Kenny asked about it, he got paddled and was told to quit snooping. By the time he was in high school, he'd done enough research in old newspapers at libraries around the county to discover that fruit cellars were good places to store and hide hooch and the tunnel system a good place to move it around if you thought you might get raided. And if you wanted to buy or sell some, you didn't have to openly carry it across the street.

"I was an investigative journalist even then. Just didn't know it. Del? Dammit, where are you?"

"Oh, come on, Abigail Staudt and Gentle Oaks weren't running bootleg hooch." Charlie tested the strength of a step.

"I can't believe anyone in this place did that or the other awful things about unwed mothers either," Elsina said.

"Gentle Oaks was built long after the days of prohibition. And Abigail Staudt bought her present house something like thirty or forty years ago from Bjorn Sievertsen, the owner of the Myrtle Pool Hall before Kenny's father."

"Charlie, that old enlarged photo up with the TV at Viagra's where the punks with sloppy grins are leaning against that ancient car? They were infamous bootleggers in Floyd County, many of them from the best families in Myrtle."

"Enough of the rural-fable stuff. I've got a plane to catch and I've found the stairs. We have to go up there and call for help. They are murdering helpless old people right over our heads. All we have to do is push up the door at the top of the stairs."

"Who is murdering helpless old people?" Kenny asked.

"The other helpless old people." Charlie reached the top of the stairs by feel—felt her head hit the door in the ceiling, actually.

Elsina Miller said, "She's right. We must go up there and stop it."

Charlie made the mistake of opening her eyes as she pushed and the door did open, but onto blinding light. Someone grabbed her arms and pulled her out of the hole in the ground. She heard the door slamming on the others trying to follow.

"Put the mat back and move that old washing machine on top to keep the others down there." Great-aunt Abigail Staudt's voice came victorious out of the blinding light.

CHAPTER 38

---◆---

CHARLIE COWERED IN the knee space under one of the nurses' stations, the one with the cat door. Where *were* the Mexicans, dammit? The only people she'd seen since being yanked out of the cellar were residents. Wandering.

Ben had let go of Charlie to haul heavy metal over the door to the cellar on Abigail's orders, and some of the attendees were wandering off even as Charlie's vision began to return. The Fatties were there in their wheelchairs grinning, minus teeth, dirty eyeglasses, and shoes.

The lunatics had taken over the asylum—with the help of Abigail Staudt and Ben the watchman. If it had been only Abigail's sisters and relatives "pillowed," that would make sense, to spare them further indignities. But that left out Darla and the nonrelatives. Abigail and Ben might have snuck through the underground tunnels to murder patients in their sleep, perhaps with the help of Marlys Dittberner inside. Or they might have talked people like Sherman Rochester into doing it for them.

Could the authority of Myrtle's witch of decency and creator of proper history be powerful enough to impose her creed upon the confused realm of senile dementia? She had apparently been bossing the town around for years. Maybe some of them remembered that much.

Sherman and Gladys had been among those straggling off when Charlie's vision had returned, he without shoes, pants, and hat, but with his oversized suit coat covering his bum and

Depends. Had he been a bootlegger once? When he was a young punk?

People were half-dressed, their caretakers underground or gone somewhere else. Charlie had slipped out of the one-time kitchen behind Gladys' wheelchair. No one came after her, which was a bit confusing. But everybody in this place, including Charlie, was pretty confused.

Once she had her bearings, she'd headed straight for the nurses' station and the phone. The jack was there but no phone. Now, would senile, demented, semimobile folks think of something like that themselves? Abigail and Ben would.

And then the lights had dimmed for sleeping and the wandering increased and Charlie had hunkered until she could come up with another idea. Ideas came fast and furious but she didn't dare dart out into the open. And of course with her luck, Dolores the tomcat chose this time to return to bedlam through the special door only he and Marlys found convenient.

Cats are true geniuses at sensing things—like which people don't like cats. Cat lovers can pat their laps for hours to entice a feline to recline there. But those who have no fondness for cats are smothered in unwanted attention from the first opportunity.

Being scrunched into the knee space of a desk area made Charlie the perfect victim of this portly critter, and because her lap was unavailable, he insinuated his considerable self into the niche between her butt, under her bent knees and the calves of her legs. His claws proceeded with astonishing ease to knead her underthighs through her jeans, and his purr sounded as if she were hand-feeding him bits of lobster and filet mignon with platinum tweezers. The grateful purring drowned out sounds coming or going or, in this place, possibly flying overhead. Sounds that could warn her of danger. There must be a way to pillow a cat—soundlessly.

Charlie and Dolores seemed to realize at about the same time that she was in added trouble. He stopped purring and started sniffing. The drawer with the critical supplies was still there if only she could dislodge the cat. Once she moved, he moaned like Elsina Miller and took off. She uncoiled frightened muscles and peered over the desktop while searching in the drawer. And watched the wandering, mesmerized.

The hall was quite full, the wanderers silent but for sniffles and grunts as they came down on sore joints and mostly bare feet. And was it getting chilly in here? Maybe it was simply Charlie's growing feeling of being trapped. Of not making her plane back to her own life, which grew more dear by the moment. She had never been good with panic.

Finally, she took off running with a stolen plug for the ladies' room, fearing the worst, not sure what it would be, dodging silent, lost souls who paid little attention to her or each other, hoping she wouldn't slip on any surprises on the way. A drug cart stood with cabinet doors left open, drawers pulled out and emptied. Loose pills and pills still sealed in bottles lay strewn all over the floor. Now the lunatics were sacking the asylum.

Those too feeble to wander called for help from every other room. Be careful what you ask for, people. Only roaming lunatics with pillows to help tonight.

Maybe the caretakers were all locked in one room and she could free them. "Illegally understaffed" didn't mean no staff at all, surely. Maybe the other nursing station had a working phone, or Elsina's office.

Charlie darted into the ladies room, only to find Sherman there, along with Flo and somebody she didn't know. They were lighting up. No wonder even the ciga-riga-rooo bird was quiet.

The first stall she tried was occupied. By the deputy sheriff of Floyd County. That's where the smokes came from. "Hi."

The next stall was empty. There were only three. Charlie locked herself in, feeling sick again. First things first. She might not get out of here alive, but—

Why the "Hi," for godsake? Even her good sense was rattled.

What was I supposed to say, "Good-bye?"

The deputy's pants had been down around his ankles, but his lap and things were covered by the pillow used to suffocate him. He was in sort of a sprawling sit Charlie would not have thought possible. Oh, boy.

She was supposed to have been next. Herman, the deputy, how many others had been sandwiched in first? The lunatics were on a rampage in this asylum. Cigarette smoke drifted over the stall door. What to do?

Well, I'm not about to stay in here and wait for the pillow, that's for sure. When she had herself together, she shoved the door open to find the trio happily puffing. Sherman even winked at her. Charlie didn't stick around to find out why.

Those people should not have matches, or stolen meds. Or pillows. The hall looked innocently the same. The calls for help had quieted, Charlie hoped not because of more pillows. Rose's walker had lost one of its green tennis balls and made screeching noises on the floor. She wore one bedroom slipper that was probably not hers and a big brown stain on the seat of her pink sweats.

"I just want to get out of here. Go home," Charlie told her and hurried to the door to the lobby. It opened before she got there when an old lady with an ankle bracelet walked in from the lobby and set off the alarm. Oh, great. Charlie tried to switch the mechanism in the cream-colored box that had turned off the racket for Harvey Rochester and Cousin Helen, but couldn't find a way to make it work.

That cold sweat again. And the dry mouth. Kraut-gin afterburn. Charlie turned to find the wanderers had stopped wandering to watch her. The smokers had come out of the john still puffing, and several wheelchairs with oxygen bottles not attached by their clear-plastic umbilical cords to people's noses less than two feet away. Most of these people weren't wearing their eyeglasses but they stared straight and true and accusingly at Charlemagne Catherine Greene. Maybe every fifth one had the black Myrtle eyes.

This place was even more terrible without staff than with it. And far more dangerous. Lunatics should definitely not run the asylum. Message there for voters.

Charlie slammed the door shut on the smelly part and rejoiced at the sound of a phone ringing from the administrator's office. She almost tripped over Gladys' extended leg.

"Gotcha now."

"Oh no you haven't." Charlie raced across the lobby and into Elsina's office, slamming the door on Gladys and her leg. Jesus watched her every move, front and back, as she watched Marlys Dittberner answer the phone.

"Because, because, because." The ancient woman still wore the ancient dress, much the worse for wear by now. She gave Charlie that toothless grin, threw the handset down on the desk and leaned over to pick up her suitcase from the floor. "I'm going home. I'm all packed."

"Marlys, may I borrow the phone?" Charlie crossed the floor as calmly as she could, Jesus' blue eyes on the wall behind Marlys following her.

"Help yourself." Marlys even handed her the handset.

Charlie, forcing what she hoped was a reassuring smile, punched nine-one-one, heard her heart pounding in her ear against the earpiece, and one ring—before Marlys Dittberner leaned over, unplugged the phone, and yanked the plastic cord from the jack.

Humming "Somewhere Over the Rainbow" sort of, the old woman calmly stuffed the phone's power to communicate in her suitcase, grabbed a pen and pencil set off the desk to add to her stash, and slammed the lid shut. But not before Charlie heard the familiar mewing of a cellular coming from the suitcase. "What are you doing, you crazy old bat? That's my phone you've got in there, probably my purse and everything. Give me that."

Charlie raced around the desk to grab the woman or the

257

suitcase, whichever she could get a grip on first, and arrived just as the ancient crone yanked the bag off the desk and swung around with it. The burden was so heavy it kept swinging and nearly toppled its owner. The sound of breaking glass inside did not bode well for oodles of dusty eyeglasses, and probably dentures and hearing aids as well. Nor did it bode well for Charlie Greene, who stopped the momentum of the swinging luggage with her stomach and went down like a pregnant hippopotamus.

"There's a land that I know of where dreams really do—" Marlys lugged the suitcase, with obvious effort and both hands, to the door but had to use one hand to turn the knob. "Come along, Toto."

Charlie had just sucked some breath back into her crushed innards and pushed herself to one knee when Dolores the tomcat dashed out from behind the desk to follow Dorothy somewhere over the rainbow.

"That's a good dog." And the door closed behind them, leaving Charlie alone. But the rheumy buzz from the lobby was ominous and she staggered across the room to lock herself in against it. One of her cracked ribs felt like it was going into remission. The lock demanded a key she didn't have and had a knob that kept trying to turn even as she held it.

There wasn't time to drag furniture over to block the door from opening inward. Jesus watched her from both walls still. The cold sweat had turned hot.

"Why then, oh why can't I?" Marlys crooned grotesquely out of tune from the other side of the door.

There was one window in the room, with a view of the front porch and the drive beyond. Two, three, and then four wanderers, half-clothed, toothless, came to peer in at her from the porch, squinting. Could they see anything? Could they remember enough to have a clue to what was happening, or care through their confusion?

Charlie turned around to hold the doorknob still with both hands behind her back, leaned her weight against the door, and dug both heels into the carpet for leverage.

And watched her heels slowly skid across the floor as the door pushed open behind her. "Oooohhhh, shit!"

"We got plenty of—"

"Oh, shut up!"

CHAPTER 39

━━━━◆━━━━

*S*HUT UP! SHUT up! Shut up!"
    "Bad girl."
    "That's naughty."
    "She should take a pill."
    "Now be a good girl and take your pill."
    It was too late to change lanes. Or was it?
    Charlie heard herself screaming and cursing as she wormed the little crushable Toyota over between two SUVs. The one in front of her climbed the semi's hood.
    "There she goes."
    "Who?"
    "The one with all the hair. Grab her."
    "Did she take her pill?"
    "What pill?"
    "The one you said to give her."
    "You old crazy woman you don't know what you're talking about. Who's that screaming?"
    Charlie screamed but managed another worm into the next lane over, where two old men in wheelchairs tried to block her way. Uncle Elmo hugged her. "Don't cry, little Charlie, this ain't none of your fault."
    "I'm so sorry."
    "You weren't raised to drive on ice. Ask old Marlys, she knows everything. She's responsible for it all."
    "All what?"
    "All the babies," Marlys said.
    "For saving them?"

"For selling them. People pay real good money for little white babies from Iowa. Edwina paid top dollar for you. Couldn't believe she had that kind of money. Being a teacher and all."

"*She is a professor*, goddammit."

"That was naughty. She should take a pill."

"White babies from Iowa come from real pure stock. Farm-fed. Pure and innocent. Top dollar."

"Bootleggers. Patriarchal murderers."

"Didn't have much protection for little girls then. They felt guilty just being born, way back. I was here serving the public long before Family Farms. Didn't use no hormones or pesticides neither."

Charlie needed food again. Probably because she hadn't kept much of her dinner down on the yellow brick road. That buzzy feeling began to overcome her fear of the wanderers, a return to her nightmare, and the pain in her middle where Marlys had slugged her with a loaded suitcase. At least her migraine had gotten sidetracked somewhere. Maybe she did take a pill.

Through the plethora of sensation and confusion, it finally occurred to Charlie that she was being herded rather than led. No one was actually touching or restraining her. Could she worm out the cat door? Was there maybe a spare snack in the drawers of the nurses' station? Could she take off running and get to a door that would open or to the storeroom that had been a kitchen and push the washing machine off the trapdoor, let the others out of the basement or tunnel to help her? Where were Great-aunt Abigail and Ben?

Marlys Dittberner, she noticed, walked beside her. Rose's uncovered walker wheel screeched somewhere behind her. Was Rose bringing the pillow? The dimmed nightlights above, staggered along the hall, made elongated shadows on the floor until you came up under the next one.

Charlie glanced over her shoulder at the shadows. They seemed to stretch forever, like all the lost souls who took forever to die had joined them, all those who couldn't walk had found a way. No going back down that hall. "I must go forward."

"That's always wise," Marlys agreed. "Everybody knows that."

"Did you really sell the babies?" Charlie decided to head for the kitchen/storeroom.

"Why not? Top dollar, white Iowa babies. Better than selling groceries. Now they go to China for yellow babies. Serves them right."

Charlie, we are going to make a run for the storeroom, and we need food.

"How did you know they go to China for babies now?"

"Saw it on the television. I'm going home, you know. I'm all packed."

"I am, too." Charlie took off, dizzy or not, and realized the alarm had stopped its cacophony. When did that happen?

She passed the door to the storeroom and had to fight her way through the first wave of wanderers and their shadows to get back to it. The light was still on. The washer was moved aside. And the mat. The door to the basement stood open. No Harvey or Elsina, no barkeep or marshal. Not even Ben or the Great Witch Abigail. The hole in the floor was dark and deep and scary. "Where'd everybody go?"

"To see the wizard. Because dreams really do come true. That's the storm cellar. I wouldn't go down there. No lights. Darker than a grave."

Sometimes Charlie was hearing Marlys Dittberner, sometimes Judy Garland. Judy Garland was dead. Marlys wasn't. Go figure.

"I just want to go home."

"Me, too."

"What if we go get your suitcase? And we can go home together." Maybe Harvey, Del, Kenny, and Elsina were in the building after all and just waiting for a chance to rescue Charlie. They could be hiding somewhere close. At least Charlie could retrieve her cell, call for help. "Marlys, where are Abigail and Ben? Besides off to see the wizard."

"Ain't seen either one in weeks."

"You and Ben were at Abigail's house today. Brought me here in the marshal's Jeep."

"That's right, we did. Forgot all about it."

"But you remember selling Iowa babies years ago."

"Groceries, too." Marlys' museum-piece dress was way too large. The skirt had ripped away from the waist and she held it up with one hand and still kept tripping on it. It had long, button sleeves that hung down over her hands. Its built-in bosom kept trying to hook her chin. Either Marlys or the dress smelled like someone's attic. "Abigail lent this to me when I lost my shirt."

"And Myrtle's grave in the cemetery, do you remember talking to me there?"

"I talk to everybody there. That's home. That's where I'm going. Told you, didn't I?"

"Why is that home? Because Myrtle's there?"

"Her and them babies that didn't get sold. Hardly any of them died, you know. I'm a good midwife."

"You buried the stillborns and those you couldn't sell in Myrtle's grave?"

"All her fault from the beginning. Her curse—why not? Some of the children who were mothers, too."

"But why is that home to you?"

"That's where I belong, and you, too. The curse must end with you. Abigail said so."

"You watch television. You must know how dumb all this is. It's not true or real or even—uh—okay, scratch the television part. But, Marlys, you are wise in so many ways—surely you can see the mistake here. How weird it is that either one of us could be responsible for or even related to a curse pronounced on the town generations before either of us were even born. And we aren't responsible for what happened before birth."

263

"That's why they have curses. So the dead can get back at the living when they need revenge. Don't you know nothing?"

This time, Charlie led Marlys by the arm, hurried her through the confusion in the hall. People made way for them because of Charlie's determination and obvious sense of purpose. She had a plan and they didn't. Why hadn't she thought of this before? These poor people were not planners or leaders. They wanted to be led.

They turned to follow her and Marlys Dittberner the other way down the hall, Rose's screeching walker right behind them again. Charlie felt so foolish to have allowed herself to be afraid of these people. Great-aunt Abigail and Ben yes, but not these poor lost souls who didn't know what they were doing even as they did it. Elsina Miller was right.

"Where do you think you're going, now?" Gladys, her wheelchair and her extended leg helped by an overturned meds cart, blocked their way.

"Going home," Marlys said.

"We're going to the cemetery. But first we have to pick up her suitcase," Charlie added.

"Didn't you forget something?"

"I always forget something, you old bat. Now get out of my way . . . oh, that's right, wait a minute."

Rose's walker finally caught up with them and stopped screeching. Charlie turned to see the pillow balanced on its top bar and noticed they'd stopped in front of the shower room.

CHAPTER 40

❖

*C*HARLIE WASN'T EXACTLY shoved into the white-tiled shower room where Darla Lempke was murdered, more like crowded into it by the sheer force of numbers eager to witness what would happen there. Or would they even know? No cheering like there would be at a football game or a public hanging. More of a mass expectation that, with this crowd, came as whispery breath, punctuated ever so faintly with the rheumy growl of weary lungs.

Charlie, get a grip here. They could be dense as dishwater but they way far outnumber us. We might try to keep our head.

The crowd had backed Charlie into the same situation she'd found Darla, the deceased activities director. Most of the faces breathing on her were blank, but the gathering was experiencing agitation from behind and leaders soon made their way forward, as they generally do.

Gladys made her way to the forefront. Somebody stepped on Dolores' foot or tail and he rose to screaming eminence somewhere back there, perched on someone's head or shoulder before he too fell from grace and disappeared.

The way cleared further for the two leering Fatties. No surprise here. They of course opened the way for Rose and her pillow. And then came Marlys.

"Marlys, help me. I'm one of the babies you saved."

"Should have buried you with Myrtle—stopped the curse. Abigail said so."

"Killing me won't stop the curse." The stark-white tile surrounding Charlie leaked icy cold through her clothes. Her jacket was gone. When did that happen? "We need to get your suitcase and go to the cemetery, remember?"

"We're going to die on her grave and stop the curse."

"Right, Marlys."

"But first we have to euthanize Charlemagne Catherine Greene, remember?" Gladys said. "Poor thing don't have any boyfriends."

"I'll be her boyfriend." One of the Fatties—all really old men looked the same to Charlie by now—wheeled up to pin her against the tile and reached for her crotch.

"Darla Lempke, Activities Director." Rose brought the pillow.

"I'll be her boyfriend, you dirty old coot." The other Fatty surged forward and cut Rose off at the knees.

The first Fatty grabbed the shower hose and tried to separate Charlie from the second Fatty, who reached for the pillow poor Rose held up from her position on the floor, and Charlie realized that most of the crowd had lost interest. Like they had with TV or Dorothy and the Tin Man. Or life. They were wandering out of the cold, crowded room to continue their journey, only Elsina Miller knew where, thinning the crowd so Charlie could see how much trouble she was really in.

Sagging biceps, forearms, jowls, cheeks, and chins, anywhere there had once been muscle and firm skin. They obviously didn't know their sad plight and looks and condition.

Charlie shoved a heel into a crotch to repay the groping finger and felt the last bit of energy leave her, leave her shaky and sagging. She fought the shower hose tightening around her neck by slipping the fingers of both hands between her skin and the ribbed plastic, watched the blaring-white tiles start jiggling, began a slow slide to the floor as the skinny, saggy Fatty with the pillow covered the light in the ceiling with his head.

"Lay still now and I'll make you feel real good. Get inside

your clothes." He disappeared behind the pillow as it covered her face.

"Darla Lempke, Activities Director."

"Well, you finally got the right one, you idiots," Great-aunt Abigail Staudt said from somewhere. "Gladys, you know what to do when it's over. Ben will help you."

"No, what? We haven't had our supper."

"We bury her in the cemetery, where dreams really do come true," Marlys said.

Charlie should have been suffocating, but there was an error in the program here. The pillow stayed pushed down on her face but nobody was holding onto her lower body or arms, so she squirmed out from under it. This should have been at least a three-man operation, but the Fatty with the hose had been distracted by a kick in the crotch. They should have held her down like Edwina, Kenny, and Uncle Elmo had after her nightmare upstairs at Viagra's. And she still had use of her arms. Maybe this had happened here before, with someone lying over the victim's middle, pinning down the arms as well as the torso, someone holding the feet below, and a third the pillow pressed on the face until the struggle was over. Was there a fourth to keep one and all focused?

Until Darla. Wrong victim but lots of wandering help, no fourth to give the orders. And Wilma Overgaard, the next victim. Something wrong there, too. Too much struggle—not enough handlers?

"Ben, stop her."

"Ben, stop her," Marlys mimicked. "I know, let's tie her in a chair and make her watch the television."

"Turn it up real loud and put in her hearing aids," Gladys agreed, "until the sound beats at her on and on for hours and hours."

Charlie knew better but couldn't help glancing over her shoulder as she staggered to the door, unable to believe they were letting her get away.

"And then make her take a pill. Lots of pills."

The Fatties had dozed off in their chairs. Even the one Charlie had kicked. They were blocking Ben, who was trying to help Rose to her feet. Abigail Staudt stood aloof, arms folded, trying to general the lunatics. Marlys and Gladys gleefully came up with more ways to torture Charlie.

"Make her sleep all night in her own shit and burn and itch—"

Charlie was out in the hall, sure that Ben was right behind her, but she had to grasp door moldings to keep upright. Lethargy overtook the buzz in her head, her heart pounded thunder, and her breath came wheezy and painful. Can you catch old age from old people?

"Que pasa?" said a muffled but urgent whisper from a dark space ahead between the dim lights.

Thank God, the Mexicans were back. The people who really ran this show. What was Spanish for "Help?" Charlie knew, but in her weakened state, her mind wasn't working well.

"Señora, you can help?" a woman said beside Charlie, who let out a startled squeak. "The door, it is locked. They go to hide and someone locks them in. I am afraid."

"Me, too. What is this?"

"The laundry."

"The Mexicans have been hiding in the laundry room?"

"Everywhere we hide, but tonight they are not many because of the troubles here. I run outside but come back to find my friends. I haf look for the keys, but—" She chatted for a while with her friends on the other side of the door as Charlie leaned against the wall to keep herself off the floor.

She tried to hang onto enough mind and strength to persuade the woman to guide her to Marlys' room to look for a phone to call for help. "I don't know where the keys to this room are, but she has the phones in her suitcase."

"Suitcase, jhes. Marlys, she steal everything. Maybe she haf keys, too."

"You'll have to help me, I'm very weak."

But they'd made it no more than a few feet when they were stopped by a *whump*, like a giant pilot light finally lit, and a poof of flame tore along the carpet toward them in the dim hall, lighting it up major big time.

❖

CHAPTER 41

*A*S HARD AS she'd tried, Charlie didn't make it out of Iowa in time.

She stood beside her mother in the little cemetery again, where the shade came from gloom rather than leaves. It turned the new-fallen snow appropriately gray.

The memorial service was a week later than planned because of the carnage at Gentle Oaks Health Care Center and the ongoing investigation. Elsina Miller leaned on Harvey Rochester's arm, one leg and foot in a cast. Harvey broke a finger when pushed from the hole in the ceiling. She'd broken a leg when he landed on her. And here, good old jaded Charlie had thought the heavy breathing and Elsina's moaning in the cellar due to other causes. She'd still be willing to bet, considering the color of his eyes, that Mr. Rochester would get Elsina pregnant before she got him redone in His image. The administrator smiled encouragement at her now. Charlie winked back. She still didn't like the woman but she could stand her. They'd lived through a lot together in a short while. If only Elsina knew why Charlie'd not gotten out of Iowa in time.

Marshal Delwood Brunsvold leaned against the red Cherokee like before, but more relaxed. There had been so much digging and publicity that the county had sprung for a backhoe rental with a professional driver. On either side of him stood his incredibly corpulent parents, making him look like a sliver of cheese in a focaccia sandwich.

After an overnight in the behemoth of a hospital, Charlie

had recuperated at the Holiday Inn in Mason City. She'd been shuttled from the emergency room to the cardiac unit for some reason and her heart was found to be fine, so she needed no further hospitalization. She'd suffered no burns, just bumps and bruises and shock that had sent her back into old nightmares. There was no emergency. Charlie figured her insurance was suspect or something, and she had no Medicare or Medicaid coverage.

But her therapy came to her. She didn't even have to charge her insurance.

The snow layer was a couple of inches, but began falling again as the three officiating ministers wound up the service—the lady Methodist minister from Floyd, a Catholic priest, and a Solemn Lutheran preacher from . . . Charlie didn't know where. She counted about thirteen newly turned graves dotting the graveyard. The carnage could have been far worse if the fire sprinkler system at Gentle Oaks hadn't kicked in. The new graves were rounded under the snow, with ripply dirt showing. The sucking earth hadn't had time to depress them yet.

Everybody was saying—even the newspapers—that in two or three weeks, the ground would have been frozen. If the fire had to happen, better now than then.

Edwina had spent the last couple of nights at Helen and Buz Bartuseks' to help plan the memorial service, and that ended Charlie's nightmares.

The earth from Myrtle's grave mounded in vast piles around it, the headstone set off to the side, still leaning. The huge root at the grave's head stood exposed and wounded by the teeth of the backhoe. It seemed the deeper they had dug, the blacker the soil, steeper patches of which had lost the snow cover, making for a black and white and gray day.

Only relatives and press joined the clergy now. All of the surviving residents had been squeezed into other nursing homes or were still hospitalized until repairs could be made to Gentle Oaks, much of the damage due to water.

Kenny Cowper stood beside her, too—more like towered. He was to drive them to the airport in Minneapolis in time to catch a red-eye West. Charlie was so happy for these people to be dead, but she teared and sniffled anyway, which kept Kenny trying to hide a smug grin, that and the last two nights. Her recovery had nothing to do with romance, but he could make even a Holiday Inn in Mason City, Iowa, erotic.

Del had found a way out of the tunnel at Orlyn Sievertsen's fruit cellar because Orlyn's dogs kept barking at the hammering and yelling beneath the cellar doors. Orlyn found a flashlight, and he and Delwood came to the rescue of the three Charlie had left behind when Ben had yanked her out of the cellar and closed the door on them. Kenny'd had to carry Elsina, but by the time they reached the Oaks, part of it was burning.

Kenny's grammy had survived. And so had the Fatties.

Sherman and Flo had taken their last smoke and managed to light up Rose, several people on loose oxygen tanks, and those too close to the resultant flames or smoke before the dousing of fire sprinklers took effect. And one died being resuscitated when overzealous ambulance types broke a fragile sternum.

The firebugs had somehow gained entrance to the liquid oxygen storage closet and the reservoir used to feed the smaller, more mobile tanks used by the less fortunate residents. It was assumed that the flames from the matches used to light cigarettes, flared by added oxygen, had spread from clothing and hair to carpet and wallboard. Perhaps Rose had read the sign on the door once too often and given them the idea.

"Did you find out who she was?" Charlie slid slanted glances at the tombstones they passed as they followed the procession out of the busy little cemetery. "And did you pay a lot of money for me because I was a white Iowa baby?"

"Your birth mother? All I know is she was Isobel's daugh-

272

ter. I don't want to know anything more," Edwina answered. "And yes, Charlie, you came dear."

"I don't want to know any more either. I want to leave all this and Myrtle far behind." What they were both avoiding was the implications of Isobel's relationship to Abigail Staudt. Talk about inbreeding.

Instead, they turned for one last look while waiting for Kenny to bring the car around. "Mom, what happens when more and more old people keep living older and older?"

"I don't know, Charlie. We can't euthanize people like we do pets. We just can't."

Great-aunt Abigail Staudt and Ben were charged with instigating just that by leading frail, senile residents at Gentle Oaks in putting "born Staudts" out of their misery. She was the instigator, Ben the liaison, and ironically one of the probable killers was a Staudt himself—Abigail's brother, the skeletal Fatty. The problem was, her dupes and those who watched them decided that there was finally an interesting activity in their limited world again. More fun than those of Darla Lempke. So they'd continued the "pillow game" haphazardly and with less organization.

Abigail suffered a stroke while under house arrest. Ben was in jail in Charles City. Abigail had arranged to put her female relatives out of their misery, but she too would now be fodder for the Oaks and take their place. Those she'd encouraged to commit euthanasia—who knew how many, or if they were always the same ones?—were supposed to forget what they'd done, like they forgot everything else. But something set off a memory, and the acts had continued without her supervision. Charlie rather suspected Gladys, whose memory seemed better than the rest. She'd also survived relatively unscathed.

"Daughters aren't going to put up with being sacrificed in the new economy. Besides, they're needed in the workforce. Economy's screwed either way," Charlie said.

"Modern capitalism will find a solution, a substitute for sacrificial daughters, perhaps. Or nature will discover how to

273

outsmart the flu and pneumonia vaccines." Edwina was a rare breed of environmental conservative.

The snowflakes came thicker, softly, with no wind in a silent world. Sad, stark, yet beautiful in black and white, and still, but for the falling snow and a lone photographer. He crouched on one of the mounds for some last shots of the enormous hole that had once been Myrtle Staudt's grave.

Probably because it had become a public mystery. Probably because no bodies had been found in or around it. No unsold babes or unwed moms who hadn't survived childbirth.

And most curious of all, not a trace or a fragment of the rebellious daughter for whom the town was named. There were no dead bodies in Myrtle's grave, nor had there been ever.

CHAPTER 42

✛

*H*ER FIRST FULL day at home, Charlie snuggled in a corner of her kitchen breakfast nook and savored a communal dinner. Mrs. Beesom's tuna noodle casserole ripe with canned peas and potato chips. A tall glass of milk. Jacob Forney's fresh-baked yeast rolls with butter. Maggie Stutzman's salad greens tossed with raspberry vinaigrette and sprinkled with raspberries. Charlie, as usual, provided the table and the entertainment.

"There's no place like home, Toto." She raised a fork of canned tuna and chips to Tuxedo, the black cat with the white chest and feet giving her a jaundiced eye from atop the refrigerator.

"My secret," Mrs. Beesom, sitting across from Charlie, confided, "is the cream-of-celery soup, Campbell's."

Luscious Libby, with the Myrtle eyes, sat beside Charlie. "Mom, you're not too old to get pregnant, right?"

"Excuse me?"

"I'm joining the Hemlock Society, first thing Monday morning." Maggie Stutzman had raspberry seeds between her front teeth. She was a lawyer and next to the birth-control pill, Charlie's best friend. Her eyes looked strangely dilated, reminding Charlie of the Floyd County deputy sheriff after he got in the med cart. "No ancient aging for me."

"I mean, not some gross guy thing like Mitch Hilsten, but you go to one of those donor clinics and buy sperm? Have it injected or whatever?"

"Why would I want another baby?"

"Well, I'll be leaving home soon. And you could use the company. And I could use a sacrificial sister to dump you on when you get to be a FROW. Works out for both of us. Right?"

"Well, I'm going to live in my house until I die in my sleep," the eighty-three-year-old Mrs. Beesom said, and Charlie and Maggie exchanged that helpless look becoming more frequent by the month. Betty Beesom had not one relative to her name—sacrificial or no.

"FROW?" Charlie asked her daughter.

"Fucking really old woman. Be glad you're not a guy or you'd be a FROG."

If it was possible to choke on mushy tuna noodle casserole, Jacob was doing so. The newest neighbor in their little condo complex of houses, attached by a high stucco wall with heavy gates to street in front and alley in back, he, along with Tuxedo on the fridge, was the only guy living here. His eyes were watering but he cleared his throat and said, "I think it a great honor to live long and prosper."

"Me, too," Libby said. "Until you get sick and your muscle and flesh and brains turn to mush."

"So the Mexicans just hid wherever and not down in the cellar and tunnels?" Maggie changed the subject with a warning look at the diplomatic Libby.

"There were only three of them the night of the fire, and few anytime. They just had such a gigantic job—you thought there were more." The two in the laundry room survived only because of the sprinkler system. "The whole situation is so overwhelming. Think of a daycare center where most of the babies and children are well over a hundred pounds, in diapers, and tormented by images and phantom memories of a life they no longer understand, their minds and bodies can no longer tolerate."

"That's why I never go near them places, even to visit," Mrs. Beesom agreed—with what, Charlie couldn't imagine.

"If these were such helpless people, how could they take

out the deputy sheriff?" Jacob Forney wanted to know.

"He'd apparently helped loot the med carts. Blood tests from the autopsy hadn't come back yet when I left, but he had a few open bottles of really fun painkillers in his pockets. The ancient smokers ignored them and went after his cigarettes."

"Hard to believe tough old Charlie Greene was born in nice old Iowa," Maggie said. "You and Edwina never looked into who your birth mom was?"

"Yeah. I might have two grandmas." Libby rearranged her Staudt hair with long fingers. Everybody watched it fall back to perfectly cup her face.

"She'd be the daughter of Isobel and Uncle Elmo?" Jacob was an accountant and, unlike his neighbors, given to detail. They had chosen him carefully.

"Problem is, Isobel was the illegitimate daughter of Abigail Staudt." Charlie vowed Libby would never go to Myrtle.

"Not that scion of propriety, too?" Maggie glanced hard at Libby Abigail Greene. "Wow, that's some curse."

"I thought the curse meant you weren't pregnant." Libby stared back.

"Which makes Great-aunt Abigail my great-great-grandmother. And Uncle Elmo, my grandfather, is also Abigail's nephew. Somehow, Edwina and I didn't want to explore this."

"Oh-oh, problems with the gene pool there." Nobody had told Jacob Forney yet that the last guy who'd lived in the compound had been murdered or that he had the same initials. "That could be serious."

"I always knew there was something wrong with you, Greene," Maggie teased, but oddly without the usual grin.

"So, do you think the curse is over?" Jacob was probably in his early forties, but he looked older. Because he was so serious.

"Which one? Gobs of fatherless babies and ruined teenage moms? Or living past the outer reaches of senility? I don't know. That many people over a hundred is sure no blessing."

"Marlys was certainly an entrepreneur. Chubby little white babies for sale, from healthy, wholesome corn-fed parents. I wonder if she advertised," Maggie said.

"She was cursed more than most. She kept trying to dig herself into Myrtle's grave to go home—Myrtle wasn't even there. And she had no luck killing herself running around naked in a very harsh climate. I think she mixed herself up with Myrtle in her dementia. And I think my great-great-grandmother witch helped that fantasy along."

Marlys Dittberner was out of luck again. She'd survived the fire unharmed but had been doused by the sprinklers and left in the cold so long, she'd contracted pneumonia. But, since she'd been given the flu and pneumonia shots three weeks before, she was recovering nicely. She would live on as a vegetable, but she would live on. Maybe into *The Guiness Book of World Records*, if anyone managed to document her date of birth. Life's not fair.

"Was there really a curse, or was one invented to explain the unexplainably long-lived elders of Myrtle?" Careful Jacob kept probing, doubting. "Or had Abigail Staudt used this lie to get Marlys to do her bidding? Marlys remembered enough to believe herself culpable and was that why she was always trying to dig her way into Myrtle's grave?" Jacob had book-shelves full of mysteries. Someday they'd have to tell him about the mystery of the man who'd preceded him in the compound.

❖

Charlie was absolutely euphoric, even giddy, her first day back in her Beverly Hills office at Congdon and Morse Represen-tation, Inc., on Wilshire. When her gorgeous assistant called into her lavish office from his tiny cubicle that protected her privacy from the hall—"The next Danielle Steel, line one"—she left her shoes under the desk and put her feet up on its top, leaned back in her leather chair and sighed.

"That's a call back, Larry."

"You are a hard-hearted woman. Okay, Paul Lazzart, Constellation Productions."

"Call back."

"Charlie, you coming to work today or what?"

"Anything else, smart-ass?"

"Yeah, some jerk from Iowa—Kenneth Cooper?"

"Oh, Kenny Cowper. I'll take it."

"Charlie, get a grip—"

"Hey, barkeep, how's it going?"

"Hi, Charlie. Just had an interesting tidbit thought I'd share with you."

"Like your book proposal."

"No. Like Delwood and I been digging because life's so boring here when you're not around. And he doesn't have enough snow to plow. We found Myrtle."

"What, you're writing fiction now? What ever happened to Dolores the tomcat?"

"Charlie, the cat's fine, not even singed. But we found Myrtle and the remnants of her baby—well, they were both remnants but in a casket together. It's her, because her bible was buried with her."

"You're kidding—in the cemetery?"

"At the bottom of the stairs in the cellar under Gentle Oaks. Going to have to revise my proposal, but you'll be the first to see it. Charlie, you still there? Charlie?"